MRS. JONES AND THE RADIUM CITY
A Jazz-Age Decopunk Fantasy
By Grace E. Robinson

Chapter 1

Cornelia Jones contemplated the dark red evening gown that hung from its hanger on the back of her closet door. She'd laid out the entire outfit for tonight's dinner party three days ago, but was now doubting her choice of this particular dress. After all, she'd worn it a mere eight months ago to a society gala at the Ambassador Hotel.

Granted, she had brand-new patent leather heels, a new pearl necklace with matching bracelet and earrings, and a gossamer gold silk wrap to wear with it. But still, one of tonight's dinner guests might recognize the dress. It wouldn't do to have anyone thinking she had a paltry wardrobe. Perhaps she should wear the midnight blue gown; it had been some time since she'd worn her sapphires, and they would complement the dress nicely. Or she could try the sultry black gown...

No, stay with the red. She'd already organized the ensemble, and more importantly, it was one of John's favorites. She pulled the gown off its hanger, running a hand across the smooth velvet; a rich red the color of her favorite wine she kept tucked away in the cellar beneath the carriage house, where it stayed hidden from the prying eyes of Prohibition officers. Wine which presumably the servants had brought up from the cellar by now so that it would be the proper temperature by the time the dinner guests arrived.

Perhaps she'd better go and make sure. After all, today was New Year's Eve and Los Angeles' finest society was invited. It wouldn't do to dawdle.

And on the matter of dawdling... Cornelia pulled a pair of silk stockings out of her bureau drawer and peered out the door of her dressing room. Across the bedroom, the door to John's dressing room was closed fast, and no light shone from under the door. She glanced at the little porcelain clock on her dressing table; the guests would be arriving in just over an hour.

Cornelia sat down to put on her stockings, then slithered into her dress, resolving to finish her hair and makeup after she'd hunted down her husband. Not that it would really require much hunting—she knew exactly where he was. When that man got focused on a project, nothing could distract him. Not even hosting a dinner party at his own home on New Year's Eve.

She pulled her white satin dressing gown on over the dress, and slipped on the matching slippers. Leaving her dark auburn hair loose around her shoulders, she hurried through the bedroom and down the hall towards the stairs. An enticing tangle of rich smells came floating up from the kitchen as she descended the sweeping staircase. Maggie was busy putting the finishing touches on all of her specialties, like the oyster cocktails and an English pudding. Never let it be said that the Joneses served bland food at their dinner parties.

Downstairs in the front hall, Joseph Rawlins, the butler, stood by the front door, adjusting his white gloves. Dear

Rawlins—Cornelia could always count on him to be fully prepared and ahead of schedule.

He looked up at Cornelia as she came down the stairs. "Good evening, Miz Jones," he said in his deep rich voice, white teeth flashing in his dark face as he smiled at her. The black man was starting to show signs of his advancing years in the gray peppering his black hair and the slight stoop in his shoulders. But he was still physically fit and mentally sharp, and kept the Jones household running as smoothly as the clocks that he faithfully wound every day.

"Good evening, Rawlins," said Cornelia. "Has Joey brought the wine up from the cellar?"

"Yes, ma'am. The wine is ready, the dinner table is set, and I've got your new record ready for playing on the Victrola in the parlor for after dinner."

"Perfect." Cornelia smiled. "Thank you, Rawlins."

"Everything is ready, ma'am, except for, um, Mr. Jones himself. I was just about to go down to the basement—"

Cornelia held up a hand. "Don't worry about it, Rawlins. As soon as I realized he wasn't in his dressing room, I came down. I'll get him."

Rawlins gave a very slight bow, really more of an incline of the head, his way of simultaneously deferring to her authority and hiding a smirk. Cornelia briefly considered letting Rawlins go ahead and fetch John—he often listened to the old butler better than he did to her. But Rawlins was better suited to managing any last-minute needs for the party, so she gave Rawlins a nod of her own, and headed toward the kitchen and the basement stairs.

The kitchen was situated toward the rear left corner of the house, near the service entrance that led outside to the driveway under a porte-cochère. Cornelia briefly peered into the kitchen as she went past. Red-faced and humming cheerily, Maggie O'Connor, the plump Irish cook, energetically stirred a steaming pot on the stove. Young Theda White, wearing an apron over her formal black maid's attire, was bent over pulling a large platter out of the ice box. All seemed well in hand.

Across the hall from the kitchen door was another door, plain dark wood, looking for all the world like another area of servants' access. Even the most curious house guest, should they make it past the dining room and into the back part of the house, would never venture through that door, thinking it merely the servants' domain. And that was exactly the way Cornelia and John wanted it.

Cornelia pulled the wooden door closed behind her as she descended the stone steps. There was no need to switch on the light; the stairwell was well-lit. As always.

The narrow staircase widened out at the bottom to give a full view of the main basement room. Four long wooden tables filled the center of the wide-open room, lined up parallel as in a university laboratory. John sat on the bench at the nearest table, facing the staircase, so if he but glanced up, he'd see her standing there. But of course he didn't.

Large sheets of paper covered the length of the table—blueprints for John's latest invention. He sat hunched over another sheet of paper, a pencil in one hand and a pair of compasses in the other. He was still dressed in his day suit, albeit jacketless. His white shirt sleeves were rolled up to the elbows, and his tie hung loosely around his neck. His light brown hair would need a good combing before dinner, and his angular jaw would need a good shave. Cornelia sauntered over and stood across the table from him, but he still didn't look up.

Glancing down at the nearest sheet of paper, Cornelia briefly studied the partial diagram of an engine and the scribbled equations around it. She tapped a smoothly-buffed fingernail lightly on the sheet of paper. "'Y to the fourth power equals eight?' Are you sure that's correct?"

"Of course it's correct," John replied in an off-hand tone, still not looking up. "And if it's not, I'll fix it later—I'm working on the air resistance calculations right now."

"In that case, all of this is wrong," Cornelia continued conversationally. "This is far too much algebra and calculus for a simple ornithopter."

"An ornithopter?" John sounded stunned. "Why would you think I'm building..." He trailed off and finally looked up at her.

Cornelia smiled at the glazed look in his blue-gray eyes. He was so endearing—if a bit aggravating—when he was this intensely focused on a project. "Good evening, dear," she said.

John blinked, the far-away look vanishing from his face as he finally smiled. "Cornelia! How long have you been standing there, darling?"

"Hours," she said sweetly. "And I know full well that you're not building an ornithopter."

He chuckled as he set down his pencil and compass. "I should hope so." He stretched his arms above his head. "*Uhng.* My shoulders feel as if I've been hunched over these diagrams for hours."

"You have been," Cornelia replied. "You need a break. And more importantly, you need to dress for dinner."

"Dinner time already?" John reached for his pocket watch, which wasn't there because he wasn't wearing his jacket, and wasn't wearing a vest, either.

"Not quite—but the guests will be arriving in less than an hour." Cornelia glanced down the length of the table, looking for his jacket. She finally spotted it, draped over the old-fashioned projecting praxinoscope that stood in the corner of the room near the stairs.

"Well, I guess I'd best pause this, then," said John, looking down at the papers scattered on the table. "I wonder where I put my jacket?"

"It's on your antique moving picture contraption."

"Ah, so it is. Thank you, dear."

As John retrieved his suit jacket, Cornelia looked back down at the paper with the engine equations. Not that she should be encouraging her husband to spend any more time down here at the moment, but there was something about that equation that she'd quoted to him...

She picked up the sheet of paper as he came around the table, his jacket draped over his arm. "Look here, John," she said, as the analytical part of her brain automatically jumped into action and began churning through the numbers. "I really don't think this is right. 'Y to the fourth power equals eight' doesn't fit with the rest of the equations here. This is for the pressure manifold, right?" She pointed at the partial diagram that filled the center of the page.

"Yes, of course," he said, "which is why this equals eight. See here, this is acceleration due to gravity, this is air pressure at sea level—" he pointed at various equations. "This isn't a simple automobile engine."

"I know that," Cornelia countered. "But if you switched the variables in these two equations here, then you still have eight—but your 'Y to the fourth power' throws it off." *Remember your dinner guests!* a voice in the back of her head reminded her, even as the lure of the mathematics problems threatened to take over her thoughts. As often as John lost all track of time down here in his lab, she really had no right to judge him. More than a few times Rawlins had to come down and drag the both of them back to reality.

John took the paper from her and frowned at it. "By gum, I think you're right. I'll have to recalculate this entire thing, which will change the manifold by—"

"Later, dear." Cornelia took the paper back from him as societal duties reasserted their dominance in her mind. "New Year's Eve dinner first, science experiments later."

"Yes, we mustn't neglect our dinner guests. But thank you for noticing that equation—that little slip could have cost me days of incorrect designs that would have been all for naught."

Cornelia laid the paper back on the messy table and took his arm. "Not for naught, John. None of your projects are ever in vain, even if they don't work on the first go-round."

John patted her hand as they headed for the stairs. "That's why I married you, dear—I knew I needed a brilliant wife to check my work."

Cornelia smiled at his joking tone, but it was the truth. No ordinary society heiress would have been able to agreeably tolerate his seemingly insane inventions or his obsessive focus, let alone join him in his work. And few men would tolerate a wife who knew more about science than most university professors and could repair a wireless radio as quickly as she could lay out an afternoon tea service.

She hugged his arm as they started up the stairs. They were indeed perfect for each other.

CONVERSATION SWIRLED around the dinner table as Theda, the maid, flitted from guest to guest, gathering up empty plates and refilling wine glasses and blessedly not spilling a drop or breaking a dish. Rawlins maintained a supervisory distance from the table unless Theda needed help, his white-gloved hands folded behind him, and his bowtie impeccably straight. The red taper candles on the table and the cedar boughs over the windows gave a festive air to the gathering, and thus far, none of the guests had started arguing. The night was still young, but as Theda and Rawlins approached the table with trays of sliced pineapple upside-down cake for dessert, Cornelia let herself relax a little. Thus far this was shaping up to be another superb holiday party for the Los Angeles elite.

John sat at the head of the long dining table, suave and debonair, with his brown hair neatly slicked down and a festive red cravat at his neck. Next to him sat Mr. Ulysses Williamson, president of the largest bank in Los Angeles, a well-groomed man far older than John but every bit as poised. Mr. Willoughby Rush sat at John's other side, a loud man whose jowls trembled every time he spoke, which was frequently. A film producer and owner of several picture studios, Mr. Rush knew more about every citizen of Los Angeles than anyone, or so he proclaimed to anyone and everyone.

Cornelia sat at the far end of the table, facing John. Next to her was Mrs. Geraldine Williamson, the banker's wife; and Mrs. Hortense Follensby. A widow of many years, Hortense served as the president of nearly every ladies' club in the city and was the unofficial matron of Los Angeles society. Mr. Rush may have claimed to know everything about everyone (he certainly knew everything about everyone in the moving picture world), but Hortense likely had a broader range of knowledge for her gossip arsenal. And like Mr. Rush, she wasn't afraid to share her knowledge at any and every moment.

The other guests occupied the remaining seats along the table. There was Miss Violet Humphries, a woman older than Hortense but a spinster, who was not shy about her fondness for modern jazz music or absurdly feathered hats. Mr. Maxwell Bentley, owner of four of the largest hotels in the city, said very little during the meal and politely refused the wine, but appeared to be enjoying himself. His wife, Ruby, was also present, which Cornelia counted as a victory for herself and her reputation as a hostess. Ruby Bentley suffered from numerous and ever-changing maladies of a vague sort, and melodramatically declined most invitations. Tonight, though, she seemed to be in perfect health as she devoured her dinner with gusto and did not share her husband's qualms about the wine.

The two youngest guests in attendance were Miss Olive Templeton and Miss Adelaide Snufflett-Frye. Olive, a girl of barely fifteen, was Hortense's niece. The girl's mother was ill and her father had been killed in the Great War, and so

9

Hortense now had the responsibility of all but raising the girl on her own. Cornelia felt a twinge of pity for the awkward Olive; she knew what it was like to have an ill mother who was not engaged in her daughter's life. But she felt more pity for poor Hortense, trying to make a proper lady out of a moody girl who aspired to be a modern flapper or a movie star.

Adelaide Snufflett-Frye was also a young woman who didn't seem overly interested in being a proper lady, although she at least knew how to behave at social gatherings. Bubbly, blonde, and a proud New Yorker, Adelaide had come to Los Angeles earlier that year to celebrate her twentieth birthday and had decided to stay. For some reason she'd taken an immediate interest in Cornelia when they first met at a bridge game some months before. Her interest had grown when she'd learned that John was an inventor and that Cornelia herself had been to college. Periodically Cornelia encouraged the girl to apply for university, as she seemed quite smart, and insatiably curious about anything and everything.

At this very moment, Adelaide was chatting with Prudence Davenport; another highly intelligent, college-educated woman, but not someone that Cornelia would have wanted an impressionable young woman to have an in-depth conversation with. Cornelia had purposefully avoided seating Adelaide and Prudence next to each other— Ruby Bentley was seated between them—but unfortunately Mrs. Bentley was so involved with her dinner that she didn't seem to mind that Adelaide and Prudence were having a conversation around her. Cornelia resolved to seat them at opposite ends of the table at the next dinner party.

Prudence Davenport and her husband, Percival, were the *nouveau riche* at the table, Percival having made his money by selling various inventions during the War. Cornelia had no problem with wealth attained by hard work—as opposed to wealth attained by inheriting from an ancestor's hard work, which was the case for many of those at the table, herself and John included. She was slightly bothered, though, by the fact that the exact details of what Percival's inventions were and to whom he had sold them were still a bit of a mystery.

The potentially dubious nature of Percival's past rankled Cornelia because both John and Percival had been recently commissioned by the federal government to work on a project together: the very same project for which John was currently sketching out calculations and diagrams in the basement. If the equation that Cornelia had pointed out was indeed incorrect, Percival would have noticed it, too, but he would have been far less kind about pointing out the error.

Cornelia pulled her attention away from Prudence and Adelaide, and thoughts about Percival, as she looked around the table, noting that everyone seemed to have finished their dessert. Dabbing at her mouth with her linen napkin, she pushed her chair back and stood up, announcing that it was time to retire to the parlor for coffee and brandy.

"Oh, I do so love good Christmas jazz," remarked Violet Humphries as everyone filed into the parlor. A modern recording of "Jingle Bells" played on the gramophone in the corner by the big bay window. No traditional holiday snow was visible outside the window, which was just fine with Cornelia; she loved the mild winters of Los Angeles.

"Such a gorgeous tree," Adelaide gushed, helping herself to a glass of brandy as Rawlins went by with the tray. Glass baubles and colored electric lights glittered amongst the silvery curtains of tinsel icicles hanging from every branch. The servants had done a wonderful job, as always, of making the Christmas tree a memorable one.

"What charming little glass cherubs," remarked Prudence, sauntering over to the tree. The hem of her diaphanous gold skirt swept against several lower branches, dislodging a few of the tinsel icicles.

"The angels are crystal, actually," Cornelia politely corrected her. "They're from Italy."

"Italy! How droll. Percival and I were just there last spring."

"Ah, Italy!" Geraldine Williamson chimed in. "Florence in the spring is simply divine."

"Isn't it, though?" said Prudence.

Cornelia turned away from them and scanned the room, looking for Rawlins and the brandy. At the moment Rawlins was across the room offering brandy to Mr. Rush and Mr. Williamson. John was just entering the room, Percival Davenport beside him. They appeared to be engrossed in an intense conversation, no doubt about their assigned government project. Cornelia caught the words "radium" and "energy output," and gave a little sigh. She wished they wouldn't talk about their work at a dinner party. It was hard enough to keep John's mind on his social responsibilities without Percival whispering distractions in his ear.

"You and Prudence are so lucky," said Adelaide.

Startled, Cornelia turned back around to find the younger woman at her elbow. "I beg your pardon?"

Adelaide sighed and patted at a well-coiffed wave in her blond hair. "You're both so lucky. Your husbands get to build modern marvels that will keep this country at the forefront of scientific development, and they tell you all about it. I wish I had a husband who got to invent harmonic resonators and plane engines and such."

Harmonic resonators? Cornelia grabbed Adelaide's arm and pulled her away from the other women now congregating around Prudence and the Christmas tree. "What are you talking about?" Cornelia demanded in a fierce whisper. "What was Prudence talking to you about at dinner?"

"Just the machine that your husbands are building," said Adelaide, her blue eyes widening at Cornelia's tone.

Cornelia drew a breath to calm herself before speaking. "Adelaide, that's classified information. No one is supposed to know about what they're building."

"Oh." Adelaide looked embarrassed. "Gee, Prudence didn't tell me that part."

Cornelia tossed a brief glance over her shoulder at the women gathered by the tree. *Prudence, what the hell are you playing at? Why would you tell this girl about a classified project?* "Adelaide," she said, working on keeping her tone calm and her voice quiet. "I don't know what Prudence told you, but it's supposed to be secret. It's a high security project for the United States military."

"I won't tell anyone, I promise. Besides, she didn't tell me how it works."

"That's because it doesn't work, not yet," said Cornelia. "They're still building it." She touched the younger woman's arm again. "Adelaide, I'm serious. Whatever Prudence told you,

you mustn't repeat it, not to anyone. In fact, just forget about everything she said."

"Well, okay..." Adelaide said slowly, giving Cornelia a puzzled frown. "But honestly, Cornelia, she didn't really tell me much of anything. She just said they were building the future. A special future, for people like us."

Now it was Cornelia's turn to frown. "People like us? What does she mean by that?"

Before Adelaide could answer, Hortense Follensby swept up to them. "Cornelia, darling, you and Miss Adelaide look far too serious for a New Year's Eve dinner party. You must have some coffee! Oh, maid!" Hortense waved a heavily braceleted arm at Theda, who was carrying the tray of coffee cups.

At this moment, Cornelia wanted something stronger than either coffee or brandy, but she graciously accepted the cup and saucer that Hortense handed to her. Hortense took another cup for herself, and after seeing that Adelaide already had a brandy in hand, she waved Theda away.

"Now, Adelaide," said Hortense, taking a delicate sip of her own coffee. "You simply must tell me where you bought those darling gloves you were wearing earlier."

Cornelia sipped her coffee and forced herself to participate in the conversation about Adelaide's latest shopping exploits. *A special future for people like us.* The words ran through her mind. Why would Prudence say such a thing? What did she mean by "special future?" And more to the point, what did she mean by "people like us?"

It was true that the Davenports, like Cornelia and John, knew the nuances of the hidden worlds of both science and mysticism. But why would she imply that Adelaide did, as well?

Unless Prudence knew something about Adelaide that Cornelia did not...

In spite of her best efforts, Cornelia was not able to get Prudence alone for the rest of the evening. Which was just as well—she needed to be a proper hostess and mingle good-naturedly with her guests, not engage in a private confrontation. However, she resolved to talk to Prudence at the next ladies' club meeting, which was scheduled for the following week.

As she struck up a conversation with Ruby Bentley about the diamond necklace Ruby was wearing, she noticed that John had broken away from Percival and was attending to his proper hosting duties, as well. He glanced up from his conversation with Maxwell Bentley and Willoughby Rush and gave her a little smile from across the room.

Cornelia returned his smile, then turned back to Ruby to give an appreciative nod as Ruby waxed poetic about the well-bred sales girl who'd sold her the necklace. Conversation buzzed cheerfully amongst the other guests, Theda circulated with her tray of coffee, and Rawlins turned the record over on the gramophone while hardly breaking stride with his tray of brandy glasses. The clock on the mantel struck eleven, signally only an hour left before Rawlins would bring out the champagne and they would welcome in the year 1924.

Prudence's worrisome conversation with Adelaide aside, Cornelia congratulated herself on another successful dinner party for the Jones family.

"ANOTHER SUPERB DINNER party, as always, my dear," said John, offering his arm as the two of them headed up the stairs.

"Thank you," Cornelia said with a smile, tucking her left arm into his and holding up her skirt with the other hand. "Good night, Rawlins," she called back down over the railing.

Rawlins was just coming out of the parlor, carrying a tray of empty glasses, and he paused and looked up at them. "Good night, Miz Jones. Good night to you, too, Mr. Jones. And happy new year."

"Happy new year to you, Rawlins," said John with a smile. "Thank you for all your work this evening. And be sure to pass a thank-you on to Maggie, too, for another perfectly prepared meal."

"I will, Mr. Jones." Rawlins smiled, inclining his head in a bow, then headed for the kitchen with the tray.

"I do wish the Davenports had behaved better," Cornelia remarked as they parted ways in the bedroom and went to their separate dressing rooms.

"Percival and Prudence didn't behave themselves?" called John from his dressing room across the room. "I thought the entire evening was smooth as silk."

"Well, yes, all things considered," said Cornelia, sitting down on her gold upholstered bench to unbuckle her shoes. "Thank goodness we didn't end up with another fiasco like the charity dinner for the War Orphans Foundation."

"How was that a fiasco?"

Cornelia stepped into her doorway, pulling bobby pins out of her hair, to see John peering out of his dressing room doorway, his cravat loose around his neck and his shirt mostly unbuttoned. "Well, first of all," she said, "Prudence said some very unkind things about Violet Humphries, and even had the nerve to insult Olive, in front of Hortense, no less." She yanked out several more bobby pins, pulling her hair. "And Percival bragged about every world power during the War had put bids in on his inventions." She went over to her dressing table and tossed the bobby pins into a pink-and-white lidded ceramic dish.

"I don't remember him talking about that this evening," remarked John.

Cornelia stepped back into her dressing room doorway. "No, that was at the charity dinner last month."

John peered out of his room, a pair of socks dangling from one hand. "Oh. Well, why are you fussing about that? It was over a month ago."

"You asked why it was a fiasco," Cornelia returned. "But thankfully, tonight was not." Hardly a fiasco, but also far from perfect. She began unbuttoning her dress, still stewing about Prudence. "However, Prudence said some things to Adelaide that worried me. She told Adelaide about your project, John. Why would she do such a thing? Does Percival know that his wife is going around blabbing about his secret projects?"

"Haven't the foggiest," said John. "That pineapple upside-down cake was delicious. Do you suppose there's any left over? Maybe Maggie could serve it with breakfast tomorrow."

Cornelia paused in the midst of pulling off her slip. She was never sure if John's refusal to engage in gossip or complaints was due to his impeccable upbringing or his constantly flitting mind.

She chuckled to herself and finished undressing. Either way, he was right. The dinner party had been a success, and grousing about Prudence and Percival was hardly the best way to spend the rest of the night. She peered out of her dressing room, but didn't see John. Then she heard water running in his bathroom, and the sound of him whistling "Jingle Bells" off-key. She smiled, and went into her own bathroom to wash her face.

The only thing that would have made the evening perfect, in Cornelia's opinion, was if her friend Charlotte de Fontaine had been there. Charlotte was her closest friend and a confidante of sorts, but unfortunately, according to the unwritten rules of high society, she was not the sort of person who should be invited to a dinner party of this stature. All of the women present this evening knew Charlotte to one degree or another, since they all had their hair done at Charlotte's salon. But despite Charlotte's reputation as the finest stylist and salon owner in the city, she wasn't a society heiress. Cornelia would just invite Charlotte over for a more informal dinner sometime soon, or perhaps for a Sunday luncheon when the salon was closed.

When Cornelia had finished washing up and changing into her gold silk nightgown and emerged into the bedroom, John was already in bed, propped up against his pillows with an issue of *The Journal of Physical Sciences and Mathematics* open in his lap.

"I think you're right about the 'y to the fourth power' in the fuel manifold equation," he said without looking up.

"Of course I'm right," Cornelia answered, laying her dressing gown at the foot of the big four-poster bed and stepping out of her slippers.

"I should get to work on fixing that equation first thing in the morning," John continued, scribbling at a page in the science journal with a pencil. "We need to begin construction next week on the—"

"Tomorrow is New Year's Day," Cornelia interrupted him as she climbed into bed.

John finally looked up from his reading and scribbling. "So it is. And I promised not to work on New Year's Day, didn't I?"

Cornelia merely smiled sweetly. She rarely wanted to discourage him from his work, regardless of the project, but a holiday seemed like a good excuse for a slight change of pace, like breakfast in bed or reading a novel together.

"Did I tell you how beautiful you looked this evening?"

Cornelia smiled again. "You did, but you may say it as many times as you like."

"You looked beautiful this evening. And you look beautiful right now." Shifting in bed to put his science journal on the bedside table, he then leaned over and placed a kiss on her forehead. Then he reached up to slide his fingers through her hair and kissed her firmly on the lips.

As she relaxed against him and returned the kiss, every thought of society gossips and mathematical equations melted from her mind. He smelled of fresh cotton and Ivory soap. She scooted closer to him on the bed and wrapped her arms around his shoulders.

Eventually they parted. "Happy new year, John," Cornelia murmured contentedly, nuzzling her face into his neck.

"Happy new year, my darling," he murmured back. "Oh, that reminds me! I have a gift for you."

He released her, grabbed a small brown box from the table, and turned back to her. "This arrived only two days ago, otherwise it would have been a Christmas gift. So it can be a New Year's gift instead."

The little brown box was about the right size to hold a necklace or bracelet, but Cornelia could never be sure when it came to gifts from John. Usually his gifts were traditionally romantic, like jewelry and furs. But then there were times like her last birthday, when he'd given her a fossilized mastodon bone and book about Victorian-era occult practices written in French. She treasured each and every gift, though, both the stylish and the obscure.

She lifted the lid. Inside on a little swatch of red velvet was a gold medallion in the shape of an ancient Egyptian *wadjet*, the Eye of Horus. About the size of a silver dollar, the medallion was solid gold except for the lapis lazuli embedded in the center of the eye. It hung from a long, thin gold chain.

"It's from the dig that we're sponsoring in the Valley of the Kings," John explained as Cornelia lifted it out of the box. "When I saw it on the manifest, I wrote a letter to the lead archaeologist and asked him to send it to me. It's supposedly a magical amulet."

Cornelia remembered seeing it on the report from the dig a couple of months ago, but had thought nothing of it. As no large statues or mummies had been excavated thus far at that dig, she saw no reason to communicate with the archaeological team. Leave it to John to be enraptured by one small amulet amongst the hundreds of artifacts.

"A magical amulet," she said, rubbing a finger across the cool smooth surface. As far as jewelry items went, it was beautiful and exotic, but she wasn't sure that it would really go with any of her outfits. "What is it supposed to do?"

"Well, according to the archaeologists, it's a talisman of protection. It protects the wearer against all manners of dangers and curses."

Cornelia raised her eyebrows at him and smiled. "And you think I need protecting?"

John's smile was almost a smirk. "Of course not, dear. You're more than capable of handling any danger or curse that might come your way." He placed a quick kiss on her forehead. "But it was such a unique item, and so beautifully engraved, I wanted you to have it."

Cornelia smoothed a finger over the medallion once more as she put in back in the box. She felt no telltale tingling warmth in her hands, as she often did when she handled a magical talisman. Magical or not, though, she appreciated John's thoughtful gesture.

"Thank you, darling. It's beautiful." She kissed his cheek, then turned to put the box on her bedside table. "I don't have a New Year's gift for you, though."

"That's all right. You're my gift, my favorite one, every day of the year." He pulled her against him in a tight embrace.

They settled down in bed, and Cornelia snuggled into him, resting her head on his chest. "I love you, John."

"I love you, Cornelia. Always."

Chapter 2

"And now before we conclude today's meeting," said Hortense Follensby from behind the podium, "Mrs. Jones will give us an update on the Girls' University Study Fund."

Cornelia rose from her seat at the table closest to the front of the room, giving Hortense a nod as she stepped up behind the podium. She scanned the room full of women gathered for the monthly Hollywood Hills Ladies' Club meeting. They met in the back room of the Orange Blossom Tea Room, and a few of the women were still sipping tea or nibbling on cookies left over from the refreshments that always opened every meeting.

"Thus far we have four applicants for the Girls' University Study grant," Cornelia began. "As always, the grant remains open for applicants until the end of January, at which time the girls must begin writing their essays for submission by March. We are also still gathering money for the fund."

The Girls' University Study Fund had been Cornelia's idea several years ago, when Hortense and Geraldine had announced that the ladies' club should become involved in another charity in addition to the local hospital and the War Widows Fund. The idea was to pay for an underprivileged girl from a Los Angeles high school to attend college. The idea had been met with a remarkable lack of enthusiasm at first, but

Prudence had jumped on board right away. Most of the society women didn't see the point of any female attending college, whether they could afford it or not, but eventually Hortense, the president of the club, had allowed Prudence and Cornelia to talk her into starting the fund.

"So many bright, eager young women dream of attending college and seeing the world," Cornelia continued in her best promotional tone, for the benefit of those who couldn't remember from meeting to meeting that the education of women was important to society. "But because of the unfortunate status of their parents—or perhaps even because some lost their father and breadwinner in the War—they cannot continue their learning past high school. Our Girls' University Study Fund allows one bright young woman to escape a future as a laundress or a factory worker and attend a college where she can study literature, science, or even medicine. The girls who receive grants from this fund are intelligent, hardworking, well-mannered, and disciplined. They are the future."

There was a smattering of genteel applause as Cornelia concluded her spiel with a gracious smile. She saw Prudence pulling her checkbook out of her purse with a flourish; several other ladies then followed suit, Adelaide among them.

Cornelia smiled again as she stepped out from behind the podium. "Thank you, ladies. The future university women of this great nation thank you."

Hortense took over behind the podium as Cornelia returned to her seat. She noted that several women who had never donated to the university fund before had their checkbooks out. She allowed herself a tiny smile as she settled back into her chair at the table with Violet Humphries and Geraldine Williamson. It was an achingly slow process, but little by little, Cornelia felt like she was chipping away at the old solid rock of higher education as a men-only club.

And as much as it rankled her to admit it, she had Prudence to thank for getting the idea off the ground.

Cornelia looked across the room to the table where Prudence sat with Adelaide and an elderly lady who looked like she was having difficulty keeping her head upright under the weight of the enormous diamond-encrusted earrings she was wearing. All three women were busy writing in their checkbooks. At the podium, Hortense gave a few more announcements and then concluded the meeting.

Cornelia quickly downed the last dregs of tea in her cup and rose from her seat the moment Hortense stepped away from the podium. She needed to talk to Prudence—alone. Ever since the New Year's Eve party last week Cornelia had been wondering and worrying about what Prudence had told Adelaide about their husbands' secret work—and why. She'd called Prudence at home several times to try to discuss the matter, but Prudence never seemed to be at home.

"Great speech about the Girls' University Fund, Cornelia," bubbled Adelaide as Cornelia approached the table. "I'm so glad that Hortense finally agreed to support that as one of our charities."

"Thank you," said Cornelia, and then turned to give Prudence a polite society smile. "It was a joint effort—I doubt I could have managed to convince Hortense without Prudence's support."

"Indeed," said Prudence, with an equally polite smile. She picked up her teacup. "Here's to the continuing education of young ladies everywhere."

"Hear, hear!" said Adelaide, tugging on her tan gloves.

"And on that note, I have something that I'd like to speak with you about, Prudence, if you don't mind," said Cornelia. "Please excuse us for a moment, would you, Adelaide?"

"Of course," said the younger woman. Their retreat was made all the easier by the elderly lady with the earrings touching Adelaide's arm and asking for assistance in standing up.

"What can I do for you, Cornelia?" Prudence asked, as Cornelia took her elbow and gently guided them over to an unoccupied corner of the room near a window. A horse and carriage rattled past outside on the street, and a motorcar rumbled by from the other direction.

"You can answer a question for me, Prudence," Cornelia said, lowering her voice. "Why did you tell Adelaide about John and Percival's project?"

Prudence dropped her polite society smile and narrowed her eyes in a glare. "And why *didn't* you tell her? You're so protective of the precocious little imp—I'm surprised you don't want her on our side."

That was certainly not the sort of answer she'd been expecting. Cornelia opened her mouth but found she couldn't think of anything to say—a rare enough occurrence by itself—and made all the more annoying that Prudence was the one who'd rendered her speechless.

"I am not protective of Adelaide," she finally managed, trying to figure out which part of Prudence's statement to address first. "I merely want to understand why you're sharing secret information with an outsider."

"An outsider?" Prudence said with harsh laugh. "Clearly you don't know her as well as you think you do. She's like you and me—she doesn't belong with these pompous society birds."

"I know that. I keep telling Adelaide that she could get accepted at any university in the country, whether they have a history of admitting women or not, if she would—"

"You're such a fool, Cornelia!" Prudence hissed. She cast a quick glance around the room, then lowered her voice. "You're a fool for not learning more about Adelaide. And you're a fool for thinking that Percival and John are the only ones who know about the project."

Cornelia took a second to glance around the room herself, to see if any of the other ladies were wondering about their private conversation. But no one seemed to be looking their way. Adelaide herself was engaged in a lively conversation with Violet over the tray of cucumber sandwiches. And Hortense, who liked to keep a close eye on everyone, was at that moment sitting at one of the tables, sorting through papers.

Of course John and Percival—and their respective wives—weren't the only ones who knew about the harmonic resonator matrix project. The United States military had commissioned the project; so there were the army officers at the lab who oversaw the work, and John and Percival had two government scientists working with them as laboratory assistants. But how would any of those people be involved with Adelaide?

Cornelia drew herself up and squared her shoulders, making the several inches she had over Prudence very apparent. Not that her height would intimidate the other woman, but still… "So who else knows about this secret military project? And what does this have to do with Adelaide? What are you not telling me, Prudence?"

"A great many things," Prudence replied archly. "A lady must have her secrets, after all. It's too bad, really, Cornelia. You and I could have been great friends."

With that, she left Cornelia standing by the window and rejoined the other women.

Cornelia almost shouted after her, but years of practiced genteel behavior at society gatherings kept her mouth shut and her feet rooted in place. She turned to frown out the window, crossing her arms tightly.

Prudence had left her with more questions, which apart from her belligerent attitude, was infuriating. Well, if Prudence wasn't going to be forthcoming with anything, then perhaps Adelaide would. The girl was curious, friendly, and liked to talk—so an invitation to a private tea at the Jones house would likely be productive.

Cornelia took a deep breath to clear the frown from her face. *All right, Prudence. You said I should get to know Adelaide better—well, I'll do just that. And together we'll figure out what the hell you're up to.*

Her polite society smile plastered back on her face, Cornelia turned from the window and glided back into the mingling crowd. Another twenty seconds of brooding alone at the window would likely bring Hortense down on her, and she certainly didn't need the president of the ladies' club asking her questions about anything.

"THANK YOU AGAIN, CORNELIA, for inviting me over for tea." Adelaide dusted her fingertips on the embroidered linen napkin in her lap.

"I'm happy that you could come," Cornelia replied. "I realized that you've been in Los Angeles for nearly a year now, but we hadn't really gotten to know each other outside of the regular society gatherings."

Cornelia had chosen the parlor for their tea, even though the sitting room was more expected for an afternoon tea for two. The parlor had a panoramic view of the back patio and gardens. Precious little was in bloom right now besides a few pastel clumps of nasturtiums, but the flagstone patio, bushes and fruit trees in the garden, and the horses grazing in the far distance made for a pleasant scene. Esther, the gray tabby cat who lived in the stables, had chosen a sunny spot on the marble railing at the edge of the patio for her afternoon nap. In the near distance a gangly Negro youth, Joey Rawlins, the gardener and stable boy, was trimming one of the dormant bushes.

"You chose such a charming spot to build your house," Adelaide remarked, picking up a ginger cookie and gazing out the glass French doors at the view.

"Have you thought about moving out of the Ambassador and finding a place outside the city?" asked Cornelia.

Adelaide had arrived in Los Angeles eight months ago, rented a room at the Ambassador Hotel, and declared that she had no desire to return to New York. Cornelia could understand that sentiment. She didn't dislike her native Chicago, but since she'd come to the west coast for university and then met John, she had been back to her childhood home only twice.

"Well, I do love the city, but there's something serene about having all this land to call your own." Adelaide finished off her cookie.

"It's easier to think when it's calm and quiet," said Cornelia. "That's why John and I chose this location up in the hills to build our house. Although other people are starting to get the same idea, it seems. The developers are selling plots of land all throughout this area."

"That's what those huge letters are up on the mountain, right?" asked Adelaide. "For the Hollywoodland neighborhood they're trying to build, right? At night you can see it from miles away, it's lit up so bright."

Cornelia nodded. "I wouldn't worry about this area becoming too developed, though. They're selling land to the movie stars and other wealthy people who, like myself and John, value their privacy and want a scenic retreat."

The horrendously tacky advertisement had been built last year. Thankfully it wasn't visible from their house, nor did their street connect with it. The garish sign was a popular destination for bored youngsters and adventurous tourists.

Adelaide looked back out the glass doors. "It's so beautiful and peaceful here, it's no wonder your husband can invent such brilliant things." She turned back to face Cornelia, and seemed to hold her breath for a moment. "If it's not too forward, Cornelia...could I ask to see some of your husband's inventions?"

It was indeed too forward, but Cornelia had been expecting their conversation to get to this point. This was, after all, her main intention for the invitation to tea. After Prudence's hinting that Adelaide was like they were, Cornelia assumed that she meant that Adelaide had knowledge of or skills in the magical arts. That still didn't explain why Prudence thought it acceptable to tell her about a classified military project, but... well, one thing at a time.

She waited a beat to give the impression that she was considering Adelaide's request.

"I suppose a small tour of a few of John's projects would be all right. I don't think he'd mind."

"Oh, how delightful!" Adelaide beamed. "Thank you so much—you're very kind."

Cornelia smiled and finished off the tea in her cup. She'd discussed Adelaide's visit last night with both John and Rawlins, and the three of them had tidied up the basement lab to make it safe and presentable. Cornelia couldn't very well invite Adelaide over with the intent to pry secrets out of her without offering up a few secrets of her own.

Cornelia set down her empty tea cup and pushed back her chair. "John's laboratory is in the basement, if you don't mind going through the servants' area to get there."

"Not at all," said Adelaide, also standing.

Cornelia led the way out of the sitting room and into the foyer, where Rawlins was waiting outside the door. "We've finished tea, Rawlins. I'm going to show Miss Snufflett-Frye the basement. She's very keen to learn more about Mr. Jones' work. We won't be long."

"Very good, Miz Jones," he said with a slight bow of his head. His impassive face told Cornelia that he was still not happy about the idea. Rawlins held an almost fatherly protective attitude towards John and his work, and the idea of a relative stranger being given a grand tour clearly rankled him. He'd protested against the idea last night, but like the proper butler that he was, he'd conceded to Cornelia and John's wishes and helped make the lab ready for show.

Cornelia cast a quick glance back down the hall as she opened the basement door. Rawlins had disappeared, probably clearing the tea things out of the parlor. She'd apologize to him later, after her idea of giving Adelaide a tour had produced results and confirmed her hunches. And if her hunches about Adelaide weren't true, she'd have to endure an "I told you so" lecture from Rawlins; and potential society gossip, if a shocked Adelaide went blabbing about all the weird items collected in the Jones' basement.

Well, it was too late to turn back now. She led the way down the narrow stone steps. Really, John's inventions filled the entire house, not just the basement. She could have taken Adelaide up to the roof turret to see the telescope and its enhanced lenses. Or to John's upstairs study to look at his typewriters that he'd modified to type out Greek letters and algebraic notations. Or out to the carriage house to see the hyper-fast, armed motorcycle that had been used as a prototype for messengers' bikes during the War.

But the basement lab was the most impressive. "Golly," Adelaide breathed as they descended the last few steps and emerged in the large open room.

Last night the three of them had removed the most sensitive projects—specifically the government project John was currently working on with Percival. They'd done some general tidying, to make the room look more like an eclectic collection than eccentric and messy. "This is John's lab, where he does his work when he's at home," said Cornelia. She made a sweeping gesture with her hand. "Please, look around."

Adelaide advanced through the room, wide-eyed, and Cornelia hid a smile. Adelaide was not shy about her awe, nor was she shy about her curiosity. She walked slowly between two long tables, pausing to look at items on each table in turn: a microscope; several wireless radios in different stages of construction; an antique copy of *Gray's Anatomy*; a Dictaphone; a tray filled with various specimens of dead moths and locusts; a topographical map of the state of California; a collection of sextants, astrolabes, and an almucantar staff.

"Your husband has so many varied interests," Adelaide remarked, picking up a chunk of turquoise ore the size of her hand. She hadn't asked what any of the items were, so far, confirming Cornelia's hunch that the girl had done some sort of scientific studying on her own, even if she hadn't been to college.

"That he does," Cornelia said with a smile. She walked along the other side of one of the tables so that she could keep up with Adelaide. She ran her hand across a large abacus, letting her fingers linger over the smooth wooden counting beads. "He doesn't use everything here on a daily basis, but he's spent years collecting and building all sorts of things, so this is where it's all kept."

Adelaide picked up an aviator's cap, with large protruding lenses where the goggles would normally be. "Opera glasses on a pilot's helmet?" she asked.

"Well, field glasses, but yes, the same concept. For the co-pilot or gunner, actually; the pilot needs to be able to focus on his plane's flight instruments as well as the sky around him."

"How fascinating. Oh, look, an automaton!" Adelaide set down the jar of potash crystals that she'd just picked up, and hurried over to the far side of the room.

Small windows dotted that wall, narrow spaces up by the ceiling to let a little daylight into the basement. A shaft of sunlight fell on a metal mannequin seated in a chair. The automaton was about three feet tall if it were standing, but was just the framework of a humanoid shape; the complex system of gears that powered it from within were clearly visible through the frame of its torso.

"I saw automatons on stage when I was a child, at circus shows and such," said Adelaide, bending over to peer at it. She traced a finger over the set of typewriter number keys embedded into the center of its chest. "Some danced, some juggled or did other tricks. What does this one do?"

"This one was designed to write and draw," said Cornelia. Which was all she knew about the thing. The automaton was one of John's ongoing projects that he tinkered with periodically when he wasn't working on something else. She had seen the machine with a pencil in its jointed metal fingers, sketching odd designs on paper while John tweaked wires and gears inside it. She wasn't sure what it was ultimately supposed to write or draw—if John himself had even decided yet.

Adelaide pointed to a heavy wooden door not far from where the automaton sat. "What's in there, if you don't mind my asking?"

"Just storage," said Cornelia. Which was true enough. There was another door on the opposite side of the room, which was also closed and locked. She and John had fully agreed with Rawlins that Adelaide did not need to see the large items storage room, the dangerous magical talismans storage room, or the room where John was working on yet another ongoing—and large-scale—project.

"John does most of his work in this room," Cornelia continued, before Adelaide could ask about what was being stored. "And his research, too." She pointed to the tall bookshelves against the wall to their right. There was another room that was the actual basement library, but she'd shut the door to that room, as well. There were plenty of books out here for Adelaide to look at.

Adelaide headed for the bookshelves, pausing briefly to examine the globe on a stand and the collection of star charts lying on a small table beside it. Cornelia came and stood near Adelaide, quietly watching the younger woman as she scanned the shelves. Books on mathematics, physics, chemistry, natural history, dictionaries, books in Latin and French and Greek. All perfectly acceptable to be in a scientist's laboratory.

Then there were the books on mythology, ancient pagan religions, medieval herbals, occult practices, and divination. Cornelia watched closely as Adelaide's scanning slowed and she cocked her head subtly as if reading each and every book's title in detail.

Finally she paused and turned to face Cornelia, but then cast a glance down at the nearest table. Of all the tables in the room, Cornelia had worked the most on this one to arrange it purposefully, rather than just tidying up general disorder. A crystal ball—the largest one they owned, nearly the size of a volleyball—sat on a black onyx stand. A set of hand-painted tarot cards lay face-up on a blue velvet cloth, next to a small marble statuette of the ancient Egyptian god Anubis. Sprigs of dried lavender and mugwort lay beside a worn copy of charms and spells written in Old English and Latin. An ancient stone tablet carved with Norse runes sat nearby.

Adelaide looked back up at Cornelia, meeting her eyes. Adelaide's blue eyes seemed to almost glow in the shafts of daylight from the narrow windows. Cornelia held her breath.

"I knew it," Adelaide said at last, her face breaking into a grin. "I thought there might be more to you than just being a scientist's wife. I'd hoped you were a witch."

Cornelia disliked the term "witch"—it evoked images of malicious hags in stories like *Snow White* or *The Wonderful Wizard of Oz*. But she smiled at Adelaide, not bothering to quibble about the word. "Science and magic are really two sides of the same coin. Both come from the natural world. A well-cast spell can be just as powerful as electricity—or just as dangerous, if you handle it wrong." As she well knew from experience. But now was not the time to alarm Adelaide with past tales of spells and science experiments gone awry.

Cornelia picked up the Old English book of charms. "A good scientist, or a good magical practitioner, studies, learns, and practices the ways of the natural world and how to use such elements for the betterment of their own lives or others. Some believe that science has taken the place of magic in our world, that modern man is now too smart to believe that the old ways still have power. But just as electricity existed before we learned how to harness it, magic still exists even if we no longer utilize it. True progress is to embrace both science and magic."

She paused, realizing that she was gripping the old charms book with enough force to bend the frail cover. She took a deep breath and relaxed her hold on the book. It had been quite a while since she'd given such an impassioned speech about the value of both science and magic. Well, that little spiel ought to impress Adelaide one way or another.

Adelaide clasped her hands and beamed up at Cornelia. "Oh, that's so true! Or, at least, I'd always thought it was true myself, or wanted it to be true. I've always known that the supernatural still has a place in the modern world."

Cornelia set the book back on the table. "I'm glad you feel that way. And I'm glad that we have that in common, now." She paused, and decided that it was now time to just ask Adelaide what she wanted to know. "Prudence knows, doesn't she? That you're a magical practitioner."

"Oh, I'm not a practitioner—I've never actually done a spell or enchantment. I've just read books and..." Adelaide trailed off, then nodded. "She knows that I've an interest in both science and magic. And I know that she's a witch, too."

As Cornelia had begun to suspect, that's what Prudence had meant at the New Year's Eve party when she'd said that Adelaide was "like us."

"I thought as much," she said aloud. "Adelaide, the Davenports may be like John and myself in that they believe in the power of both science and magic, but...I would ask you to use caution if Prudence offers to teach you anything. She's a very intelligent and skilled woman, but an important element of practicing magic is one's motive. Selfish or malicious intent can get you into a world of trouble."

"You think Prudence has malicious intent?" Adelaide's eyes widened. "I know she's snobbish, and I know you two don't really get along, but—"

Cornelia held up a hand. "Perhaps 'malicious' was too strong a word." Although it wasn't. "What I meant was that if you want to learn more about magic, just use wisdom in who you take advice from."

"Will you teach me?"

That was not where Cornelia had meant for this conversation to go. Everything she knew—for both magic and science—was self-taught or she'd learned from being married to John. She was hardly mentor-quality for teaching most anything.

"Well...ah, perhaps I could give you some pointers or advice, on an occasional basis," she managed. "But let's not worry about that right now. I do have another question for you, though, this one not about magic. What exactly has Prudence told you about the project that her husband and my husband are working on?"

"She said it's called a Magnetic Resonator Engine. She said it's a flying engine, but not for a regular airplane."

"Well, that's not quite accurate." Cornelia was grateful that Prudence had apparently skimped on the actual specifics of the device, although she'd probably done so in order to pique the girl's curiosity.

Cornelia was confident at this point that Adelaide would neither judge her nor gossip about John's experiments or her own magical knowledge. However, she had no business knowing anything about the secret gravity engine project for the government. Unfortunately, with her interest aroused and Prudence trying to exert some sort of influence over the girl, sooner or later Adelaide was bound to learn more about it. Cornelia would rather Adelaide learn the truth now, rather than whatever Prudence might tell her later.

"The engine uses controlled magnetic harmonic resonance to create a gravity matrix field," said Cornelia. "Or it will, once it's finished."

Adelaide blinked at her.

"What that means is that it uses a combination of magnetism and sound waves to create a pocket of space around objects that will disrupt the connection between the relative density of the object and the density of the earth."

Adelaide still looked confused.

Cornelia tried again. "It's an anti-gravity engine. When finished, it will enable objects to fly through the air at unprecedented speeds, regardless of the object's size, weight, or the principles of friction and lift. It could change modern aeronautics as we know it."

"Golly," breathed Adelaide. "Prudence never told me all that."

"Well, now you know. The idea was first developed during the War, but the War ended before anything was even begun. A few months ago the government scientists who'd developed the concept recruited John and Percival Davenport as the lead scientists to make the idea into a reality."

"Quite the honor," said Adelaide.

"Yes, indeed," Cornelia agreed. "But that's why I told you before that their project is classified. It's not something that the general public—or even the general scientific community—should know about. At least not until it's finished and working properly. When the president of the United States of America asks you to keep a secret, you keep it."

The president himself had not actually said such a thing to them personally, but both men had been required to sign papers swearing them to silence. The papers had not specifically forbidden them from telling their wives, John had said—although that was probably implied. Most scientists didn't tell their wives about their work, even if they wanted to, since most wives wouldn't understand or care.

But now, not only did both wives know everything, but now so did Adelaide. Cornelia's implication about the president personally requesting silence, though, seemed to do the trick for Adelaide. She pursed her pink lips together and nodded furiously.

"I won't tell a soul, Cornelia. I won't even tell Prudence that you told me anything."

Good girl. "I know you won't, Adelaide," she said with a smile. "Now, you've seen John's lab, and it's getting late. We'd best get back upstairs before Rawlins comes down after us."

Adelaide's tight face relaxed as she followed Cornelia between the rows of tables back towards the stairs. "Thank you, Cornelia. For showing me your husband's lab, and for telling me...the secret. And for telling me about magic. Now I know who I can come to if I have a question about anything."

Cornelia gave her another smile as they started up the stairs, but she quivered inside. She'd certainly rather have Adelaide coming to her with questions than going to Prudence. But if Adelaide wanted a bona fide teacher? Whatever it might take to be a teacher of magical disciplines, Cornelia wasn't sure she had it.

"WE'LL TAKE OUR COFFEE in the basement, please, Rawlins," said John.

They'd finished dinner and dessert, and John pushed his chair back from the table as Rawlins stepped forward to begin clearing away the dishes.

"Certainly, Mr. Jones," he said, setting the empty dessert plates on a silver tray. "I'll be right down with it."

Cornelia got up from her seat and followed John down the hall towards the basement stairs. "Well, it sounds like your tea with Miss Adelaide was a success," he said, holding the basement door open for her. Over dinner she'd told him everything about Adelaide's visit and their conversation in the basement. Well, almost everything.

"It was," she said as they descended the steps into the wide room. "And see? Nothing out of place. She was inquisitive, but polite. She didn't try to operate anything, and she didn't press about the closed doors."

"Splendid. I should like to get to know her better." John meandered through the room, his eyes roving over the tables. He paused and reached down to pick up a black fountain pen from one of the tables. "Was this here when we were arranging things last night?"

"It was. It seemed an appropriate prop to leave on an inventor's work table. Why, have you been missing it?" Probably. John owned more pens, pencils, and chalk than an entire university—and still complained frequently that he couldn't find a writing implement.

"No, no," he said absently, setting it back on the table. "It's the blue one I'm missing—the one with the gold filigree."

"The one with the dull nib that you refuse to replace?" Cornelia asked. "I last saw it on your dressing table in the bedroom."

"Ah! I remember now. What would I do without you, darling?" He turned and gave her a peck on the cheek. "Now, what were we talking about?"

"Adelaide's visit for tea." Cornelia smiled as she watched him pick up the pen again and put it in his breast pocket.

"Ah, yes. She's alone here, is that right? No family?"

"That's right. Her family is back east in New York. She wanted to travel, but she says that she really likes it here."

"Then we must encourage her to stay here," said John, heading for the back of the room and the locked door that led to the rest of the basement.

Cornelia paused as he pulled the key out of his pocket and unlocked the big wooden door. "What makes you say that?" she asked.

"Well, she seems clever. More than clever, from what you've said, after your tea today. It would be a shame for her to get bored with Los Angeles and run off to London or somesuch to join the crowd of Bright Young Things and lose herself to pointless revelries."

"You're quite right." Cornelia hadn't really imagined Adelaide doing such a thing, but after all, she was young and full of adventurous ideals, and seemed disinclined to attend a university. But she was interested in learning magic.

"And on that subject," Cornelia said slowly, stepping down the two stairs and following John as he headed down the windowless corridor to the back part of the basement. The floor was lower in this section of the basement to create a higher ceiling for accommodating larger equipment and constructs. John stopped a moment to open the door and peer into the large equipment storage room. "Nothing's out of place in here," Cornelia said. "We didn't leave the main room."

"I know," said John, shutting the door. "What were you about to say?"

"Well, now that I've confirmed my suspicion that Adelaide knows the ways of magic," she began carefully. "And she's confirmed her suspicion that I do, as well..." She trailed off again as they stopped in front of another closed door.

John paused with his hand on the knob. "Yes?" he prompted.

Why was she so reluctant to tell him her fears? And why, for that matter, was she so fearful of the idea of teaching Adelaide? She took a deep breath. "Well, Adelaide asked me to teach her. About magic."

John smiled, his teeth a white flash in the dim corridor lighting. "That's wonderful. What a splendid idea! And that's a good way to be sure to keep her around—and away from Prudence, too."

"Yes, you're right. I'd thought of all of that..."

John opened the door and went into the small room, punching on the light as he did. Cornelia stepped in after him. She didn't bother to reiterate that she hadn't let Adelaide into this room. He knew that; he just liked to make the rounds of his domain sometimes, often after they'd had guests over or he'd had a stressful day. It was his way of reminding himself of the order of his world.

This was a small room, made all the smaller by the enormous cylindrical tank in the center. The tank, clear glass panes supported by a metal framework, sat on a dais about two feet in the air. The tank itself was seven feet tall, leaving just enough clearance between the top of it and the ceiling for the lid that John was building. The walls of the room were covered in instrument panels, more complex than an airplane's dashboard.

This project, an ongoing experiment that he'd been working on for a few years now, John had dubbed an "artificial womb." The purpose was to create a clean, safe, and nurturing environment, much like the safety of a womb, to protect a body that had been severely injured or had contracted an incurable disease. John believed that with the right mixture of chemicals, tubes for breathing and electrical wires to stimulate the brain, and fluid in the tank for low-pressure support of the body, a sick or injured person could be preserved in a sort of stasis until a cure could be found.

John walked through the room, stepping over cables that lay across the floor, pausing a moment to peer inside an open panel and poke at the tangle of wires inside. Cornelia knew that he wasn't likely to actually work on this project tonight—he didn't have any tools with him, and half of the blueprints were in his study upstairs. She stood patiently by the door, since it was rather cramped in the room, and waited for him to finish his perusing.

After a few minutes he finished his circuit of the room, and they stepped back out into the hallway as he shut the door. Cornelia stayed silent as they walked back down the hall, and up the two little steps into the main lab room. Rawlins had brought the coffee down—a silver tray with two cups sat on the corner of the table nearest the stairs.

"Is something wrong, darling?" John asked, glancing at her as they walked between the tables back towards the stairs. "You look anxious."

"I'm not anxious. I'm just…" She stopped walking. *Nervous, not anxious,* she thought to herself. But was she more nervous about being a magical tutor or confessing her fears to John?

John stopped, too, and turned to face her. "Cornelia?"

Now *he* looked anxious, his narrow eyebrows creased together and his blue eyes intense and bright. "What's wrong?"

She smiled at his concern, relaxing a little, and put a hand on his chest. "I'm being silly, I suppose. When Adelaide asked me to teach her about magic, I…I don't know that I could. At least, not very well."

John laid his hand over hers and clutched her hand tighter against his chest. "Why not? I think you teaching her the ways of mysticism is a wonderful idea."

"I'm not a teacher, John. I have no idea how to instruct someone—especially a beginner. And I'm practically a beginner myself! Just because I've read a lot of books doesn't mean I have any practical knowledge or application—"

"Oh, hogwash," John interrupted. "If you've read more than she has, and done more than she has, then you know more than she does—and you can teach it. You're not instructing a university course in the art of practical magic—just teaching a curious young girl about Gaelic pronunciations and which herbs to avoid mixing with which oils."

Cornelia gave a little laugh in spite of herself, and John laughed, too. He was of course referring to the time that she had nearly burned the house down with an incorrect attempt at brewing an herbal potion. It had happened long ago enough that they could laugh at it now, but what if she made a similar mistake while trying to instruct Adelaide?

"But John, what if—"

He interrupted her again, this time with a kiss. She didn't try to fight it, and let him hold her; his lips were soft and gentle, and his arm strong and supportive as he slid it around her waist.

He released her slowly. "You'll do fine, darling," he murmured.

"But I don't know that I can truly be responsible for someone else, not in a mentorship sort of way. What if I make a mistake?"

"Then you'll correct your mistake, and move on. Like with anything. No scientific undertaking goes right on the first try, and magic is the same way. And if something gets set alight, then you know where the sand buckets are, just like last time." He grinned.

She had to smile. "But what do I teach her? And how?"

"Just answer her questions, to the best of your ability. You said the girl's curious—now that she knows you're a magic practitioner, she's bound to have at you with questions any

45

chance she gets. Give her some reading material. We have a huge library—find the best books to give her a general understanding of what she needs to know."

He was right, of course. She had gotten herself overly worked up over nothing. He could always calm her down and bring her mind back to center with just a few words. She slid her arms around his neck and leaned her head against his shoulder. "Oh, John, what would I do without you?"

He tightened both arms around her and kissed her temple. "I love you, my darling."

"I love you, John." She hugged him tighter. "More than anything."

EYES CLOSED, CORNELIA tilted her head back and enjoyed the feel of warm water and strong fingers running through her hair. Charlotte de Fontaine, the owner and lead stylist at Salon de Fontaine, stood on the other side of the sink, expertly rinsing the shampoo out of Cornelia's hair.

Cornelia had found Charlotte's salon shortly after moving to Los Angeles years ago, and had never had her hair or nails done anywhere else since. Anybody who was anybody came to the Salon de Fontaine—politician's wives, movie stars, and the Los Angeles societal elite all appreciated Charlotte's class and skill. Charlotte staffed her salon with only the most talented women, most of whom she trained herself. A Cajun born in the Louisiana Bayou, Charlotte had lived with relatives in France since her teenage years and had learned the art of cosmology from skilled stylists in Paris.

Charlotte hand-crafted the finest shampoos and skin creams, which she easily could have sold to all the best department stores across the country—but she kept her creations in her salon, exclusively for her personal clients. She was a brilliant chemist, and more than a few times Cornelia had sought her advice for one of John's projects, if it involved chemistry more complex than what either of them normally worked with. Cornelia also sought Charlotte's help with magic potions—especially after the time she'd nearly burned the house down with her own potion-brewing.

"All finished!" Charlotte chirped from behind Cornelia, turning off the water and wrapping a towel around Cornelia's head.

Cornelia sat up, securing the towel around her head, and got up to follow Charlotte to a different chair to have her hair dried and styled.

"So, Miss Adelaide, she's interested in learning the fine art of magic from you, *oui?*" said Charlotte, pulling a comb through Cornelia's wet hair.

The salon was empty of other patrons at the moment—a rare occasion—and Cornelia had told Charlotte all about Adelaide's visit the day before. "Yes, apparently so," she said. "So I may be calling on you a bit more often if Adelaide wants to know about brewing any concoction more complex than chamomile tea."

Charlotte gave a tittering laugh, her blond curls bouncing. Her hair was platinum blond and styled in a curly bob like Clara Bow's. Between her hair style and her petite, delicate build, she came across as a good ten or fifteen years younger than she actually was.

"I'm happy to help in whatever way I can, darling," said Charlotte. "And as we talk about helping, are you yet convinced to try a little something new this time? May I help you see how you would look with a bob? A straight cut, lying here at the chin." Charlotte held her ivory comb against the bottom of Cornelia's jaw.

Cornelia met Charlotte's gaze in the gold-rimmed mirror, and smiled at the other woman's impish grin. "Not this time, Charlotte," she said with a little chuckle. Cornelia still kept her auburn hair long, though not nearly as long or elaborately coiffed as had been the fashion a decade ago. Her hair reached her shoulder blades, which was enough for a small bun and finger waves; or for a simple braid at home in the evenings.

"Ah, well," said Charlotte with a melodramatic sigh. "There is always next time, yes?"

"Perhaps," Cornelia smiled. They had this same exchange nearly every week.

The etched glass door of the salon opened, and a young woman with a boyish bob, not unlike the style that Charlotte wanted to give Cornelia, walked in.

"Welcome, Mademoiselle Moore!" Charlotte sang out. "I shall be with you in a moment!"

"Please, there's no hurry, Charlotte," the woman replied. "I'm quite early for my appointment—I can wait."

Judging by the woman's appearance, and Charlotte's address, Cornelia assumed that she was Colleen Moore, the actress. One of the salon girls scurried forward from the back room to take Miss Moore's coat and hat, and offered to make her some tea.

Miss Moore seated herself in one of the pink-upholstered Queen Anne's chairs that were gathered in a corner near a large window hung with voluminous lace curtains. The entire salon exuded an air of French glamour and florid art nouveau, without feeling old-fashioned. Charlotte's unique style touched everything, from the Persian rugs on the polished marble floor, to the cut-glass bottles and decanters of hair ointments on the shelves, to the chandeliers made of rose-colored crystal and elaborate curls of brass. Cornelia enjoyed Charlotte's carefree taste in decorating, even though she would never have her own house done in such a flamboyant style.

Charlotte prattled about the weather and the latest issue of *Vogue* as she toweled, combed, and styled Cornelia's hair. They didn't discuss Adelaide or anything having to do with magic now that there was another person in the salon. While Charlotte was well-known among her clients for offering her unique herbal tonics of various sorts, she kept the actual witchcraft aspect of her work close to the chest.

"A wonderful job, as always, Charlotte," Cornelia said as Charlotte pulled the towel from her shoulders and turned her back to face the mirror. Silky perfect waves, tidier than she ever managed by herself or even with the maid's help, framed her face, the waves held in place by a few of Charlotte's trademark rhinestone crystal bobby pins.

"*Magnifique,*" said Charlotte with a wave of her comb.

The bell over the front door tinkled again as it opened, and a policeman entered. Cornelia, Charlotte, and Miss Moore all turned to look at him—a police officer was an unusual sight in this part of town, especially inside a women's salon.

Charlotte stepped forward, comb still in hand. "May I help you, *monsieur?*"

"Good afternoon, ladies," he said. "I'm looking for a Mrs. John Jones."

Cornelia rose out of the salon chair, an odd discomfort fluttering in the pit of her stomach. "I am Mrs. Jones."

The officer pulled off his hat and glanced at the other two women. "Could I speak privately with you, ma'am?"

Charlotte waved them towards the back corner of the salon, and went over to speak with Miss Moore. Cornelia followed the officer over to the corner framed by tall glass shelves full of bottled ointments and tonics.

"I'm Officer Andrews with the Los Angeles Police Department," the man said. "I called at your house, and your butler said that you were at the Salon de Fontaine. I'm afraid I have some bad news."

"What's happened?" Cornelia managed to ask, her throat feeling suddenly tight and dry.

"There was an accident at the Santa Monica Research Facility," Officer Andrews said. "Your husband has been badly injured, and has been taken to the Sisters of Mercy Hospital."

Her heart shuddered, and she laid a hand on the glass-topped telephone table that stood next to one of the shelves.

"I'm very sorry to have to tell you the news, ma'am. I'd be happy to escort you over to the hospital immediately. The doctors aren't sure that he's going to make it."

Chapter 3

The waiting room at the Sisters of Mercy Hospital was quiet, the only sounds the rhythmic ticking of the clock on the wall and the uneven clacking of the receptionist hitting the keys of her typewriter. Cornelia sat on the edge of a hard chair, her purse in her lap and her black-gloved hands folded tightly on top. She'd been here nearly thirty minutes now. When she'd arrived, the receptionist informed her that the surgeon was working on both men and would be finished soon. *Soon* couldn't come soon enough.

Both men. She assumed that meant Percival had been injured, as well. Questions swirled in her mind about what could have happened and what condition John was in. But the police officer who'd taken her to the hospital had no details, and neither did the girl behind the typewriter.

John had been injured a few times over the years while conducting experiments or building inventions. And then of course there was the time that Cornelia had nearly blown up the house with her miscalculated potion-brewing. But John had never been hurt so badly that he'd needed to go to the hospital. This couldn't be happening.

Cornelia finally stood up and began pacing. The polished wooden floor creaked beneath her shoes, adding to the discordant noise of the ticking clock and the typewriter keys.

A moment later the outside door opened and Prudence rushed in.

"Prudence." Cornelia halted her pacing as the other woman hurried over.

"Cornelia. What's happened?" Prudence's narrow face was pinched even thinner with worry. "The police said there was an accident at the lab."

"That's as much as I know, too," said Cornelia. She waved a hand at the typist. "She said that the surgeon was working on both of them."

"Surgeon?" murmured Prudence. "God, what happened?"

Cornelia twisted her purse in her hands. "I wish I knew." She felt a pang of sympathy for Prudence. The other woman looked stricken and deflated, all of her normal cockiness gone. No matter how asinine she could be, she didn't deserve to be standing in a hospital in fear, waiting to hear about her husband.

Neither of them deserved it. Cornelia started towards the receptionist, even though she knew that the poor girl had no new information. At that moment, a wooden door across the room opened and a thin middle-aged man in a white doctor's coat stepped out.

"Mrs. Davenport? Mrs. Jones?"

"Yes?" said Cornelia, stepping forward. Prudence came up beside her.

"I'm Dr. Landers. I've finished the surgeries. Both men suffered burns, abrasions, and some broken bones. Mr. Jones was the more severely injured of the two—he suffered numerous internal injuries, and a concussion, as well. Mr. Davenport should make a full recovery, though he should remain bedridden for several weeks while his broken ribs mend. As for Mr. Jones, he's stable for now, but not out of the woods yet."

Cornelia opened her mouth, but Prudence asked the question first. "Can we see them?"

The doctor nodded. "Yes, but just for a moment. Both are heavily sedated right now." He turned and opened the door he'd just come through, motioning for the women to go through.

They stepped through into a long corridor, then followed the doctor past closed doors. "Doctor, do you know what happened?" Cornelia asked in a hushed tone.

"Some sort of explosion," he said, glancing back at her.

Cornelia looked at Prudence, her own concern and puzzlement mirrored in the other woman's face. An explosion? There were so many parts to their project—the explosion could have been anything from an electrical generator to the gravity matrix engine itself. Her chest felt tight.

Cornelia halted as Dr. Landers opened the door to the men's hospital room. Two beds were at the far end of the room, one on either side of the single window. Percival lay in one bed, his face pale and a bandaged hand lying outside the coverlet. Which meant John was in the other bed...

Prudence hurried to Percival's side, while Cornelia slowly approached the other bed. John's head and face were fully wrapped in bandages, and he had a rubber mask over his nose and mouth, with a tube leading to a bulky breathing machine next to the bed.

"There was some bleeding in his lungs," said the doctor quietly. "He's on the respirator for now just to make it easier for him to breathe. He received a burn to the right side of his face, although not a severe one. It should heal with minimal to no scarring."

Cornelia stopped beside the bed. Her legs trembled and she wished there was a chair she could sit down in. She wanted to touch him, but his coverlet was pulled up to his chin, and not even his hair was visible through the bandages around his head.

"John, what happened?" She barely heard her own voice over the whirring of the respirator. Had he known what was happening as the accident occurred, or did he never know what had hit him?

The doctor was speaking again. "I'm afraid I have to ask you both to leave now, Mrs. Jones, Mrs. Davenport. The men have just come out of surgery and their conditions need to be monitored closely."

Cornelia cast a lingering glance back over her shoulder as she followed Prudence and the doctor out of the room. *You'll be all right, John,* she thought, clenching her jaw. *You have to be.*

"Do you know when they might be awake?" Prudence asked as they went back down the hall to the waiting room.

"I really can't say just yet. They both are on heavy painkillers right now, which will keep them asleep for many hours. You're welcome to come back tomorrow during the hospital's open hours. The secretary on duty will be able to reach me, and I can tell you if either is awake yet."

"Thank you, doctor," said Prudence, pulling a handkerchief out of her purse.

Cornelia felt no sting of tears, not yet. Right now her mind still whirled with shock and questions. She would contact the federal officer in charge of the laboratory facility just as soon as she got home, she decided. She had to find out what had happened at the lab.

CORNELIA PLACED THE phone receiver back in its cradle and let out a sigh. After nearly an hour of telephone calls, she'd finally reached someone who had both the authorization and the willingness to allow her access to the Santa Monica Research Facility. Since no one would tell her anything, she'd demanded to see the lab for herself—which had not been a popular idea with the police officer or the first three government officials she'd spoken to.

She'd also inquired as to why John hadn't been taken to a military hospital—not that she doubted the abilities of the doctors at Sisters of Mercy, but she figured that the military would want to look after their own. That question had been easily answered, though—John was a civilian. Never mind that he was injured while working on a military project...

Cornelia leaned back in the heavy wooden chair and swiveled away from the cluttered desk to stare idly out the front window of the house. She'd chosen to use the telephone in John's upstairs study instead of the one in the main hall downstairs. She'd rightly judged that this telephone battle wouldn't be a short one, and she didn't want to be standing in the front hall the entire time. Although at this point her neck ached and her arm was tired from holding the receiver. But those pains were minor compared to the strangling tightness of worry in her chest.

She heard a tap at the door, and swiveled the chair around to see Rawlins in the doorway.

"Any success, Miz Jones?" he asked.

"Yes, finally." She rubbed a hand wearily across her face. "No one seems to know anything, and no one wanted me to go and find out anything, either—but I did at long last reach a major who granted me permission to view the lab. The police and their own workers are still investigating the scene, he said, but he grudgingly said I could come by tomorrow morning at ten."

"That's good news," said Rawlins. "I'll tell Ronald to have the car ready."

"Thank you, Rawlins." She closed her eyes and slumped in the chair. If the government investigators did figure out exactly what had happened, would they share it with her? She wasn't technically supposed to know anything about the project. And would there be anything to see after their investigation and clean-up today? What was she hoping to find? And if she did learn anything, how could that help to aid John's recovery?

"Miz Jones?" Rawlins' voice sounded closer, and she lifted her head to see him standing by the corner of the desk. "Dinner is ready, ma'am. Would you like to eat now, or shall I have Maggie keep it warm for later?"

"Dinnertime already?" Cornelia looked over at the bookshelf. The clock that normally sat on the top shelf was gone. "What happened to the clock?"

"Mr. Jones took it down to the basement this morning before he left," said Rawlins. "He said he wanted to fix the chime."

Just last night John had complained—as he did periodically—that he didn't like the sound of the chime on that particular clock. Cornelia had told him absently—as she had several times before—to take it downstairs to his lab so he'd remember to work on it. He'd actually listened to her this time. And now he couldn't work on it because he was unconscious in a hospital room.

The tightness in her chest spasmed and suddenly tears blurred her eyes. She shouldn't cry in front of Rawlins, but she couldn't stop. She turned away from him and buried her face in her hands.

His warm hand pressed gently against her shoulder. Breaking down in front of a servant was most improper, but now it didn't matter. And Rawlins was more than a just a servant, especially to John.

She turned back around in the chair and grabbed Rawlins around the torso, burying her face in his chest. Sobs rattled through her, uncontrollable, as Rawlins' hands held her shoulders in a gentle embrace.

After a few moments she finally wrestled enough control of her crying to lift her head and release Rawlins. He produced a handkerchief, which she gratefully accepted and mopped at her face.

"I'm sorry about that, Rawlins," she choked out.

"Don't be, Miz Jones." His voice was soft. She looked up at him and saw tears glistening in his dark eyes. He touched her shoulder again. "It's been a long day. Should I have Maggie fix you a tray so you can eat in your room?"

Cornelia managed a weak smile. "Yes, thank you. You're so good to me, Rawlins."

He smiled and offered his arm to help her up from the chair. She clutched his arm and let him escort her down the hall to the bedroom, appreciating his comforting presence.

"I'll bring up your dinner in just a few minutes, ma'am," he said, opening the bedroom door for her.

"Thank you." She gave him another little smile, then noticed the damp smudge on his white shirt front that she'd made with her crying. "I'm sorry about your shirt."

He glanced down and gave a small chuckle. "Don't worry about it, ma'am. You get some sleep tonight, and tomorrow you can find out everything that happened. And Mr. Jones will be on the mend, too."

She could only nod to that. She gave his arm a grateful squeeze before releasing him and going into the bedroom. *Tomorrow I'll find out what happened*, she thought as she shut the door behind her. *And John will be on the road to recovery.* She prayed that Rawlins was right.

CORNELIA LOOKED OUT the window of the Rolls-Royce as her driver, Ronald, pulled the car up to the unmarked door.

The gray metal door matched the gray metal bunker that was built into the mountainside. John had described the Santa Monica Research Facility to her before, but of course she'd never been allowed to see it.

A grim-faced, broad-shouldered man in military dress stood outside the windowless door. The instant Ronald brought the car to a halt, the man stepped forward and opened the back door.

"Mrs. Jones," he said, not offering his hand to help her out. "I'm Major Brandt."

"Good morning, Major Brandt," she said, tightening her fur coat around her as she climbed out of the car. A thin layer of clouds covered the sun, giving the cool January breeze an extra nip.

He opened the metal door, and wordlessly led the way down a narrow hallway. They passed a few doors, all closed, all dull gray, all windowless and unmarked. How did John manage to work in such a cheerless place?

Major Brandt finally stopped in front of a door that looked identical to all the others, and pushed it open. "This is where the accident occurred, ma'am," he announced flatly.

This room felt much less claustrophobic than the corridor, with its wide floorspace and high ceiling. Three long work tables, not unlike the arrangement in the basement lab at home, sat together at one end of the room, covered in papers, hand tools, and bits and pieces of equipment. A chalkboard, freshly washed and blank, hung on one wall.

A rope ran from wall to wall down the center of the large room, dividing the work tables from the charred, smoke-blackened other half of the room. Cornelia walked over and stopped at the edge of the rope. The air smelled like a mixture of greasy smoke and antiseptic soap.

"What happened?" she asked, scanning the empty charred area. Whatever had been here—whatever had exploded—had since been removed. The only evidence that anything had occupied the space—beside the smoke damage on the walls, of course—were a few scattered shards of broken glass, and the drag marks across the metal floor where something large and heavy had been hauled away.

"There was an accident," Major Brandt replied.

Cornelia did her best not to give him a withering glare. "I'm aware of that. But what was the nature of the accident? It looks like an explosion. But what exploded? What was the cause? Who else was working here at the time besides Dr. Jones and Dr. Davenport?"

"I'm afraid that's confidential information, ma'am."

"Major, my husband is dying in a hospital room. He was injured working on *your* project. Don't I have the right to know what happened to him?"

"It's not my project, ma'am," the major said in his expressionless tone. "Everything in this facility is property of the United States government."

"The government which my husband was working for!" Cornelia replied. "I deserve to know what happened!"

"I'm not at liberty to discuss that, ma'am."

Cornelia bit back a string of swear words, and instead turned her back on the man and stalked back towards the work tables. Yes, she knew that Major Brandt was just following orders, but she'd hoped that because of his rank, he'd be able to tell her *something*.

She looked at the sheets of calculations and schematics that littered the work tables. Maybe there was a clue here about what they'd been working on yesterday. She scanned the pages, picking up several sheets to study them.

"You're not allowed to touch anything, ma'am," Major Brandt informed her.

This time she let herself glare at him. "I can't touch anything?" She waved a sheet of paper in the air. "These are my husband's notes, that he wrote himself. Why am I not allowed to look at them?"

"Everything in here belongs to the United States government," Major Brandt repeated.

Cornelia dropped the sheet back onto the strewn pile on the table. "I can't touch anything, and you won't tell me anything about what happened yesterday. So why did you even bother to let me come here?"

"Out of courtesy for your husband's current condition."

She had to give a derisive laugh at that. "Some courtesy. May I at least *look* at the papers?" She held up her purse in both gloved hands, and clutched it to her chest to show that her hands were fully occupied.

The major seemed to ponder her request, then finally gave a curt nod.

She walked slowly down the length of each table, scanning the visible papers and trying to glean some inkling of anything. She really needed an hour or two to sort through every single sheet, but apparently that was out of the question. The blank chalkboard had clearly been recently cleaned, so whatever the men might have been working on minutes or hours before the accident was gone.

Cornelia paused at one section of a table, and squinted down at the edge of a diagram that was peeking out from underneath a book about the magnetic field of the earth. She glanced over at the major; he was still standing near the door, where he'd been, but was staring directly at her. She frowned back at the table. Next to the diagram she noticed a familiar-looking pen—the blue-and-gold fountain pen that John had been looking for the night they talked about Adelaide. Apparently he'd found it, no doubt on his dressing table where she'd told him it was; but now it was forever trapped in this federal government tomb. She swallowed the sudden lump in her throat.

Footsteps sounded on the metal floor, and she glanced up to see a young officer step into the doorway. He spoke quietly to Major Brandt. As the major turned his head to talk with the younger man, Cornelia impulsively snatched up the blue fountain pen and slipped it into her coat pocket.

"Mrs. Jones," Major Brandt announced. "I'm afraid I am required elsewhere. Lt. Shaw will see you out. Good day, ma'am." He gave a nod and stepped out of the room.

The young Lt. Shaw gestured towards the door. "Mrs. Jones?"

And just like that, visiting hours were over. Not that she'd accomplished anything with this visit except to be further frustrated. Working for the government back during the War had been one thing, but if only John hadn't agreed to start working on this project for them again...

But playing the "if only" game was useless. Cornelia followed the young lieutenant back down the narrow corridor to the outside door. She'd call the hospital as soon as she got home, she decided, unless Rawlins already had a message from the doctor waiting. When she'd phoned this morning before leaving the house, Doctor Landers had reported no change in John's condition.

In the back seat of the Rolls-Royce, Cornelia pulled the fountain pen out of her pocket. John's notes would have been far more valuable, but there was no way she could have surreptitiously taken even one sheet of paper. Idly she pulled off the cap, and couldn't help smiling—the nib of the pen was rusted and dull, just as before. John had taken the pen to work, but still hadn't bothered to change out the nib.

How could he have even written with the thing? She tweaked at the pen's nib with the tip of a black-gloved finger; not only was it dull and sporting a touch of rust, but it was inserted into the pen crooked. Her tweaking loosened the crooked nib, and it fell out of the pen into her lap. As she examined the pen more closely in order to put the nib back in, she realized that it wasn't screwed closed properly. No ink was leaking out, but she held the pen upright anyway and unscrewed it completely. The pen looked like it had been empty of ink for some time, but there was something else inside it. She tipped the pen over and a small cigarette fell out.

That's odd, she thought. On the rare occasions that John smoked, it was a pipe, not cigarettes.

Laying the empty pen in her lap, she pulled off her gloves and then picked up the roll. It wasn't a cigarette after all, she realized, but nothing more than a tightly rolled scrap of paper. Carefully she unrolled it.

A string of numbers was written, in John's handwriting: *54° 11′ 5″ S, 115° 33′ 19″ W*

Cornelia stared at the paper, her heart beating faster. A geographic location. A location for what? And why had John secreted it inside a fountain pen?

Whatever this was, it was her first clue. She leaned forward over the back of the front seat. "Drive as fast as you safely can, Ronald," she called. "I need to get home quickly."

"Yes, ma'am," the young blond man replied. The car sped up.

She settled back against the seat and stared at the scrap of paper. *Oh, John. What are you trying to tell me?*

AS THE CAR PULLED THROUGH the open iron gates and down the gravel driveway, Ronald cocked his head and called into the back seat, "Mrs. Jones? Would you like me to drop you off at the side entrance today?"

Cornelia looked up and met his eyes in the rear-view mirror. "Thank you, Ronald, but no. The front entrance will do."

"Yes, ma'am." He guided the car around to the pillared front porch of the house.

Cornelia appreciated his consideration in asking. Occasionally she did want to be dropped off at the side entrance near the kitchen, because it was closer to the basement stairs. But right now, she needed to talk to Rawlins, and he was usually waiting by the front door.

"Thank you, Ronald," she said to him again as the car stopped. She didn't give him time to get out and open the door for her—she climbed out and hurried up the front steps.

Rawlins opened the right-hand side of the double front door for her. "Welcome home, Miz Jones," he said. "Was your trip successful?"

"Mostly no, but perhaps not a total loss," she replied as he helped her off with her coat. "Any phone calls while I was away? Did the doctor call?"

"No, ma'am. But Miss Adelaide telephoned. She wanted to express her sympathy and asked if there was anything she could do."

"That was thoughtful of her." Cornelia pulled off her gray cloche and handed it to him. "Remind me to call her back later today."

So the hospital hadn't called, but perhaps no news was not bad news—if John's condition had worsened, she would have received a call. "I'm going to call the doctor and get an update on John," she said. "And while I do, I need you to go downstairs and find an atlas or a world map—specifically one that shows detail of the southern hemisphere. I'll join you in a minute."

"Yes, ma'am." Rawlins finished putting her coat and hat away in the coat closet, then headed down the hallway towards the basement stairs.

Cornelia stayed in the main hall and used that telephone to call the Sisters of Mercy hospital. The answer was the same as earlier that morning when she'd called: John's condition was—for good or ill—unchanged. "Thank you very much," she said to the secretary. "Please tell the doctor that I will be in this afternoon to visit."

Retrieving her purse from where she'd laid it on the telephone table, she went down to the basement. Rawlins was in the library room. Numerous maps and atlases were spread out on the large rectangular mahogany table in the center of the room.

"I'll be going to the hospital after lunch," she informed him. "John's condition is apparently unchanged, but hopefully I can get more details from the doctor." She opened her purse and pulled out the blue fountain pen. "And speaking of details—the lab facility had been completely cleaned up. All of the equipment they'd been working on had been removed from the room, and any evidence of equations or projects that were in progress or might have led up to the accident were erased. And Major Brandt was more tight-lipped than a speakeasy owner in front of the police. If anyone does actually know what happened, they're not saying."

She held up the pen. "There is, however, this. The major wouldn't let me take any of John's notes, but on a whim I grabbed this pen off one of the tables. And I'm glad I did." She unscrewed it and dumped the little roll of paper onto the table.

Rawlins raised one bushy eyebrow. "What is it, ma'am?"

Cornelia unrolled it and showed him the paper. "Coordinates. I have no idea why John would have written this down, nor why he stashed it inside a fountain pen. But it must mean something."

They both bent over the maps, and spent the next several minutes measuring, cross-referencing, and double-checking the coordinates. Rawlins laid a wrinkled dark finger on one of the maps, in the middle of the southern Pacific Ocean. "There's nothing there," he said.

Cornelia looked at one of the atlases, where they'd circled the spot in pencil. "Dead center in the middle of nowhere," she said. "It's hundreds of miles away from Cape Horn, Antarctica, even Easter Island."

"Mr. Jones wouldn't have written down coordinates to nowhere," said Rawlins. "He never mentioned anything to you about having to travel somewhere?"

"No, he didn't." She met Rawlins' eyes. "His journal. He may have written something down in his journal."

Rawlins glanced out through the doorway of the library into the main room of the basement lab. "I don't recall seeing his journal lying around for a few days. I can look for it, though."

"I think it's upstairs in our bedroom," said Cornelia. "I'll get it."

As she hurried up the two flights of stairs, she hoped and prayed that he'd written some other clue in his journal. His journal wasn't a secret diary—it was merely his record of ideas, plans, and nightly musings. Out of simple respect, Cornelia didn't habitually read his journal—unless he asked for her to read him a passage that he'd written about an idea for a project or somesuch. He wrote in it nearly every evening, but he hadn't mentioned to her what he'd written about for several days now. Which was not unusual or worrisome. But now, there was a chance that he'd written something that might help them.

Sure enough, the worn leather journal was lying on his bedside table under a stack of science magazines and a volume of Shakespeare's sonnets. Cornelia swallowed the lump in her throat as she moved the poetry book aside. She and John had been reading Shakespeare to each other the evening before the accident. Blinking away tears before they could form, she grabbed the journal and went back downstairs.

Rawlins was sitting on a padded bench against the wall in the library, under one of the small windows up near the ceiling that let daylight into the basement. He set aside the atlas he was studying and stood up as she came into the room.

Cornelia waved at him to sit back down, and took a seat beside him on the bench. "Let's see if his journal has anything to tell us," she said, thumbing through it to find the most recent entries.

January fifth, four days ago, consisted of numerous equations for the gravity matrix resonator. Cornelia skimmed through them briefly, not immediately noticing anything that seemed out of place or odd. Most of the equations pertained to magnetism, as far as she could tell, and appeared to be nothing more than John's constant tinkering and refining of his ideas.

The next entry, January sixth, offered more details. First there were a few more scribbles of equations, then John had written: *"I overheard Percival and others talking about a location for the project. We're not at the testing stage yet, and I'd already put forth a location out in the desert for the first test. Unsure about this other location that they mentioned, will try to inquire further."* Then at the bottom of the page, after a couple of more partial equations, he'd written the word *"Caelum."*

Cornelia and Rawlins looked at each other. "Caelum?" said Rawlins. "What does that mean?"

"It sounds Latin," said Cornelia. She handed the journal to Rawlins as she stood up and headed over to one of the shelves. She pulled down the heavy "C" volume of an encyclopedia set and laid it on the table. Rawlins came over to stand beside her.

"Here it is," she said. *"Caelum, a constellation in the southern sky. Listed as one of fourteen southern hemisphere constellations by the eighteenth-century French astronomer Nicolas Louis de Lacaille. It is also known as* Caelum Scalptorium, *Latin for 'the engraver's chisel.'"*

She looked at Rawlins. "A southern constellation. Caelum would be visible from this location." She gestured at the maps they'd been looking at.

"It would be visible from most anywhere in the southern hemisphere, though," Rawlins countered. "And even a bit north of the equator. See, here's the right ascension and declination of the constellation." He pointed to the celestial coordinates listed in the encyclopedia.

"Hmm." She peered at the entry. Rawlins was right, of course. And there didn't appear to be anything else remarkable about this rather minor set of stars.

"Let's see what he wrote for the next day," said Rawlins.

They went back over to the bench. Cornelia picked up the journal and read aloud John's last entry, made the night before the accident. *Mrs. Davenport came by for a visit again this morning. She didn't stay long, but Percival seemed upset after she left. I haven't told Cornelia yet about Prudence's visits, tho perhaps I should as they've been increasing in frequency these past few weeks. I don't want to make things difficult between Cor. and Pru. in their social circles. Poor Cor. puts up with enough as it is, bless her. Drat, I left my blue pen at the lab. Must remember to get it tomorrow.*"

Cornelia felt an odd chill sweep through her. Prudence had visited the lab the day before the accident? And not for the first time? How had she managed that when Cornelia had had to pull eyeteeth just to be allowed to look at an empty room?

"He mentioned the blue pen," said Rawlins. "He must have written down those coordinates and was planning on bringing it home to show you."

Cornelia stared at the journal page in silence for a moment, her thoughts in a knot. "Why didn't he tell me about Prudence?"

"He was trying to protect you," Rawlins said gently. "He said so, see? He didn't want you getting kicked out of every ladies' club in Los Angeles because you had a shouting match with Prudence at a dinner party."

"Who said I'd ever have a shouting match with her?" Cornelia said with a glower. "Right now I've half a mind to drive over to her house and punch her in the face."

Rawlins chuckled softly. "That won't help either, ma'am."

"Perhaps not, but she more than deserves it." Cornelia shut the journal with a smack. *Damn it, John,* she thought. *What else do you know that you didn't tell me, or bother to write down?*

Rawlins pulled his watch out of his vest pocket. "Maggie ought to have lunch ready by now, ma'am. I'll have Ronald ready with the car when you're finished, to take you to the hospital. And remember to call Miss Adelaide back when you return later this afternoon." He stood up, and then offered her his arm.

With a sigh Cornelia set the journal on the bench and stood up to take Rawlins' arm. "Thank you for keeping me on track, Joe," she said as they exited the library and walked through the lab to the stairs. "And if you're ever in the same room with Prudence and myself again, I expect you to hold me back; otherwise I may ruin the Jones family's good name with one smooth swing."

He laughed. "Yes, Miz Jones. I promise."

She gave his arm a grateful squeeze as they headed up the stairs to the dining room.

Chapter 4

"Right this way, Mrs. Jones." A nurse in a white gown and starched cap held open the door to the interior of the hospital.

Cornelia rose from her seat in the waiting area and followed the nurse. It was the same room as before, so she remembered the way, but she obediently followed the nurse down the long corridor. The nurse stopped outside the door.

"Right in here, madam. The doctor will be along in just a few minutes." The nurse gave her a reassuring smile, and went on down the hall.

Cornelia hesitated before reaching for the doorknob. Since apparently John's condition was not improved, then she would be seeing him again as an unrecognizable form mummified in bandages and hooked up to an oxygen apparatus. She took a fortifying breath, stepped up to the door, and noticed that it was already open a crack.

She put her hand on the knob to push it open, then paused as she heard voices inside. It sounded like Prudence. She was talking with Percival. Cornelia stayed with her hand on the knob, and leaned her head forward to hear through the small opening.

"...behind schedule," came Prudence's voice.

"We're not behind schedule, Prudence," Percival replied. His voice sounded strong, healthy, and more than a little annoyed. "I'll be healed up and out of here in a few more days."

"A few days," huffed Prudence. "That's too long. There's a lot of work to be done."

"We have plenty of time, and everything's being handled. I'll take care of it."

"Like you've taken care of it so far?" Prudence snipped.

"I said that everything will be fine," Percival replied sharply. "Mrs. Jones!"

Cornelia looked up and saw the thin form of Dr. Landers coming down the hallway towards her.

"I apologize for keeping you waiting," he said. "You're welcome to go inside—it's not locked."

Cornelia pushed open the door and preceded the doctor into the room.

A curtain on a frame had been set up between the two beds, and the curtain was drawn to give each patient and their visitors a bit of privacy from one another. But since the beds sat against the far wall, both were fully visible from the door.

John lay still fully bandaged up, and still attached to the breathing machine. On the other side of the curtain, the Davenports must have heard the doctor's voice in the hall, because Prudence was standing next to Percival's bed and gathering up her purse from the chair.

"I'll see you tomorrow, dear," she said tenderly, and bent over to kiss him on the forehead. She gave Cornelia a polite nod as they walked past each other in the room.

She also nodded at the doctor. "Thank you, Dr. Landers," she said, her voice oozing sorrow and appreciativeness. "I'll be in tomorrow to see him."

"Very good, Mrs. Davenport," said Dr. Landers.

Percival lifted a hand in a feeble wave at his wife, then let it fall to the blanket as he turned his head away and closed his eyes. He heaved a loud, exhausted-sounding sigh.

Cornelia glanced back at Prudence as she exited the room. What was their conversation about? Was the gravity matrix engine project still going ahead, despite the explosion, and without John's participation? If so, why hadn't she been informed?

She quickly pushed those questions away, though, as she approached John's bed. A chair had been provided this time, and Cornelia sank into it. She laid her hand on the edge of the bed, afraid to touch the outline of his arm under the blanket in case there was a wound or burn that shouldn't be disturbed.

"I should be able to remove some of the bandages in a few days," said Dr. Landers quietly. "The minor burns and skin abrasions are healing nicely."

Cornelia sensed a "but" hanging in the air. "He's still on the respirator," she said.

"Just until he's stronger."

Cornelia looked up at him. "Please be honest with me, doctor. I don't want sugarcoating and empty promises. I want to know all the details of his condition, and the realistic chances of recovery. I have some knowledge of human anatomy and I promise I won't faint at anything you tell me."

Dr. Landers pursed his thin lips and looked like he was about to protest, but then nodded. "Let's step into my office.

You'd be more comfortable there, and we don't want to disturb Mr. Davenport while he's trying to sleep."

Mr. Davenport was not trying to sleep in the least, Cornelia was sure. A quick stab of jealous anger went through her as she realized that Percival seemed to be already on the mend and John was still bandaged and unconscious. Grateful for the doctor's offer of privacy, she followed him out of the room, her heartbeat quickening.

Down the hall in his small and somewhat jumbled office, Dr. Landers showed her to the stuffed leather chair in front of the desk, then went around behind the desk to sit.

"Mrs. Jones, I spoke the truth before. His burns, cuts, and other minor surface abrasions are healing as I would expect them to on any man of his age and health. I can remove some of the bandages in a few days, and there should be very little scarring from those injuries."

He folded his hands and set them on the desk in front of him. "It's his internal injuries that concern me. Or rather, the condition of his internal organs, even though they appear to be uninjured."

Heart still pounding harder than she wished it would, Cornelia blinked at him, then leaned forward in her chair. "What do you mean?"

The doctor sighed and shook his head. "I hate to have to tell you this, but I am at a complete loss. I was able to repair his internal injuries with the surgery I performed—some minor damage to his lungs, and his left kidney. He should be healing now. And he is, except... Except that all of his organs appear to be shutting down. There's no cause that I can determine. A slower metabolic rate is normal for someone mere days out from sustaining life-threatening injuries. But it's more than a slowing of organ function."

Cornelia held her breath and waited for him to continue.

"I called in another doctor—a specialist in the field of organ dysfunction, from Seattle. He arrived early this morning. He has run every test there is, and from what he can determine, it appears that your husband's internal organs have become too heavy, or dense, to function properly. There is very little swelling or inflammation, so that is not the cause. His organs are simply too heavy for his body, too compacted internally to function as before."

"How could this have happened?" Cornelia asked, hearing the unsteadiness in her voice. She wondered if she should ask for another opinion from another doctor—but Dr. Landers was an experienced surgeon and had already brought in a specialist. Dr. Huett was their family physician and a good doctor, but his skillset lay in treating Cornelia's bout with influenza last year, or the time their gardener Joey had broken his arm.

Dr. Landers was speaking again. "I'm sorry to say, but I'm afraid we have no idea what could be causing it, nor how to reverse it." He rubbed his forehead and sighed. "I am sorry to bear such bad news, madam, but there's nothing we can do. We have him on the respirator, and have started giving him nutrients with a feeding tube; but I'm afraid that if his organ function continues to slow, I estimate that he has a week to live. Ten days, perhaps, but certainly no longer than that. I'm sorry."

The room grew small and dark around her. "Thank you for telling me, doctor," she heard herself say. *A week to live.* How could this be happening?

Dr. Landers stood up. "Again, I am very sorry. We will keep him here sustained and comfortable for as long as we can." He came around the desk. "Allow me to personally escort you out, madam."

"Thank you, doctor," Cornelia repeated. She started to stand and found that her legs suddenly wouldn't work. She allowed Dr. Landers to help her up, and to walk her back down the hospital corridors, through the waiting room, and out to the sidewalk where Ronald waited with the Rolls.

In the backseat of the car, she clenched her jaw and stared out the window, refusing to draw out her handkerchief. Sobbing all over Rawlins the other night was one thing, but she was not about to break down in front of the chauffeur. Or the doctor, or anyone else. Her mind roiled with questions, and her heartbeat still hadn't returned to normal. The doctor's words rang in her ears. *A week to live.*

"You can't die, John," she whispered to herself, too softly for Ronald to hear in the front seat. He couldn't die, he just couldn't. She needed a miracle cure, or more time to figure out how to heal him, or both.

THE NEXT MORNING CORNELIA was supposed to be attending a dress exhibition from one of the local couture designers, showcasing their new "mid-winter" line of fashion. She called Hortense Follensby as soon as she got out of bed to beg off attending the show. Ordinarily she enjoyed a classy fashion exhibition, but right now she just couldn't handle idle chatter about hats and gloves.

"Of course, dear," Hortense said on the other end of the line. "We all understand. You must be dreadfully upset. You can't be expected to attend every event at a time like this. Stay home and rest, but do keep us posted about your husband's recovery."

Recovery. If only. "Thank you, Hortense," Cornelia said, managing to keep the strangled tightness she felt out of her voice.

"You take care now, Cornelia," Hortense said in a grandmotherly tone. "Good-bye, dear."

"Good-bye, Hortense." Cornelia hung the earpiece back on the hook and let a few hot tears slip out. Then she swiped her hand across her eyes and went downstairs to the dining room.

She had spent a sleepless night thinking, crying, and cursing into her pillow. She'd even gone down to the basement library for a couple of hours and pored over numerous spell books, hoping to find an incantation or potion that could help John in even some little way. But she'd come up with nothing.

After forcing herself to eat breakfast, Cornelia went to her desk in the upstairs library. She needed to distract her mind for a little while, and the mail had been piling up for a few days now.

A half dozen of the correspondences were letters of sympathy from Hortense, Adelaide, the Williamsons, and others. As Cornelia scanned the letters, it occurred to her that one sympathy letter she would not receive—at least not yet—was from her father. John had no close living relatives left, and she was in no hurry to inform his distant third cousins whom she'd never met that he was in the hospital. But her father would want to know.

Know what, though? That John was dying? Dying due to an unknown condition, caused by an unknown accident. She didn't want to worry her father, but he was fond of John and would be very upset if John died and Cornelia didn't tell him until after it happened.

No. She squeezed her left hand into a fist, and tears blurred her vision of the letter in her other hand. She would not let John die. Somehow, some way, she'd find a way to save him. She usually wrote to her father about twice a month, and they'd just exchanged Christmas and New Year's letters, so she could wait. Besides, her father would probably want to come out here to be with her, which Cornelia would appreciate, but she didn't want her father traveling from Chicago and through the snowy western states in the middle of winter.

She set the condolence letters aside, forced her attention back to the rest of the mail and distracted herself with writing checks. First she wrote out checks to the various charities that they regularly supported: the children's hospital, the Negro hospital, a war veterans' program, the Salvation Army. Then she wrote the checks to the other projects they sponsored: the archeological dig in Egypt, a local motion picture studio, a literary foundation in Chicago that her parents had helped to found years ago, and a scholarship at the Crandell Institute of Sciences.

Then she busied herself with reading over the financial statements from their various investments, and then reviewing the checkbook ledger. While she wrote the checks for the charitable giving and other financial support, she let Rawlins handle the day-to-day payments like the staff wages, household expenses, and other bills. All was in order, as per usual.

The telephone rang. Cornelia froze, waiting for Rawlins to answer it downstairs. Perhaps it was Dr. Landers calling with good news. Or not-so-good news...

She heard Rawlins' slow footfalls at the top of the stairs, and she rose from the desk to meet him in the doorway of the library. "Miss Adelaide is on the phone for you, Miz Jones."

Simultaneously disappointed and relieved, Cornelia gave a small sigh. "Tell her that I'll call her back later."

"Yes, ma'am." Rawlins turned back towards the stairs.

"Wait." A conversation with a sympathetic ear might do her some good. "Never mind, Rawlins. I'll speak with her. I'll take the call in John's study."

"Very good, ma'am."

Cornelia went through the open informal sitting area outside the library and turned left into John's study.

In the study, Cornelia picked up the telephone receiver and leaned against the edge of John's wooden desk. "Adelaide?"

"Cornelia!" the younger woman's voice sounded anxious. "It's good to hear your voice. We've all been so concerned for you."

"I appreciate that. I was just reading all the letters, actually, from you and Hortense and Violet and everyone. Please tell all the ladies that I'm most grateful for their kind words." She paused, and heard a faint buzz of what sounded like conversation and music in the background. "Are you calling from the dress exhibition?"

"I am," said Adelaide. "We've taken a break while the models put on their next outfits and we consume all the delectable *hors d'oevres*. The hostess said I could use their telephone. You're missing a lovely show, though I don't blame you one bit for sitting this one out."

Cornelia had not been intending to tell Adelaide everything, especially not right now, but she found herself saying: "John is dying. The doctor said he has a week to live."

"Oh my God. Oh, Cornelia, I'm so sorry. I wish—is there anything I can do to help? I mean, I don't know what I could do, but...I'm so sorry."

"Not unless you know a magic spell that can reverse organ density," Cornelia said, trying to keep the bitter edge of frustration out of her voice.

"I don't know any spells for anything," said Adelaide, sounding sorrowful. "Um, organ density? What's that mean?"

"Dr. Landers said that John's internal organs are failing because they've become too dense and heavy to function properly. And it's not due to swelling or any other medical condition he's familiar with. He says there's nothing he can do. And I don't know what to do, either." Cornelia drew a shaky breath. She felt a strange blush of relief, telling Adelaide the full truth.

"I think that the gravity matrix resonator machine was on and functioning in some way when the accident—whatever it was—occurred," she continued. "And somehow it hit John and has altered the density of his body." She'd come to that conclusion sometime during her sleepless night. It was the only explanation that made any sense.

"Golly," said Adelaide. "Is that what happened to Prudence's husband, too?"

"I doubt it. Percival will probably be out of the hospital in a few days. What has Prudence told you?"

"Nothing. She hasn't been to any gatherings or talked to anyone, either." Adelaide paused, and Cornelia could hear that the background sounds had shifted, and the music had stopped.

"Do you need to get back to the show?" Cornelia asked.

"No, it's all right. The telephone is around the corner in the hallway here, so my conversation isn't disturbing anyone. Are you...are you going to be all right, Cornelia? I wish there was something I could do to help. But I don't know any spells. I wish I could help you heal him, or reverse the gravity, or even just buy you more time. A week...gosh, Cornelia, I'm so sorry."

Buying more time... An idea tickled at the back of her mind. She straightened up, cradled the phone receiver between her shoulder and ear, and began shuffling through the papers that lay piled on the desk.

"Adelaide, you're brilliant," she said hurriedly into the phone. "You've given me an idea. I don't know why I didn't think of this before...where is it..." John had papers and notes for about six different projects scattered all over this desk.

"I am?" said Adelaide. "I have? What idea? What have you thought of?"

There it was—the folder with the blueprints for the artificial womb. The preservation chamber in the basement, John's idea to buy more time for someone with an "incurable" condition. The machine was almost complete—if she and Rawlins could just finish building it in the next few days, then....

"Cornelia?" came Adelaide's voice. "Are you still there?"

"Yes," she said finally, staring at the blueprints, her mind racing. "I'm still here. Adelaide, I think I have a way to save

John. Or, at least, to buy more time until I can figure out how to save him. One of his own inventions."

"A time machine?" Adelaide asked, sounding awed.

Cornelia gave a small chuckle in spite of the situation. "Not quite. But the next best thing—a way to preserve his body in a static state until a cure can be found. Thank you, Adelaide, you're a genius. I must go—I've got a lot of work to do. Thank you again." Without waiting for Adelaide's reply, she hung up the phone and ran out of the study.

"Rawlins! Rawlins!" she called, hurrying out into the hall.

"Yes, Miz Jones?" came Rawlins' voice, and then he appeared on the landing at the turn of the stairs. "What's wrong?"

She gripped the newel post at the top of the stairs with one hand and held the folder full of blueprints aloft in her other hand. "I think we can save him."

"Ma'am?" Rawlins looked up at her in confusion.

She headed down the stairs towards him. "John's artificial womb. It can preserve him and buy us the time we need to find a cure. We just need to finish building it."

Rawlins took the folder from her as she stepped down beside him. He flipped through the pages, then looked at her with a gleam in his dark eyes.

"I think you're right, Miz Jones. We'd best get to work right away, then."

AFTER AN EARLY BREAKFAST, Cornelia walked through the basement lab, through the door at the back of the room, and down the corridor into the chamber where she and

Rawlins had been working for the past two days. Maggie and Theda had been given the temporary extra responsibilities of covering for Rawlins' duties, and Maggie was preparing quick dinners and cold sandwich lunches so that they could keep working.

Rawlins, dressed in a gray work shirt and brown overalls instead of his usual black and white butler's livery, stood on a ladder tinkering with an instrument panel high on the wall when Cornelia entered the small room. He glanced down at her. "I'm just about finished wiring this one, ma'am. Then this set of electrical gauges will be all set up."

"That's good news," she said. "I wish I had better news."

He looked down at her again. "The military men at the research lab giving you the runaround again?"

"Not exactly. I haven't been able to reach anyone at all." Cornelia drew a deep breath to calm her mounting frustration. "I called all of the numbers that I'd called before when I was trying to gain access to the facility right after the accident. The operator said that three of the numbers had been disconnected—Major Brandt's among them—and the others just rang with no answer. I had her call multiple times, but still nothing."

"Numbers disconnected?" said Rawlins. "That doesn't make sense."

Cornelia stepped over a pile of rubber hoses on the floor as she came closer to Rawlins' ladder. "I'm not sure what to think. Even with the project halted because of the accident, they wouldn't just close down the entire facility, would they? And I have a right to John's personal belongings that are still there." She rubbed a hand across the back of her neck to ease the tension from her fruitless time spent on the telephone. "We have to get that radium."

They were making good progress with completing John's preservation machine. The blueprints were complete, and most of the necessary pieces, tools, and equipment they already had in the house. Yesterday they'd taken inventory of what they still needed, and Cornelia had telephoned several of John's regular suppliers to order some specialized wires, gears, chemical compounds, and other items. Some of it had already been delivered that morning, with the rest on the way.

The only thing they were still missing was the most vital piece of all: a rare isotope of radium that was the power source for the machine. John had ordered the radium months ago, and had had it sent to the Santa Monica lab for storage until he was ready to use it, since they had a better facility for storing radioactive materials. He had gotten all the proper permissions from the military officers in charge at the lab, and Cornelia had all the signed paperwork to prove it. She just needed to contact someone about it.

She sat down cross-legged on the floor and picked up a screwdriver. Climbing ladders and scooting around on the floor was much easier in pants than a dress, so that morning she had dressed in a pair of tan trousers and an old floral blouse that she didn't mind getting dirty or torn.

"I guess there's no other way to power this thing but the radium?" said Rawlins from up on his ladder.

Cornelia craned her neck to look up at him. "We already discussed this. And I did some math last night. This machine requires too much energy to be run off of electricity. Even if we turned off every light in the house, I don't think the circuits could take it. The same with a gasoline engine. We'd need an engine the size of this room. And besides, we have no way of attaching this machine to any sort of power source besides the radium. John already built the chamber for it, with all the right pipes and wires. And the lead sheets for the outside of the housing should be delivered tomorrow."

Rawlins said nothing, but he nodded and continued his work. Cornelia turned back to the open panel at the base of the tank's platform. She tested all of the connections inside the panel, giving each screw a savage twist to make sure they were tight. They had to get that radium.

"If no one will answer the telephone," she said at last, "then I'll drive over there and knock on the door."

She half expected Rawlins to protest, or at least to encourage her to try the telephone again, but all he said was, "Shall I go tell Ronald to bring the car around?"

"No, you stay up there—I can call him." She finished tightening all of the screws, then placed the metal cover over the open panel and screwed it on. "This panel is finished," she said as she got up. "The wiring connections for the temperature regulation coils."

Rawlins glanced down. "Very good, ma'am. Good luck to you."

"Thank you—I have a feeling I'm going to need it."

She walked back through the basement, then once upstairs she crossed the hall to the kitchen. Maggie was there washing dishes in the large white sink, up to her elbows in soapsuds.

"Mrs. Jones!" said Maggie. "What can I help you with? I was about to bring luncheon down just as soon as I finished me washin'. D'you need Theda? She's upstairs doin' her cleanin'."

"No, it's fine," Cornelia said to the Irishwoman. "And I'll be out of your way in just a moment. I just need to call Ronald."

She went through the kitchen and into the butler's pantry, situated between the kitchen and the dining room. There was a telephone in there that connected only with the carriage house.

Cornelia lifted the earpiece off of the hook and after just a second, Ronald's voice answered. "Hello?"

"I need the car, Ronald. We're going back to the Santa Monica Research Facility in the mountains. I'll be ready to go in ten minutes."

"I'll be there, ma'am," said Ronald briskly.

She hung up the phone and hurried upstairs to change. Nine minutes later, properly attired in a blue dress, gloves, and hat, she poked her head back into the kitchen. "I'm going out, Maggie," she said. "Rawlins knows where I'm going. I'm sorry to miss lunch. You can go ahead and bring Rawlins his food whenever you're ready."

"Very good, ma'am," said Maggie, who was drying her hands on a towel as the sink drained its suds. "Will you take a bite wi' you? It's ham an' cheese." She hurried over to the icebox and pulled out a platter of sandwiches.

Cornelia consented to taking a sandwich, thanked the cook, and headed for the foyer.

Ronald was waiting just inside the front door for her. He opened it for her, then hurried ahead to open the car door. "Anywhere else you're going today besides Mr. Jones' research lab, ma'am?" he asked as he climbed into the driver's seat.

"No, nowhere else, Ronald. Thank you."

It was a good thirty-minute drive, which felt much longer. As she ate her sandwich, Cornelia tried to distract herself from her anger at the military officers in charge of the lab and ran through the list of what they still needed to do to the machine to make it operational. If she'd calculated it right, and if she and Rawlins worked non-stop with only short breaks for food and sleep, then everything should be complete in another two days, three at the most. According to Dr. Landers' report when she'd called the hospital this morning, John's condition was deteriorating at the rate that he'd predicted. They'd be cutting it close, but the artificial womb should be ready in enough time to preserve John's body and save his life.

All they needed was the radium.

At last the car pulled onto the winding dirt road that led to into the hills, and then the metal wall and entrance of the research bunker came into view, tucked into a hillside.

"Looks like no one's here to meet you, ma'am," said Ronald after bringing the car to a stop in front of the door. "Were they expecting you?"

"No," said Cornelia. "Which is why I'm here. I couldn't reach anyone by telephone, so I came to knock on their door."

Ronald hopped out of the car to open the back door for her.

The bunker door had a keyhole and a large metal handle, but no window, knocker, bell, or anything else. Cornelia rapped sharply on the door. When no immediate answer came, she hammered on the door with a fist.

She tried the handle, not expecting it to turn, which it did not. She bent down and peered through the keyhole. The light was on inside; she could make out the featureless tunnel, but no people. She banged on the door again.

"There might be another entrance, ma'am," said Ronald. "The road continues on up that way, around the mountain."

Cornelia looked where he was pointing, seeing the narrow dirt road winding up around the hill that the bunker was built into. There had to be another entrance—a larger one, for transporting equipment and supplies.

"I'm sure you're right, Ronald," she said. "Drive on."

They got back in the car, and he drove on up the road. Sure enough, a moment later the road opened up into a large parking and loading area. The parking lot, a wide flat space of dirt rimmed by scraggly bushes and the side of the hill, was empty.

So this was where John had parked his car every day when he came to this lab. The dusty lot seemed as bland and cheerless as the interior of the bunker had. John always drove their older car, a green-and-black 1916 Packard, to the lab, so that she could make use of the newer silver Rolls-Royce for her errands and societal duties. The police had brought the Packard back the day after the accident.

"Funny that no one's here today," said Ronald as he steered the car towards the wall of the bunker against the hillside. "I know it's Saturday, but I thought those military types worked every day."

Funny indeed. And vexing. And suspicious. She'd had a niggling in the back of her mind ever since the accident, but with every passing day, more and more bizarre evidence seemed to be mounting that something else was going on. Prudence and Percival's conversation, Prudence being allowed access to the lab when Cornelia was not, John's strange injuries while Percival was relatively unharmed... Not to mention John's bizarre note that he'd hidden inside the fountain pen. And now this.

Ronald parked in front of the large double doors. Cornelia banged on both doors, tried the handles, then walked over to the smaller personnel door next to the equipment doors, and tried that one. All locked, no answer.

"I doubt this place has any windows," she said, "but perhaps there's a hidden emergency entrance that we've overlooked." She secured her hat pin against the brisk breeze coming down the mountain, and set off into the bushes along the bunker wall.

"Um, Mrs. Jones?" Ronald hurried after her. "What are you looking for again?"

"Another entrance. A window. An escape hatch. Anything. Anything that might give us access, or give us a clue as to where everyone is."

They searched the bunker area for close to an hour, scrambling through bushes and over rocks. Ronald climbed up onto several precarious rocks on the hillside and even up into a small tree. The only evidence they found of any recent human activity at all were the tire tracks in the parking lot, and the occasional cigarette butt.

Cornelia was about to give up when Ronald called to her from above, higher up on the hillside. "Mrs. Jones! I think I found something."

She started up the steep slope, all but crawling, pulling herself up by grabbing the scrubby desert bushes. Ronald slithered back down the hill to come up beside her and help her along. He led her up to a round metal hatch built into the ground, fully hidden from view below by the bushes and the uneven landscape of the hill.

The hatch had a wheel latch like a bank vault. Ronald grabbed the wheel with both hands. "It turns, Mrs. Jones. Should I try opening it?"

"By all means."

As Ronald grunted and cranked the wheel, Cornelia abruptly realized they were doing something rather illegal. If someone was waiting on the other side of that hatch, she could hardly excuse herself by saying she just "dropped by" or had "accidentally" opened the hatch door.

But that didn't matter, she told herself with resolve. John's life, and her legal right to the radium that was stored in that bunker, mattered more than anything. At this point she didn't care about a scandal in the papers or even being thrown in jail—just as long as she could finish building John's preservation tank and get him into it first.

With another grunt, Ronald heaved back on the circular door and it lifted open with a rusty creak.

A dark tunnel descended straight down into the hillside, the metal rungs of a ladder built into the wall of the tunnel. Leaning on the steep hillside, Cornelia shifted her hip and her elbow against the rough ground as she peered into the hole, her heart beating faster. If this place was truly as deserted as it looked, this could be a way in.

"I keep a flashlight in the car," said Ronald. "Should I go get it, ma'am?"

Cornelia looked at his earnest young face, grateful for his willing assistance. She nodded.

He scurried down the hill to the car. No one emerged from the dark tunnel while he was away, and Cornelia heard no sounds coming from inside, either. Ronald returned, out of breath and with his black chauffer's cap askew, and switched on the flashlight. The beam of light glinted on the metal floor of the bottom of the tunnel and what looked like another door, perpendicular to the tunnel and leading into the hill.

Before Cornelia could say anything, Ronald swung himself into the opening and began climbing down the ladder, flashlight waving erratically as he went. Cornelia held her breath. If a guard were to appear at this moment, she would make sure that Ronald was not charged or held responsible in any way. And she'd also make sure that she didn't leave till she'd gotten John's radium. Somehow.

She heard Ronald banging on the door at the bottom of the tunnel, and then a moment later he started climbing back up the ladder. "I guess that second door is to keep folks from breaking in from the outside like we're trying to do," he said in a disappointed tone as he emerged. "It's locked up tight."

Cornelia sighed in both frustration and relief. "Well, this place is nothing if not secure," she quipped. "Let's head back home."

They clambered back down the hill, Ronald's uniform in need of a good wash, and Cornelia's stockings shredded beyond repair. When they got home, she decided it was time for another set of telephone calls.

Chapter 5

Back at home, Cornelia changed into clean, undamaged clothes. She laid her dress out for Theda to repair the snags in the skirt, hung her coat on the bedpost to remind herself to have it sent to the cleaners, and tossed the stockings into the trash can.

The first telephone call she made was long-distance to the company in New York where John had ordered the radium from. It was a long shot if they had any more of that particular isotope available, but Cornelia had to try. As she waited for the connection, belatedly she remembered the time difference between Los Angeles and New York. The company would probably be closed by now.

Surprisingly, someone answered the telephone. However, as she had suspected, because of the rarity of that radium isotope, it would take at least six months for their facility in Germany to come by a sample of any decent size. Cornelia thanked the secretary for working late and answering her call promptly, and hung up.

The next call she made was to the Davenport household. If Percival somehow had enough clout to allow Prudence access to the lab, then perhaps they could help her get ahold of the radium. She hated the thought of asking either of them for a favor, but she was getting desperate.

"Davenport household, West speaking," the butler answered.

"I need to speak with Mrs. Davenport. This is Mrs. Jones. It's an urgent matter."

"I'm sorry, Mrs. Jones, but Mrs. Davenport is not here. May I take a message?"

"Where has she gone?"

"I'm not at liberty to discuss that, madam."

Not at liberty to discuss that? What the hell kind of answer was that? Cornelia gripped the phone receiver tighter. "When will she be back, then?"

"I really couldn't say, madam," West replied.

Cornelia blew air out between her teeth, not caring if the butler heard it. "Very well. Take a message, then. Please tell her that Mrs. Jones called and has a very urgent matter to discuss with her. Please have her call me back the moment she gets in, no matter how late it might be."

"Very good, madam."

Cornelia hung up without thanking the butler. When she'd looked at the clock in the bedroom while changing clothes, it had been nearly dinner time, so visiting hours at the hospital were over. And if Prudence had missed every ladies' gathering, as Adelaide had said the other day, then where was she at this hour of the evening?

Still fuming, Cornelia went downstairs to the basement. Maggie had laid out two trays of food in the main room, and Rawlins was sitting at one of the long tables eating.

"There you are, Miz Jones," he said, rising up from the bench as she descended the steps. "I was just about to come find you."

She sat down on the bench opposite him and took a swallow of wine from her glass before picking up her fork. "I think I'm going to need something stronger than wine tonight."

"Your trip didn't go well, ma'am?" said Rawlins, sitting back down.

While they ate she told him about what she and Ronald had found, and about her fruitless calls to the Davenports and to the radium supplier.

"What are we going to do, Joe?" she said. Panic was starting to rise now, and she laid down her fork as she looked at Rawlins. "Without that radium, the machine won't work and John will die." She squeezed her napkin fiercely in her left hand.

"Mr. Jones isn't going to die," Rawlins said firmly, with far more confidence than Cornelia felt right now. "Are you sure that the radium is still at Mr. Jones' lab in the mountains? You said the place looked abandoned."

She shook her head. "No, I'm not sure. And I'm not sure if the facility has been cleared out or not. It's just that no one was there today. I can't imagine why the radium John ordered would have been moved, but then, nothing about any of this makes any sense." She twisted her napkin. "I could see through the keyhole that the light was on in the main corridor, at the front door to the place. Surely they wouldn't have left the light on if they had cleared everything out and closed up shop."

"Maybe you need to go back and try again, then," said Rawlins.

"Oh, I intend to. First thing tomorrow. Have Ronald ready with the car at eight in the morning."

He nodded. "Yes, ma'am. Only, I was thinking..." He put down his fork and dabbed at his mouth and thin, close-cropped moustache with his napkin. "Well, what I mean is, it sure seems like they don't want you there."

"I quite agree. Which is precisely why I need to go back." She frowned at Rawlins' odd expression. "What are you getting at? You have another idea, don't you?"

"Well, it's not quite proper and all, ma'am," he said, slowly laying his napkin down beside his plate. "But maybe you should go back when you're sure nobody's there." He stared at her intently with his dark eyes.

A strange feeling swept over her as she realized what he was trying to say. "You mean...break in? Rawlins, you've been reading too many detective novels. You can't seriously be suggesting that I try to break into a locked military facility."

He didn't flinch. "You have a better idea, ma'am?"

She stared at him. Her butler was actually encouraging her to commit a crime—and a potentially dangerous crime, no less. She ought to be offended, or horrified, or...or...

"But how?" she finally managed to say.

"I've never broken into any place myself, ma'am," Rawlins said, all proper and pious again. "But I know you have."

She felt her face redden. "John told you about that, did he?" she said after a pause.

"Yes, ma'am," said Rawlins, his face serious. "Many years ago."

"I'll bet he did." Cornelia wished she weren't flushing so fiercely. "Once we save his life and heal him, remind me to kill him."

"Yes, ma'am." Rawlins' face was still solemn and serious, but his eyes were twinkling.

Cornelia cleared her throat. "More to the point, that was a completely different situation. We were in college. And it wasn't a secure, clandestine military bunker." She tapped a fingernail on the tabletop. "I can't do something like that alone. I wouldn't even know where to begin." She looked at him. "Are you offering to help, since this was your brilliant idea?"

"In any way I can, ma'am," he said with a definitive nod. "Although I don't have the breaking and entering experience you do, ma'am."

She glared at him. "I'll thank you not to keep reminding me of my youthful escapades, Rawlins."

He pursed his lips in a dead serious expression. "Yes, Miz Jones."

She tapped the tabletop again as her mind raced. The small hatch up on the hill that Ronald had found would be the perfect entry point, but she couldn't just go clambering in with no plan. And no tools. What did one need for a break-in? She couldn't believe she was seriously considering this—but then, as Rawlins had pointed out earlier, they were out of ideas.

"Charlotte," she said suddenly.

Rawlins peered at her over the rim of his wine glass. "Miss de Fontaine knows how to break into a military bunker, ma'am?" he asked, setting the glass down.

"No. Well, I doubt it. But what I mean is, she might have some ideas. And she knows everybody. All the right people, of course, and all the not-so-right people who might be the right people to help us in this situation." Or so she hoped. Charlotte didn't exactly go around talking about connections to the Mafia or something absurd like that. But Cornelia knew that being a magical practitioner of Charlotte's level of skill likely meant that she had connections outside of just the world of high society and the Hollywood elite.

Cornelia downed the last of her wine as she stood up. "I'm going to call Charlotte. Bring me a drink, if you would, and then get back to work on the artificial womb. I'll join you again as soon as I've spoken with Charlotte."

Rawlins also stood. "Yes, ma'am," he said, loading their dishes back onto the tray.

She used the telephone up in the main hall so that she wouldn't have to climb another flight of stairs up to John's study. Rawlins appeared with a teacup on a small silver tray just as the operator was connecting her with Charlotte's residence. She nodded at Rawlins as she took the cup and saucer. Scotch, judging by the smell. An appropriate choice after the day she'd had.

"Cornelia, *ma chérie!*" came Charlotte's voice over the line.

"Charlotte, I'm sorry to bother you late in the evening like this, but I have a question for you."

"It's no bother at all," Charlotte said brightly. "What can I help you with?"

"Well, it's rather complicated, actually," Cornelia said, suddenly reluctant to just announce to Charlotte that she wanted to burglarize a military facility. "Well, you know about John's condition, right? And that he's not improving."

"*Oui,*" said Charlotte sadly. "My heart cries for you, darling."

"Thank you. Well, I..." She squeezed the candlestick telephone in her hand. She didn't really want to go back out again, but this conversation seemed too serious—and potentially dangerous—to be having over a telephone line. "I hate to impose, Charlotte," she began again. "But could I come over? I want to talk to you about something, and I'd rather do it in person."

"*Oui,* but of course, darling. Come over right away, do."

"Thank you," said Cornelia. "I'll be right there."

She hung the earpiece back on the hook and set the phone down. Then she picked up the teacup that was sitting next to the telephone, and tossed back a swallow of scotch. Ignoring the burning in her throat, she hurried down the hall towards the basement again to tell Rawlins and have him alert Ronald.

She had a feeling—or at least a passionate hope—that Charlotte was just whom she needed right now.

RONALD PULLED THE CAR up to the curb in front of the Salon de Fontaine. The sidewalk was empty and the salon dark as Ronald hopped out of the car and opened the back door for Cornelia.

"I'm sorry to keep you out late like this, Ronald," she said as she climbed out. "But I don't know how long I'll be."

He touched his chauffer's cap. "It's no problem, Mrs. Jones."

Between the salon's large glass windows and the equally ostentatious display windows of the women's shoe store next door was a small white door that led to the second story of the building. Cornelia pressed the buzzer next to the door.

"*Allo,* who is it?" chirped Charlotte's voice through the tinny speaker.

"Charlotte, it's Cornelia."

"Cornelia, darling! Do come up."

Cornelia opened the door and ascended the gray marble stairs to Charlotte's apartment. Charlotte easily could have afforded to own a home in a wealthy hillside community, but she chose to live in the apartment above her salon. It was hardly a pauper's dwelling, though. The spacious suite was as full of pink finery and lace as the salon below.

Charlotte greeted her at the door, dressed in a voluminous white dressing gown. She ushered Cornelia into the sitting room, then went into the kitchen.

"Tea, *ma chérie*? Or wine? Or something stronger, perhaps?"

Cornelia definitely wanted something stronger than tea, but she'd already had that scotch before leaving the house. "Wine will do nicely," she said.

"Wine it is," called Charlotte from the kitchen. Cornelia heard her clattering glasses in one of the cupboards. "So tell me your troubles, darling."

"It's about John," said Cornelia as she cleared a space for the glasses on a nearby tea table by moving aside heaps of dried herbs, a bowl full of crystals, and a long coil of hemp twine. "I didn't want to continue our conversation over the telephone—it felt unsafe, somehow. I don't know how or why, and I have no proof of any sort, but I have a strange gut feeling that John's accident at the lab might have been more than an accident."

"*Mon Dieu!*" exclaimed Charlotte as she returned to the living room, carrying two wine glasses.

"I don't want to worry you, Charlotte," she said as they sat down. "And as I said, I have proof of nothing. However, that's sort of what I wanted to talk to you about."

"*Oui?*" said Charlotte, handing her a glass.

Cornelia took a sip of the rich red wine to steady herself before speaking. She'd mulled over various ways of explaining the situation to Charlotte, but had finally decided that the direct approach would be the best. Charlotte might be surprised, but not horrified or offended.

"I need your help to commit a crime," Cornelia said finally.

Charlotte cocked her head to one side, her short blond curls bouncing. "Come again, *ma chérie?*"

Cornelia launched into the tale of John's mysterious injuries, building the preservation tank, and the search for the radium. "And so," she finally concluded, "I need to get into the Santa Monica bunker. I'm not asking you to accompany me—just because I'm sinking this low doesn't mean I intend to drag anyone else down with me. But I was hoping you might have some ideas. I have no idea where to begin." She took another sip of her wine, and waited to see Charlotte's reaction.

The other woman had been calmly sipping her own wine while Cornelia talked, and now she set her glass down on the table. "You poor dear," she said sympathetically. "This is so very terrible, that such a tragedy continues to grow worse." She shook her head, her expression sorrowful. "Tell me, do you still order wine and spirits from the Arrows Through the Heart Nightclub?"

"I do." Should anyone besides Charlotte inquire about such a thing, Arrows Through the Heart was a respectable nightclub and all she ordered from there was ice.

"Have you ever met Lou Vincini, the owner?"

Cornelia shook her head. "I've never actually been there. Ronald occasionally picks up the drink order, but usually their driver brings it when he delivers the ice."

"Selling illicit beverages is only one of Lou Vincini's talents," said Charlotte. "He's quite knowledgeable when it comes to the magical arts. Not so much a practitioner himself, but he knows how magic works, how to find things, and who to talk to."

Cornelia was not surprised by this news. When nationwide Prohibition had officially begun, Charlotte had referred Cornelia to the Arrows Through the Heart Nightclub as the most trustworthy and secretive speakeasy in the city. She might have known that Charlotte had more reasons for supporting the place than just liking the liquor.

"Charlotte, I've never been to a speakeasy before."

"Oh, piffle—don't look so worried, Cornelia!" Charlotte said with a laugh. "Lou is a good man, once you get to know him. Just be sure to take a lot of money to encourage him to talk to you—and a talisman or magical trinket for barter wouldn't hurt, either. And be sure to tell him I sent you—we've known each other for years. Now, as for how to find the place..." Charlotte then launched into a long string of directions, until Cornelia asked for a pencil and paper to write it down. Most of the streets were in a part of town that she'd never been to before, far away from the districts of elite shopping and Hollywood homes.

"I probably shouldn't show up to this place in a shiny Rolls-Royce driven by a chauffeur," Cornelia remarked, reading over the directions she'd copied down.

Charlotte gave a tittering laugh. "Something more subtle would be better, yes. Doesn't your husband have a motorcycle?"

"A modified old Indian, used as a scouting bike during the War. John taught me how to ride it, although I usually just ride it around our property or on the empty roads outside the neighborhood."

"*Très bien*," said Charlotte. "For this, a woman on a motorcycle will attract far less attention than a woman in a Silver Ghost."

"I can hardly believe I'm doing this," Cornelia said, folding up the paper with the directions and putting it into her purse. "But I can't thank you enough for listening to me and helping me, Charlotte."

"Anything for you, darling. And to help you save John."

The nervous flutterings that had begun while Charlotte talked about visiting the speakeasy abruptly stilled. It didn't matter how strange, inappropriate, dangerous, or even terrifying anything might be—she would do it all and more to save John. She reached out and grabbed Charlotte's hand, giving it an appreciative squeeze.

The clock on the mantel struck ten. Early still, for an evening out on the town—or at a speakeasy—but she had a long night ahead of her. "Thank you for the wine, Charlotte." She stood up. "I'd best get going, so I can transform myself into a brazen motorcycle-riding gin mill flapper," she said with a dry chuckle.

Charlotte laughed, too, and air-kissed her cheeks before walking with her to the door. "*Bonne chance* to you, darling,"

Charlotte called as Cornelia descended the steps down to the sidewalk outside.

NEARLY TWO HOURS LATER, Cornelia turned the motorcycle into the alleyway behind the low brick building with the faded lettering of *Chas. H. Printing House* painted on the side. She pulled up behind a row of trash cans to park, and switched off the engine. The alley was dark, cold, and smelled like a latrine. Hardly the sort of place she'd expect Charlotte to frequent, but apparently Lou Vincini was a diamond hiding in this rough.

Well, this was certainly an evening of firsts. Her first time skulking around outside a military bunker, the first time she'd ridden the motorcycle in city traffic, and the first time she'd been to a speakeasy. John would be shocked at her behavior, she mused. But she'd have plenty of time to apologize to him after she'd saved his life.

Climbing off the bike, she adjusted her clothing—not that she had any hope of looking decent in this getup. She had on her black riding pants and tall black boots that were reserved for the very rare occasions that she went horseback riding. But instead of a white blouse with hunter green wool jacket, like proper equestrian gear, she'd put on a black blouse and a black leather jacket. She slipped the motorcycle key into a pocket as she descended the concrete steps to the basement entrance of the building.

Cornelia rapped on the door as she pulled off her driving goggles. She started to pull off the snug aviator-style cap so she could straighten out her hair, but then thought the better of it. The less she looked like herself here, the better. She kept the cap on, covering her auburn hair, and let the goggles hang loose around her neck.

A little window in the door slid open and a pair of black eyes squinted through.

Cornelia met the steely gaze. "Cupid is dead," she said, reciting the password that Charlotte had told her.

The window slid shut, then the door opened—just partway, barely wide enough for her to slip through. A small, wizened old Chinese man closed the door behind her.

"I need to speak with Lou Vincini," she said to him.

His gaze was unblinking and fierce, and he made no move to indicate that he'd even heard or understood her question.

The secrecy of a speakeasy, Cornelia reminded herself, and made her way across the dimly lit room to the bar. A scattering of people sat at tables tucked in far recesses of the smoky haze in the room, and she felt their eyes following her.

A large balding man stood behind the bar, wiping down a glass. Gold and bejeweled rings flashed from his fingers. That had to be Lou Vincini. She stopped directly in front of him.

He looked at her intently, but didn't stop with his slow wiping. "What'll it be, doll?"

"I'm not here to drink," she said, pulling off her black gloves.

Still smoothing his rag over the glass in his hand, he looked her up and down, his eyes lingering over her chest. Cornelia forced herself to stay motionless and not slap him. She was grateful for the dim lighting, which she hoped didn't show her flush of mortification.

"This ain't that kind of joint, doll," he finally said, when he was finished perusing her body. "Try the brothel across the alley."

Cornelia clenched her jaw. This night was just getting better and better. She unbuttoned one of her jacket pockets, pulled out a folded fifty-dollar bill and slid it across the counter to him. "I'd like to speak with Lou Vincini. I have a very...delicate problem, and I need his help. Charlotte de Fontaine recommended him."

The man finally stopped wiping the drinking glass and set it and the rag on the counter. He took the folded bill and slipped it into his vest pocket, then angled his head to the right. "Step right into my office, doll. Lou Vincini, at your service."

He lifted a section of the bar to let her through, and then ushered her into a small stuffy room. Crates of liquor bottles were stacked all around, leaving only a narrow walkway from the door to the paper-strewn desk.

Lou switched on the desk lamp. The dim bulb shaded by dark-green glass gave a sickly pallor to the cramped room. He pulled a rickety wooden swivel chair out from behind the desk, gestured for her to sit, and then leaned against the edge of the desk.

"So what's this delicate matter you need help with?"

Cornelia sat down carefully in the unsteady-looking, battered chair. "I need to retrieve a rare and dangerous item from a military bunker in the Santa Monica mountains," she said. Might as well cut to the chase right away.

He paused in lighting a cigarette. "You don't do things small, huh, doll? Well, first of all, I don't tangle with the Feds or the military." He struck a match and puffed on his cigarette a moment.

Cornelia pulled another fifty-dollar bill out of her jacket pocket, and then a thick pan of amber as long as her hand. "That's Baltic amber," she said, handing them both to Lou. "The finest quality, and it's been used for spell-casting for close to a century. Very imbued with magical energy."

Lou pocketed the money without looking at it, and turned the flat chunk of amber over in his hand. "Hmmp," he grunted, blowing out smoke. "I got half a dozen lumps of amber." He set it on the desk. "Look, doll, just because I've got the local cops in my pay doesn't mean I want to deal with government men. And certainly not the military. I did my part during the War, you know. What've you got against our boys?"

"Nothing," she said. "I'm as much of a loyal American as you are." Whatever that might mean, considering he was a gangster. "Look, Mr. Vincini, I'm not asking you to do anything. I just need either the means to get into this facility myself and retrieve what I need, or for you to point me to someone else who can help me."

Lou took a drag of his cigarette. "That's going to cost you way more than a hundred bucks and a lump of amber."

Cornelia sighed. "I'm already a paying customer, Mr. Vincini. I buy two to three bottles of spirits from you nearly every week. I'm Mrs. John G. Jones."

Lou pulled his cigarette out of his mouth and straightened up. "Mrs. Jones. Well, it's a real pleasure to make your acquaintance." He picked up the cigarette box from the desk and held it out to her.

She shook her head. "No, thank you. We've been very pleased with the quality of your beverages, Mr. Vincini. And Charlotte de Fontaine also speaks very highly of you and your ability to find out information that others can't."

"This joint don't look like much, but I take pride in offering only the best stuff," said Lou. "No bathtub gin here. You and Miss Fontaine are some of my best customers, and I'm happy to serve my best customers in any way I can. Especially with the 'special' stuff that most speakies don't do."

"Glad to hear it. So you can help, then."

Lou took another puff. "Well, like I said, I'm not going to do nothing to get on the bad side of the Feds, if you know what I mean. What sort of information are you wanting to find out?"

"How to get into a secure military base."

"Look, Mrs. Jones, I'd love to help, but I already told you I ain't going to tangle with that."

"And I already said that I wasn't asking you to *do* anything," she said, trying to keep her growing frustration out of her voice. "Just help me figure out how to do it myself, or show me to someone who can help."

He squinted at her over his cigarette. "A good set of lock picks and an invisible cloak oughtta do you just fine," he said with a deadpan expression. "I can loan you my lock picks."

Cornelia glared at him and stood up. "This is not a joke, Mr. Vincini. I'm sorry to have wasted your time. Keep the money and the amber, but consider next week's liquor order to be my last."

He put out a hand and grabbed her arm as she started to move towards the door. His grip was surprisingly gentle. "Wait, Mrs. Jones. I'm sorry." He snuffed out his cigarette in the ashtray, then laid his other hand on her shoulder and guided her back down into the chair. "I was only fooling. I think I can help you. I was serious about the lock picks, though. You know how to pick a lock?"

She gave a reluctant nod. John had a very elaborate set of lock picks that he used for numerous sorts of tinkering—including picking locks to trunks, cupboards, and other things in their own house whenever the keys went missing. Rawlins had gotten good at making duplicate keys to anything and everything in the house after having to help John pick the lock to his own dressing room. And then there was that time she'd picked the lock to the science lab when she was at college, as Rawlins had so gleefully reminded her earlier.

"Good," said Lou with a nod. "So the invisible cloak thing's a gag, obviously, but a confusion spell might work. You know, in case you run into guards or whatnot. Know any confusion spells?"

"Not offhand," said Cornelia. "But I do know that I have at least one spell book with befuddlement charms."

"Good, good." Lou gave her a smile—a genuine, kindly smile, even though it was punctuated by several gold teeth. "Now we're getting somewhere. I gotta ask, though—why would a society dame like you want to break into anything, especially a military base? What's so important?"

Cornelia swallowed the sudden lump in her throat. "My husband's life is at stake."

Lou nodded solemnly, and Cornelia was grateful that he didn't ask her to elaborate. "Okay, so you got lock picks and a confusion spell. So now, let's see..." He lit another cigarette. "Are you better with crystals or plant magic?"

"Either, I suppose, though I have more experience with plants and herbs. I'm not very good at brewing potions, though." She'd need Charlotte's help if she had to mix potions.

"You could take along some plants for protection and good fortune," he said. "Whatever you've got on hand that's the most powerful. I got some dried herbs myself, if you need anything." He pulled his cigarette out of his mouth and jabbed at the air. "Mistletoe. That would be good to have in case the lock picks ain't enough."

"Mistletoe opens locks," Cornelia said, remembering the various herbals that she'd read recently.

"Exactly."

The mistletoe ball that hung in the sitting room doorway had been taken down a few days ago, along with the rest of the Christmas decorations. Cornelia wasn't actually sure what happened to all the greenery each year after the holidays, but she felt confident that Joey the gardener would be able to get her a sprig of mistletoe.

"You also probably shouldn't try to do this all alone." Lou's voice brought her mind back to the present. "Clearly you ain't no fainting wallflower, but it's always a good idea to have someone watching your back. Especially if you ain't had much experience with this sort of thing." He took a puff of his cigarette. "You got someone who could watch your back? If not, I can recommend a couple of guys who could help you out—for a fee, of course. And if the operation goes south, you don't know me and them guys don't know me, either, you understand?"

Cornelia nodded and swallowed nervously. She did not at all like the idea of using hired thugs as her backup. She'd rather go it alone, in that case. But what he said made sense—a venture of this magnitude would be easier and safer with an extra set of eyes and hands. Rawlins had sworn to help in any way he could, but there was no way she could ask him to help break into the bunker. Besides, if something went wrong, she'd need a steady mind at home to handle things. Ronald would be a better choice, since he was younger and already knew the lay of the land.

"I have someone who can help me," she said to Lou. She hated to ask any of her staff to participate in such a venture, but it was the best choice right now.

Lou nodded and shifted his large bulk against the edge of the desk. "Sounds like you've got the makings of a swell little hit lined up, then. Don't forget to take along some regular weapons, too, not just all the spells and stuff. You know, some knives or a gun or something."

"Yes, I was planning to take weapons and tools with me," she said. She was starting to feel a little more confident about getting into the facility, but the next step would likely be harder than that—locating the radium. "Mr. Vincini, I appreciate all the suggestions you've made, but I have a feeling that getting into this building will be the easy part."

"Probably so," he said, puffing on his cigarette. "Shouldn't be too bad if you know how to use the lock picks and the mistletoe."

She frowned at him. "What I mean is that once I'm inside, I need to know where I'm going, how to find what I'm looking for."

Lou took a long drag and didn't answer right away. Cornelia wondered if she'd need to produce some more money.

The amber was the only non-monetary item she'd brought along as barter, since she had no idea what he would consider valuable.

"If you're asking for a map of the place, I can't help you," he said finally. "Like I told you, I don't tangle with the military. I ain't sending any of my boys to scope out the place."

"Then do you know someone who might know their way around? I can pay, of course." She unbuttoned her jacket pocket with the money in it.

He blew out a slow puff of smoke. "Are you looking for a person, an object, or information inside this place?" he asked.

"An object. A fairly small object." She held up her right fist.

"Hmm." Lou snuffed out his cigarette in the overflowing ashtray on the desk. "I think I might have just the thing for you." He went around behind the desk and began rummaging in one of the liquor crates in the corner. "Ah, here we are." He came back around the desk.

"I think this can help you, Mrs. Jones." He held up a tiny glass vial, barely as long as a pinky finger. It had a small cork stopper, and was filled with an inky black liquid. "This is all I've got left. It's a rare concoction, made with some pretty exotic ingredients. It's a seeker's potion—helps you find what you're looking for. Just uncork the bottle and speak out loud what you're searching for. Be sure to be real specific. The fumes that float out of the bottle will show the path to what you're looking for." He held the little vial in front of the desk lamp and squinted at it. "I'd wager there's about two or three uses left in here." He held it out to Cornelia.

Gingerly she took the tiny bottle. Could she trust him? Was this potion in fact what he claimed?

"It ain't a gag," Lou said, as if he could sense her doubts. "I don't sell bathtub gin, and I don't sell snake-oil magic potions. It's the real deal."

Charlotte would not have recommended him if his potions were suspect. She carefully put the vial into one of her jacket pockets. "Thank you. What do I owe you for it?"

"Well, normally a potion like that would be worth at least its weight in gold. Got some pretty rare and expensive ingredients in it. But if you've got another fifty in your pocket, we can call it square. I'm always happy to help out a friend of Miss Fontaine's."

Cornelia pulled out another fifty dollar bill and handed it to him.

"Oh, and one last tip," he said as he put the bill in his vest pocket. "The outfit you're wearing right now is perfect for a job like this. I'm not sure what you were planning on wearing, but don't try to break into nothing all dolled up in your glad rags."

Cornelia managed a smile. "I was saving my new couture ball gown for another occasion, so I'll wear this. Thanks for the advice."

He gave her a gold-toothed grin. "Glad to be of service. Before you go, let me give you one more thing." He went around to the other side of the desk and rummaged in one of the drawers. "Free of charge, just because I like you and I appreciate your business." He came back around the desk and handed her a small flat stone. The soft grayish-white mineral had a Celtic knotwork design carved on both sides. "Protection token," he said. "I've used it before so I know it works. Just as some added help in case you come across armed guards or booby traps."

Cornelia squeezed the small stone between her fingers before slipping it into her jacket pocket. "Thank you."

She should be able to gather all the supplies she needed fairly quickly, even the mistletoe. That would give her all day tomorrow to help Rawlins with the rest of the work still needed on John's machine; and then after dark tomorrow night, she'd head into the mountains.

She stood up from the chair and extended her right hand. "Thank you for your help, Mr. Vincini. My butler will be calling in a few days to place my regular order."

Lou took her hand in a firm but gentle grasp. "A pleasure doing business with you, Mrs. Jones. And good luck to you."

She swallowed. "Thank you." She would more need than a little good luck to pull off this insane plan.

Chapter 6

"I'm glad we finally finished connecting all of the hoses today," Cornelia said to Rawlins. "Will you be able to finish connecting the pressure gauges this evening?"

"Yes, ma'am," said Rawlins around a bite of food.

They were seated at a table in the basement lab, eating an early dinner of cold ham sandwiches. They'd been in the preservation tank room all day, working feverishly on the machine. Only a few small tasks remained to be finished, and then it would be ready for the radium. Which she should have later tonight.

"I have no idea how long it will take to get the radium," Cornelia said. "But Ronald and I will certainly be back before morning."

"Yes, ma'am," said Rawlins again. "Are you sure you want to do this?"

Cornelia narrowed her eyes at him as she chewed a bite of her sandwich. "This whole insane escapade was your idea, Rawlins. Don't you dare try to talk me out of it now."

He shook his head. "Of course not, ma'am. I just want to make sure you're prepared, is all."

"Of course I'm prepared," she replied, a bit more snappishly than she meant to. She was as prepared as she could be: tools, spells, and clothes were all laid out and ready. The only trouble was that she was absolutely terrified—but it was too late to turn back now.

Footsteps sounded on the slate steps, and Cornelia turned around on the bench to see Theda slowly descending into the basement.

"Yes, Theda?" said Cornelia, as the girl paused on the bottom step. The poor maid was very nervous around most of John's inventions, and avoided the basement as much as she could.

"Um, there's someone here to see you, ma'am," said Theda. "Miss Snufflett-Frye."

Cornelia raised her eyebrows. "Adelaide? Why would she be visiting? She didn't call earlier, did she?"

"No, ma'am," said Theda. "She insists on speaking with you, though. She told me to tell you it was urgent, ma'am."

Rawlins rose up from the bench. "I'll speak with her, Miz Jones, and send her away."

"No, don't bother." Cornelia waved at him to sit back down. "You're a builder right now, Rawlins, not a butler. Just finish your dinner and keep working." She dabbed at her mouth with her napkin and stood up. "I'll talk to her, and be back down shortly."

Cornelia followed Theda up the stairs and down the hallway to the foyer. Adelaide, her gloves in her hand but still wearing her coat and hat, stood examining the French impressionist painting on the wall above the telephone table.

"Cornelia!" said Adelaide, turning to smile at her. "I'm sorry to drop by unannounced, but it's very important. Could we talk for a moment?"

"Just for a moment," said Cornelia, showing her into the sitting room. "Forgive my attire—" she gestured at her dirty trousers, rumpled blouse, and messily pinned-back hair "—but I wasn't expecting callers."

"It's all right," said Adelaide, sitting down on the gold mohair sofa and pulling off her cloche hat. "I should have telephoned you first. I'm sorry to interrupt you while you're working." Her tone was polite and easy-going, as always, though Cornelia noticed a flicker of surprise in the girl's eyes as she took in Cornelia's appearance. Women of their social class didn't usually "work" at anything.

Cornelia perched on one of the russet-colored upholstered armchairs, hoping that the seat of her pants wasn't too dirty.

"Cornelia, what's going on?" Adelaide said as soon as they were seated, the relaxed tone gone from her voice now. "I know you're up to something."

Cornelia sighed. "Adelaide, I appreciate your interest and concern, and I'm sorry that I've been so reclusive, but what I'm working on is important and time is of the essence."

"I know," said Adelaide. "That's why I'm here. I want to help."

"Adelaide, now is not the best time for magical tutoring."

"I know you're working to save your husband. I know you're about to do something very dangerous in order to save him, and I'm here to help you."

"What?" said Cornelia in surprise. "How could you possibly know that?"

"I was at the salon earlier this afternoon, and Miss de Fontaine told me that I should go see you."

"What?" Cornelia said again, stunned now. How could Charlotte have broken her confidence like that? "What did Charlotte tell you?"

"Only that you were about to do something very important tonight and that you'd need my help for it."

"Why would she tell you that?"

"Charlotte is like us, isn't she?" Adelaide said earnestly, her blue eyes sparkling.

Cornelia pursed her lips and frowned at Adelaide. "Yes, she is," she said. But what was Charlotte trying to accomplish by getting Adelaide mixed up in all this mess? Cornelia always appreciated Charlotte's wisdom and insights—but this? She was tempted to call Charlotte right now and question this betrayal of her secrets.

"So, what are we doing?" Adelaide's bright voice interrupted her inner grumblings.

"What? No—*we* are doing nothing." Cornelia stood up and went over to take Adelaide by the arm. "*You* are going home right now. I'll call a taxicab for you—"

"No." Adelaide's voice was suddenly fierce as she stood up and yanked her arm out of Cornelia's grip. "Charlotte is worried about you, and so am I. I don't care if you're casting the world's biggest spell tonight or committing the crime of the century. I'm staying."

Cornelia stared at the younger woman for a moment, angry at her defiance, but also feeling a strange wave of gratitude. "Why?" she finally said. "Why do you want to help me? Why such a determined loyalty to someone you hardly know?"

"Hardly know?" Adelaide echoed. "I think I'm getting to know you pretty well." She smiled. "I want to help because I want to learn. And because I know that you actually care. You've been kinder to me in the short time I've been in Los Angeles than my family has been my entire life. I've always been the black sheep of my family, but you've shown me a place where I can actually fit in."

Cornelia swallowed the sudden lump in her throat. Her simple encouragements about scientific and magical pursuits had truly meant that much to this girl? She felt as if she ought to say "you're welcome," but that seemed a paltry reply to Adelaide's heartfelt confession. She swallowed again.

"And besides," Adelaide said into the silence. "We cunning women have to stick together, right?" She grinned.

Cornelia gave a wry smile. "Cunning women indeed." Apparently there was no fighting this girl—or Charlotte, for that matter, the devious little Cajun. "I'll need every ounce of cunning I can muster tonight. You guessed correctly—I'm preparing to commit the crime of the century."

"Really?" Adelaide's eyes widened. "Golly! What are we doing?"

Cornelia shook her head at her use of 'we.' "I'm breaking into a secret military bunker."

"Golly!" Adelaide breathed again. "So when do we leave?"

"Adelaide, I can't allow you to come with me. What I'm doing is dangerous, not to mention illegal."

"I figured that, since you said it's the crime of the century."

"Adelaide—"

"Cornelia." Adelaide stepped closer and looked into her eyes. "We're doing this together."

She stared at the younger woman's fierce expression, still feeling that bizarre blurring of shock and intense gratitude. This was a monumentally bad decision, she was sure—but right now, she didn't have the time or the will to fight it.

"All right," she said with a sigh of defeat. "Come on down to the basement and I'll give you all the details. Let's go."

CORNELIA HUNCHED LOW over the handlebars of the motorcycle as she sped up the winding mountain path. The chilly, dusty wind bit at her face, a stark contrast to the warm pressure of Adelaide's arms around her midsection.

Three people wouldn't fit on the bike, and bringing the car was a bad idea, so with reluctance Cornelia had left Ronald behind and brought Adelaide instead. Ronald had protested, Rawlins had protested, and Cornelia herself protested again—and yet here she was, bringing Adelaide into her own problems.

Ronald had suggested attaching the side car to the motorcycle so they could all three go, but that would have made the bike a lot slower, as well as more noticeable. A car would have been the fastest, as well as potentially the most secure—but also the most recognizable, even if they drove the older Packard. Then Adelaide had remarked that, should they be caught, the police or military authorities would likely be more lenient on two upper-class women than any men who might be in their party.

Her logic was sound, and so here they were, two women about to commit the crime of the century. Of all the magic that Cornelia might have considered teaching Adelaide one day, lock-picking and befuddlement charms were not what she'd wanted to start with.

About half way up the mountain, Cornelia switched off the motorcycle's headlight. There was no way to disguise the noise of the engine, but hopefully the lack of light would make the bike harder to pinpoint right away, should someone hear the echoing roar of the motor. The moon was bright enough for her to see the dirt road as it wound up the hillside around to the back entrance.

As before, there were no vehicles parked and the place appeared to be deserted. Cornelia pulled over to some bushes at the far edge of the parking lot and switched off the engine. After they'd climbed off, she pulled the front end of the bike up behind the bushes. The bushes hid the chrome handlebars, and the rest of the bike was painted black, so hopefully it wouldn't be easily spotted.

"What a rush!" Adelaide said in an enthusiastic whisper, pulling off her goggles. "I've never been on a motorcycle before."

"Glad you enjoyed it," Cornelia quipped. Normally she loved the rush of motorcycle riding as well—unladylike though it was—but right now she was far too nervous to have enjoyed the ride.

Since Adelaide had ridden behind Cornelia, she was wearing the leather satchel that had all of the breaking-and-entering tools in it. Cornelia took the satchel from Adelaide as she pulled off her driving goggles. Stashing them in the satchel, she slung the bag over her chest, and pointed up the hill. "The entrance hatch we're going to use is up there."

They crossed the dusty parking lot and began climbing up the hill. Adelaide lagged behind as the hill grew steeper.

"Are you going to be able to manage in those shoes?" Cornelia said in a low voice as Adelaide caught up to her.

"I'm fine," the younger woman replied, her voice full of confidence.

Cornelia did not have another set of black horseback-riding livery, but she'd found a pair of black trousers and another black blouse for Adelaide to wear, and Ronald had donated his chauffeur's coat. The only thing Cornelia didn't have was another pair of suitable boots, so Adelaide had opted to wear the black buckle pumps that she'd been wearing with her dress.

They finally reached the round metal hatch in the hillside, and together they managed to turn the wheel.

Before pulling open the hatch, Cornelia reached into the satchel and pulled out one of the guns she'd brought. "Just in case someone is waiting in the dark on the other side of this door," she whispered, handing it to Adelaide. "Now remember, this gun doesn't use bullets. Twist that knob on the side, then point and squeeze the trigger."

Adelaide nodded and licked her lips, and held the bulky gun pointed at the hatch.

Cornelia had brought her regular revolver, but the gun she'd given Adelaide was one of John's inventions, which they called a Tesla gun. A miniature Tesla coil inside the barrel of the gun discharged an electrical field, which was useful in both incapacitating a person and in disrupting certain types of magic spells.

With a quiet grunt of effort, Cornelia heaved up on the hatch's wheel, and the door creaked open. Nothing emerged from the tunnel below them. Cornelia pulled out the flashlight and shone it down into the empty passage.

"There should be another door at the bottom of this tunnel that leads into the bunker," Cornelia murmured to Adelaide. "So once we get down there, keep the Tesla gun ready, because I'll probably have to pick that lock."

Cornelia put away the flashlight and dug in the satchel for a different set of goggles, these much larger and heavier than driving goggles. A wire attached the eye pieces to a bulky battery pack which Cornelia fastened around her waist with a belt. Another of John's tinkerings, the goggles converted just the tiniest bit of ambient light as well as infrared wavelengths into the visible spectrum. This way she could navigate the dark tunnel without having to use the flashlight and potentially alert any guards.

They climbed down the ladder, leaving the hatch above open so they could get back out. At the bottom of the ladder was a solid metal door, locked tight, just as Ronald had reported when they were here yesterday.

Picking the lock was an easy matter. After just a few seconds of probing, Cornelia felt the springs and levers shift, and the lock turned with a loud click. She froze, but then hearing nothing else, she pulled out her revolver and tugged open the door.

They were somewhere deep inside the bunker, and at this point there was no ambient light and apparently little in the way of infrared beside the two of them, so the night-vision goggles became useless. Cornelia switched off the battery pack, put the battery and the goggles back in the satchel, and turned on the flashlight.

A gray, featureless corridor stretched in both directions, silent, cold, and blessedly empty.

"Which way?" Adelaide whispered.

Cornelia unbuttoned one of her jacket pockets. "Let's find out."

Time to learn if Lou Vincini's seeker's potion was worth the one-hundred-fifty dollars and the trip to a speakeasy. She handed the flashlight to Adelaide and gingerly uncorked the tiny vial.

"Show me the path to John's radium," she said, raising her voice above a whisper and hoping no one was nearby.

A wisp like black fog rose out of the little bottle and floated down the corridor. They hurried after it. The wisp stayed about two feet ahead of them, leading them around several corners and down long hallways. Cornelia tried to remember the turns. *Left, left, right, second left...* She had no idea the bunker was this big. This much space was certainly not needed just for the gravity matrix resonator engine project. What else was this bunker laboratory used for?

Finally the dark wisp stopped in front of a solid metal door, just like all the others they'd passed, then floated through the keyhole. Cornelia corked the bottle and tried the door handle, just in case. Unsurprisingly, it was locked, so she dug out the lock picks again.

Once the lock clicked, Cornelia took the flashlight from Adelaide and motioned for her to take out the Tesla gun. She'd put her little silver revolver in one of her pockets for easy access, and after giving the door a push, she transferred the flashlight to her left hand and pulled out her gun.

The room was dark and silent. Quickly she flashed her light around the room, tracking the movement with the gun in her right hand. A storage room of some kind—a very large one, from what she could see of the rows upon rows of metal shelves. She didn't immediately see any windows or other exits, so after closing the door behind them, she found the light switch with her flashlight and flipped it on.

Adelaide made a little noise and held up her hand to shield her eyes. Cornelia squinted in the sudden brightness as she looked around. Definitely a storage area—easily as large as a factory warehouse—with boxes and crates stacked ceiling-high on shelves. The magic wisp of fog had ceased when she'd corked the vial, but now she realized she should have left it uncorked—otherwise they'd be here all night if they had to go through every shelf and crate in this enormous room.

"We're looking for a small box, right?" whispered Adelaide, a dismayed tone to her voice.

"The amount of radium John ordered should be smaller than my fist, and it would have been shipped in a secure lead box—so yes, a small metal container, perhaps ten inches long or so. Heavy, but it should still fit in this satchel."

Putting away her gun and flashlight, she held up the seeker's potion. The vial was about half empty now. She uncorked it again. "Show me John's radium," she said.

The black wisp floated out of the vial and down a long row of shelves. They followed it till it stopped at a set of shelves that lined the back wall of the room. The wisp settled on a small metal box on a shelf just above their heads.

Cornelia corked the vial and put in back in her pocket.

With a grunt of effort, she reached up and pulled the small heavy box down from the shelf, grateful for her black leather gloves as the corner of the box scraped against her fingers. Several labels were pasted all over the box, saying "Danger: Radioactive Material Inside." On the top of the box was the shipping label with John's name and the date it was delivered, back in August.

Cornelia felt a wave of relief, but she needed to make absolutely sure—she couldn't afford to have this be a wasted trip. She unclasped the lid. Inside the thick lead walls of the box was a smaller box. She pulled the lid off that one. A small chunk of rock was tucked in a nest of black cloth. The rock was a dullish silver overall in color, but held an odd faint sheen of greenish light.

She let out a long sigh as she closed up the box. "This is it," she murmured. "We can go now."

"Are all of these boxes radium?" Adelaide asked. She was looking up at the shelves in front of them.

Cornelia scanned the rows of large metal crates that lined the shelves. Each one was stamped with "Danger: Radioactive Material Inside" as well as the label of "Ra-197."

"How strange," Cornelia said. "Yes, according to the labels all of these contain radium—the same isotope that John ordered, radium-197. It's very rare. John chose this particular isotope of radium to power his conservation tank because it produces both beta and gamma radiation. It also has a half-life period of nearly one hundred years, making it relatively simple and predictable to work with—as far as radioactive materials go."

She reached for one of the boxes on the lowest shelf and slid it off onto the floor. Adelaide helped her to open the clamps and lift off both sets of lids. Inside was a lump of radium—packaged the same way that John's was, except that this chunk of rocky material was at least as big as her head.

"Golly, that's a big hunk of radium," said Adelaide as they closed up the box. "Is this to power the gravity machine that John was building?"

"No," said Cornelia as together they heaved the metal box back onto the shelf. "At least, not all of this. They'd discussed the idea of using radium-197 to power the gravity matrix, but I don't think they'd settled on it. But even so, it would need a piece of radium only about half that size." She gestured at the box on the shelf. "But this..."

She looked up at the shelves again and felt an odd chill. There were a dozen metal boxes this size just on the shelves directly above her. Looking both to her left and her right, as far as she could see, boxes labeled "Ra-197" lined the wall.

"If a lump of radium half that size could power an engine that cancels gravity," said Adelaide slowly, "then what would anyone be using this much of it for? This would be enough radium to...to power a city bigger than Los Angeles and New York put together."

"I don't like this," Cornelia said, half to herself. "Radium-197 is such a rare isotope that I didn't know there was even this much in the entire world. And here's half a warehouse full of it."

"We could look around some more," said Adelaide. "It doesn't seem like anyone is here."

Cornelia started to protest, as she knelt down to wrestle the heavy box of radium into her leather satchel. They got what they came for and they'd been strangely fortunate—they should quit while they were ahead and just leave. But even as she started to say that aloud she saw Adelaide's logic.

She'd been trying to get access to this lab for over a week now, wanting details about the accident and the current status of the gravity engine. She'd never get another chance like this.

Reaching into her pocket for the seeker's potion, her fingers brushed another vial. Before leaving the house, she'd burnt a collection of star anise, bay leaves, and chamomile for protection and good luck. She'd put the ashes into two small vials, for each of them to carry. She clutched the little tube of burnt herbs, then pulled out the seeker's potion.

"All right," she said, standing up and slinging the now-heavy satchel over her shoulder. "We shouldn't pass up this opportunity, but we must be careful. And you must promise me that if anything happens, you'll take this satchel and run. Don't wait for me."

Adelaide nodded as they started back down the row of shelves towards the door. Cornelia grabbed Adelaide's arm and halted them in the middle of the row.

"Adelaide, I mean it. If something happens, if guards show up—I'm going to give you this satchel and tell you to run. You have to do everything you can to get out and get home. I can pay lawyers to get myself out of prison if need be—but John will die without that radium. Promise me that if I tell you to go, you'll go."

She kept a tight grip on Adelaide's arm—probably too tight—until the girl gave a solemn nod. "I promise, Cornelia."

Back at the door, Cornelia switched off the light in the room, plunging them into blackness. They listened at the door, then Cornelia peered out with her flashlight—the hallway was empty as before. With her lock picks she re-locked the door—oddly more difficult than unlocking the door—and then she uncorked the seeker's potion.

"Show me the path to the magnetic resonator gravity matrix engine," Cornelia said. No wisp of black fog appeared in the beam of her flashlight.

"Maybe it doesn't know what that means," suggested Adelaide.

"It took us straight to the radium," said Cornelia. "We shouldn't have to give it a science lesson for it to find something—it's magic." She sighed. "All right, let's try this. Show me the path to John's anti-gravity machine." Maybe the potion needed a personal connection in order to find something.

Still nothing. She held up the vial in the beam of light—it was still nearly a third full of the inky black liquid. Based on what they'd done so far, that should be enough for at least one more use.

"Now what?" said Adelaide, sounding worried.

What now, indeed? They could simply break into each room one at a time, to see what else this facility was being used for; but that seemed dangerously time-consuming. What she needed was more solid information.

"Show us to the office of the leader of this place," she said.

Black fog drifted out and floated down the hall. They followed the floating wisp, and Cornelia looked over at Adelaide.

"It was worth a try," she said. "Major Brandt—or whoever is actually in charge of this place—ought to have an office here, and maybe that's where we can find John's notes. Or information about what all that radium is for, or something."

The wafting potion led them down several more turns and halted at a door just like all of the others in this place. This door boasted the only labeling she'd seen: the word "office" was painted above the door frame.

So the potion was not faulty. If it couldn't find the gravity machine, then that must mean that the device was no longer here—or was so damaged that it was no longer recognizable as what it was supposed to be. Cornelia felt a flush of frustration as she knelt down to work on the door lock—that meant she wouldn't be able to examine it to learn more about the accident. But the leader's office was the next best thing.

This lock proved to be far more stubborn than the others she'd worked on thus far. She glanced up to make sure that Adelaide had the Tesla gun out and ready, and then dug in the satchel for the sprig of mistletoe.

She traced the outline of the doorframe with the little plant, then held the sprig over the keyhole, visualized lock pins and springs loosening in her mind, and muttered, "Open." Then she tried the door with the picks again, and within seconds it unlocked.

Cornelia switched on the light. The room was austere and tidy—tall wooden file cabinets lined the far wall, and a large wooden desk sat in the center of the room, with a solitary chair. Several neat stacks of papers, a telephone, and an empty ashtray were the only things on the desk. The only decoration in the room—if it could be called that—was a large world map on the wall.

Cornelia went over to look at the map while Adelaide headed for the desk. There appeared to be nothing unusual about the map—it showed both topographical formations and political boundaries, and had latitude and longitude lines. No other markings or anything to indicate that it was anything more than a decorative reference tool.

"Look at these letters," said Adelaide from over by the desk. "Judging by the postmarks, they would have arrived here either yesterday or today, and they've all been opened. So I don't think this place has been abandoned."

"It certainly looks that way," said Cornelia, joining her at the desk. She picked up a stack of envelopes. At a quick glance, all of the papers on the desk all appeared to be correspondences. She dreaded going through all of the file cabinets, but that was the next most likely place that any records or notes about the gravity matrix project might be.

"See if there are any letters for John," Cornelia said, gesturing at the pile Adelaide was looking through. John had never mentioned receiving mail at this lab, but it couldn't hurt to look. All of the envelopes in her stack were addressed to people whose names she didn't recognize.

She replaced the envelopes on the desk, then crossed the room to the file cabinet. The drawers were all locked. She sighed and dug for the lock picks again.

"Look at this," said Adelaide, turning towards here with a letter in hand. Apparently she'd decided to open each envelope. Cornelia opened her mouth to tell the girl that they shouldn't waste time reading every personal letter in the office, but

Adelaide held the paper out towards her. "This looks like some kind of secret code."

Cornelia crossed back over to the desk and looked at the sheet of paper Adelaide had unfolded. Pairs of letters were arranged in a grid-like pattern across the page, reading apparent gibberish. "Yes, that does look like a coded message. Any indication that it's been decoded?"

Adelaide flipped the paper over, then checked the envelope. "Doesn't look like it. Based on the postmark, it probably arrived earlier today, so maybe they didn't have a chance to decode it yet. The return address is a post office box here in Los Angeles. Funny to send a secret code just across town."

Funny indeed—and more. Cornelia couldn't shake the growing sense of apprehension that she'd felt ever since finding the immense stash of radium. If that message had been decoded, perhaps the solution had been put somewhere more secure than the envelope on top of the desk. She pulled open the top desk drawer, which was blessedly not locked.

And she could see why. Nothing of importance: two pencils and one pen, lying in a neat row, a magnifying glass, an ink blotter, and an embossed stamper with a pad of ink. She picked up the stamper and peered at the end of it, expecting to see the backwards imprint of the name of the facility, or perhaps the owner of the desk.

Instead, the embossment was merely four raised dots, arranged in an uneven line. A bizarre sense of déjà vu went through her; why did that strange arrangement of dots look familiar?

"That's a funny thing to put on a stamp," said Adelaide, peering over at it. "It's not a braille letter, is it?"

"Caelum," said Cornelia, abruptly remembering. She'd seen that pattern in the encyclopedia in the basement, when she and Rawlins had been trying to decipher John's journal notes and the strange clue he'd left in the fountain pen. "This pattern of dots is the constellation Caelum," Cornelia said aloud. "A minor constellation in the southern hemisphere."

"Again, a funny thing to put on a stamp," said Adelaide. "What does it mean?"

Cornelia put the stamper back, closed the drawer, and picked up a stack of envelopes. "I'm not sure. But it must mean more than just a set of stars in the night sky. Perhaps it's a person, or the code name for another project."

"Maybe this coded message has the answer," said Adelaide, flapping the envelope.

"Maybe. I wish we had the time to try to decode it. Perhaps we can find a sheet of blank paper and copy it down—we shouldn't take anything from this room. We don't want them to know we were here."

Just then a loud alarm clanged out in the hall. Adelaide yelped and dropped her stack of letters.

"Too late—they know we're here." Cornelia dropped her stack and pulled her gun out of her pocket. "Time to go."

Adelaide snatched up a fistful of envelopes from the desk as they hurried back over to the door. If anyone was coming down the hall, it would be impossible to hear footsteps now over the clanging of the alarm.

Cornelia yanked the door open and whipped up both the flashlight and the gun. The hall was still dark and empty, but probably not for long.

As they ran down the hall the way they'd come, Cornelia tossed the flashlight to Adelaide and pulled out the seeker's potion. Only a few drops remained in the bottom of the vial.

"Damn," she muttered, uncorking the vial. "Show us to the nearest exit."

They hurried after the black wisp, rounding several corners, until the fog finally faded out and vanished. The vial was empty.

"Now what are we going to do?" Adelaide said loudly over the clanging alarm bell, her eyes wide.

"We keep going," Cornelia shouted back. "Look for a door with a light switch on the wall near it—in a windowless place like this, they'd need to be able to turn on the light as soon as they entered. And we left the door to the hillside hatch unlocked." She gave each door they passed a quick shove to see if it rattled or opened, just in case they were back to where they'd started. All of these corridors looked the same.

Two flashlight beams suddenly appeared on the wall behind them, coming from around the corner. "Oh no," panted Adelaide.

Cornelia slowed down long enough to pull the satchel off her shoulder and sling it over Adelaide. "Remember what I told you," she said as they hurried on down the hall, Cornelia still giving a shove to every door they passed. "Don't be afraid to use the Tesla gun, and if I give you my revolver, don't be afraid to use that, too. I will gladly sacrifice myself to make sure that you can get out. You *have* to get out with that radium."

As the light beams shone behind them, Cornelia risked a glance back over her shoulder to gauge how far away the guards were. She almost stumbled in her shock.

"What in the world are those?" gasped Adelaide, also looking back and actually stumbling.

Two mechanical contraptions on wheels were barreling down the hall after them. Each sported a vaguely humanoid torso with a head, but where a face might have been on a mechanical mannequin, there was a bright flashlight beam. Small discs spun on the top of the heads, possibly either sound receivers or radio-wave receivers. The hinged mechanical arms had pinchers rather than hands. The bodies looked to be about human-sized, but instead of a lower torso and legs, each mechanized mannequin sat on a boxy three-wheeled base. The metal wheels had deep tread built in—or perhaps were covered in small spikes?—and rattled noisily down the hall.

"Automata," said Cornelia. What the hell kind of place was this that had not only created mechanical guards, but felt the need to use them?

"Guard automatons?" Adelaide all but shrieked. "What are we going to do?"

"Keep going!" She shoved her shoulder against Adelaide, spurring her to movement again. They jogged down the hall, Cornelia kicking at every door they passed.

The automata were catching up. "Keep going!" Cornelia shouted again as she spun back around and brought up her gun. She fired the revolver, but the bullet missed and ricocheted off the walls farther down the hall. It had been a very long time since she'd done any target practice—and even then it wasn't against moving mechanical targets in a dark hallway.

She jogged backwards for several steps, aiming again with the gun, focusing on a spot in the center of the chest of the nearest machine. She paused just long enough to squeeze the trigger. This bullet hit the automaton dead on. It ground to a halt, electronics sputtering, and its light beam flickered and faded.

"You got one!" Adelaide crowed as they ran.

"Not for long," Cornelia gritted. Up ahead another light beam shown on the wall, about to round the corner in front of them. The alarm bells were still clanging, giving her a headache and fraying her already jangled nerves. That was probably the idea.

The automaton she had shot appeared to be immobilized, but the other one behind them was still going strong—and fast. Its pincher hands were out in front of it, and a blue arch of electricity jumped from one pincher to the other. She suspected the voltage was likely a lot stronger than the stun setting of her Tesla gun.

She fired off another shot at this one. The bullet grazed one of its arms. Sparks flew from its arm and pincher, but it kept rolling, unaffected.

"Cornelia!" hollered Adelaide, waving with the flashlight at the automaton that had rounded the corner ahead of them and was now coming down the hall towards them from the other direction. There were no cross-corridors between them and either automaton, and only two doors that were at all close by. Cornelia probably didn't have time to pick the lock of either one before the machines got to them. "Do you know any spells that can stop them?"

Cornelia tried to swallow her rising panic. Every spell she'd ever learned seemed to have left her mind, but even so, she'd never learned any sort of magic that could stop something like this.

She'd burnt the herbal blend ahead of time for protection and good fortune, but that was a minor and generalized spell. She doubted the ashes in their pockets would protect them from high-voltage electricity and mechanical guards that wouldn't be susceptible to a befuddlement charm. She was also wearing the Eye of Horus pendant that John had given her on New Year's Eve, tucked it inside her shirt. The Celtic knotwork amulet from Lou Vincini she'd given to Adelaide. But were ancient amulets enough to protect them from being electrocuted?

Electricity... A sudden idea came to her. "Give me the Tesla gun," she snapped, thrusting her revolver at Adelaide.

They traded weapons. Cornelia held up the bulky gun and twisted the knob on the side to charge the coil, and fired at the nearest automaton.

It halted, gears grinding and its headlamp flickering. The gun took about three seconds for the coil to cool down and be ready for another charge. During that three seconds, the other automaton was fast approaching. Then the one she'd just shot started to move again.

But she'd used the lower setting on the gun. She twisted the knob twice in a row to put the gun on its highest charge.

"Adelaide, stand in front of me," she ordered. "Hold tight to me, and put your toes on top of my boots."

"What?" stammered Adelaide, moving to face her.

"Just do it!" Cornelia wrapped her left arm around Adelaide to keep her close, and felt the pressure as the girl stepped onto the toes of her riding boots.

"Hold still," Cornelia instructed, and fired the Tesla gun at the floor.

She felt a faint tingle as the electrical blast raced through the metal corridor. Both automata skidded to a halt in a burst of sparks.

"That may not incapacitate them for long," said Cornelia. But hopefully it would hold them for at least eight seconds, which was the amount of time needed before she could use the Tesla gun again after a discharge on the high setting.

"Cornelia," said Adelaide, still standing on her feet and hugging her. "Behind you. There's a light switch by that door."

She released Adelaide as she turned around. About two yards away was a door; she kicked at the door, and it rattled. Yanking on the handle, she pushed it open. A ladder built into the wall showed in Adelaide's flashlight beam.

"The hatch. Go!" Cornelia pushed Adelaide through the door, then stepped through and slammed it behind her. They scrambled up the ladder.

"You must have rubber soles on your boots," Adelaide panted as they climbed.

"I do. And I assumed that your shoes had leather soles and celluloid heels, which is why I had you stand on my feet."

"I felt a little tingle, but it worked."

Below them, a clanking came from the door. "Not for very long," muttered Cornelia. "Faster! We're almost out."

They burst out into the chill night air. Cornelia slammed the hatch shut, and they half slid-half tumbled down the hill to the open parking lot. There appeared to be no activity—automata or otherwise—out here right now, but that could change at any second.

The motorcycle was right where they'd left it, and in a moment they were speeding back down the mountain path. Since secrecy was no longer a concern, Cornelia switched on the headlight so she could drive faster. John had modified this bike during the War, and one of his additions was a long gun barrel attached to the side, just under the seat. It fired rifle bullets, and the controls for the gun were by the handlebars so that one could drive and shoot at the same time. The gun mechanism hadn't been used since the War, and it fired only ahead of the bike. She prayed that she wouldn't have to figure out how to use it.

Cornelia checked her rearview mirror every few seconds, and tried to keep her eyes looking all around while still focusing on the road, but no pursuit came. Adelaide was gripping her far tighter than on the ride up here, but Cornelia didn't mind the squeezing pressure. Back on the city streets, as they sat stopped at one of the newly-installed traffic signals, she felt Adelaide's arms tighten even further and felt the younger woman shuddering against her back. She wondered if she was crying. Her own nerves were still far too high for tears right now—or even to feel terror over the events of the night. There would be time to unwind her emotions later, once they got home with the radium.

Two police cars went racing past, sirens blaring, heading in the way they had just come. The police could have been on their way to anywhere in the city—or the outskirts—but Cornelia was glad that they were far removed from the Santa Monica hills at this point. Right now they were just two women joyriding through the city on a motorcycle—an unusual and improper activity, perhaps, but hardly illegal.

All things considered, they'd been strangely fortunate. Apparently the burnt herbs and the protection amulets had done their job, providing them with safety and luck. There were so many potential ways that the night could have ended differently.

Cornelia felt her heart rate starting to return to normal as she drove up through the quiet streets of the Hollywood Hills. Adelaide was still clutching her tightly, but her shuddering breathing had calmed. The open gates of Ivystone Hill Manor shone in the headlight as Cornelia turned into her driveway.

"We did it, Adelaide," she said over her shoulder. "We're home."

Chapter 7

Cornelia stood in the preservation tank room, looking up at John.

He was alive. Unconscious, and still slowly dying, but alive—and would be alive many months longer than what the doctor had predicted. They had bought time. Cornelia could now devote all of her time and energy into finding a way to reverse the effects of gravity engine on his body.

As soon as she and Adelaide had returned last night, she'd sent the girl upstairs to the guest bedroom, and she and Rawlins had installed the radium. A dry test run of the machine two days ago had showed that John's designs were flawless and their execution of his designs were also, mercifully, flawless. The radium had been the only missing piece, and now they had it.

It was nearly three in the morning when Cornelia had finally gone to bed, but she was up again at seven and called the hospital. She knew that they would grant her request of having John brought home so he could "pass in peace." After the ambulance orderlies had arrived with John and placed him on the cot they'd set up in the sitting room, Rawlins and Ronald had carried him down to the basement.

Then she and Rawlins had placed him in the empty tank, hooked up all of the wires and hoses, closed the glass door in the side, and filled the tank with water and the chemical mixture that John had designed. And now she could breathe again. The artificial womb, powered by the radium, was doing its job, and John was alive and protected.

She heard Rawlins' quiet shuffling footfalls on the slate floor behind her, and he stepped into the room. "He looks good," Rawlins remarked softly.

Cornelia nodded, not taking her eyes off of John and the tank. "He does." Considering that he'd been fully swaddled in bandages at the hospital, she was expecting to see him maimed and disfigured. While he still had some patches of blistered and burned skin on his face and hands, for the most part his body looked healed and fine—at least on the outside.

The cylindrical tank was over six feet tall, enabling him to float in the enclosure, fully suspended by the buoyancy of the pale blueish fluid. He was naked, save for the pair of briefs they'd put on him for modesty's sake. A rubber breathing mask covered his nose and mouth, and a strap went around his chest, holding the cables and wires that monitored his heart rate, breathing, and other vital functions.

All along the walls of the tiny room, lights pulsed on the instrument panels, gauges ticked, and the oxygen recirculator whooshed air gently though the respirator hose. Cornelia had circled the room, checking each and every gauge and instrument reading, at least six times since they'd gotten him into the tank. Now, as she stood next to Rawlins, looking up at John, she abruptly realized that she'd been on her feet for hours without a break. She wished she had a chair.

As if he could sense her thoughts, Rawlins gently put an arm around her shoulders. She leaned against him, letting her body relax just a little. Dear Rawlins, always such a solid rock.

"We did it, Joe," she murmured. "I haven't seen his face for a week. And now I can look at him again. I..." She trailed off. John was home, he was safe, and she could see his face, but his blue-gray eyes were closed, and she couldn't run her hands through his sandy brown hair, or hear him speak to her... She felt tears starting to trickle down her cheeks, but she didn't care.

"He's safe now," Rawlins said quietly, his arm still strong and supportive around her shoulders. With his other hand he pulled a handkerchief out of his jacket pocket. "We'll find a way to cure him. We have time now."

Cornelia dabbed at her face with the handkerchief, and finally turned away from John to look Rawlins in the face. His black eyes were glistening with tears, too. She managed a tiny smile as she handed his now-damp handkerchief back to him. "I think you need this, too," she said.

He returned her teary smile. "Yes, ma'am." He dabbed at his eyes.

After a few moments, Rawlins said, "Luncheon will be ready in a few minutes, ma'am."

She looked at him again. "It's mid-day already?"

"Well, I took the liberty of asking Maggie to prepare lunch a bit early," Rawlins said. "Miss Adelaide didn't eat much breakfast, and you haven't had anything all day except two cups of coffee."

That's right—she hadn't had any breakfast. Or any food last night as she and Rawlins stayed up late finishing the installation of the radium.

"Thank you for looking after me, Joe," she said, giving him another smile, a warmer one this time. "I'm quite hungry, now that you mention it."

They walked through the basement towards the stairs. "I know the machine is working fine," Cornelia said as they emerged from the stairs and crossed the hallway into the dining room. "But I feel like someone should check on it frequently, at least for the first few days, just to make sure there aren't any hiccups or problems."

"I'll go back downstairs just as soon as I've served the lunch, ma'am," Rawlins said.

Cornelia smiled gratefully at him as he pulled out a chair for her.

Adelaide entered the dining room, dressed in her tan blouse and dark green skirt that she'd arrived in yesterday evening. "Cornelia!" she said, hurrying over to join her at the table. "Did it work? Does the radium make the preservation machine work? How is he?"

"Everything is working," Cornelia said. "The radium is powering everything properly, just as it should." She took a breath. "And John is alive."

"Oh, I'm so glad." Adelaide smiled, digging into the plate of cold cuts that Rawlins had just laid on the table.

Cornelia delicately took a few sips of her tomato soup, but then realized that she was indeed famished, and joined Adelaide in devouring the cold cuts and buttered bread.

They ate in silence for a few minutes. "I never thanked you properly, Adelaide," Cornelia said at last, finishing off another piece of bread and returning to her soup. "You risked your life to help me, to help John." She paused in her eating as Adelaide looked at her. "I don't know that I'll ever be able to properly repay you." Whether Adelaide had fully understood the dangers when she insisted on joining Cornelia's quest or not, the girl had kept her head and performed admirably. Cornelia was now very glad that Adelaide had been with her.

The younger woman grinned at her. "Well, you're welcome, I suppose. I'm just pleased that I could help. I'm glad I got to do something in my life that actually mattered. Social clubs and charity work are all well and good, but I've always wanted to do something different, something more."

Cornelia stared at her a moment. The more she was getting to know Adelaide, the more she was starting to realize why, perhaps, the girl wanted to be involved in Cornelia's troubles: she was so very much like Cornelia herself was at that age. Twenty years old, with a scientist's curiosity and a thirst for adventure—if Cornelia hadn't married a scientist and inventor, she herself might have wound up racing hell for leather on a motorcycle and battling automatons just to keep herself entertained.

"And speaking of something more," Adelaide said slowly, after chewing a bite. "I need to show you something after lunch."

Cornelia looked at her again, wondering about the odd change in her voice. "All right," she said. "What is it? Is something wrong?"

"I'm not sure. I took some letters from the desk in the bunker last night."

Cornelia nodded. She'd seen Adelaide grab a handful just as the alarm had gone off, but she'd quickly forgotten about it during all the activity after that. "I remember," she said.

"I've spent the morning reading through them. I think you need to read them. And that coded message, too."

Cornelia laid down her soup spoon. "You decoded that message?"

"It was just a standard Playfair cipher. Pretty simple once you know the key word. I used 'Caelum' as the key word and worked it out pretty quickly."

Cornelia decided not to mention that the last time she'd unraveled a Playfair cipher it had taken her nearly an entire day. As impressive as Adelaide's talents were, the serious tone in her voice and the heavy look in her blue eyes made Cornelia's heart start to pound. She pushed her empty soup plate away and pulled her napkin out of her lap. "I'm finished. Let's go look at those letters."

CORNELIA SAT DOWN IN one of the high-backed leather chairs in the upstairs library while Adelaide went to the guest bedroom to get the letters. She rejoined Cornelia a moment later, sitting down beside her in another chair.

"This is the coded message," she began, handing Cornelia two sheets of paper.

The first sheet was the original message—indeed written as a Playfair encryption, now that Cornelia had time to pay attention to the sets of coupled letters arranged in a tidy five-by-five grid pattern. Adelaide's decryption was on the other sheet, printed in capital letters across the bottom of the page, amid numerous scribblings and notes.

Cornelia read it aloud. *"City ready for launch 31 Jan. Send remaining radium."*

"What does it mean?" Adelaide asked.

"I'm not sure." Cornelia stared at the paper, feeling the chill of apprehension creeping through her again. "This says 'the remaining radium.' That would mean that the radium we found at the bunker is only a portion of what they've collected. And 'city ready for launch.' I'm not sure about that, but it doesn't sound good. Who was this addressed to? Did you take the envelope, too, or just the encrypted message?"

Adelaide handed her the envelope. It was addressed to "Director Van Hopper." Cornelia shook her head—not a name she recognized.

She took the next envelope that Adelaide handed her. This one was addressed to "Dr. P. Davenport." So apparently Percival received mail at the lab, even if John did not. She pulled out the letter.

Dr. Davenport—

I trust this letter finds you fully recovered. The delay after the removal of Dr. Jones was unfortunate. You are expected at the launch site before the final phase is complete. Your work thus far has been invaluable to the Caelum, and we expect your continued service as we usher the people into this bold new era of progress. Coordinate with Director Van Hopper to ensure that there are no further delays or impediments.

We anticipate your timely arrival.

Executive Commander Ravenstock

Cornelia stared hard at the letter. The paper rattled as her hand started to quiver. "The removal of Dr. Jones," she said, her voice suddenly hoarse. "What the hell does that mean?"

"I think it means just what it sounds like," said Adelaide soberly, handing her another letter. "This one is from Prudence."

"*From* Prudence?" Cornelia echoed. The name on the envelope was "Director Van Hopper" again. With trembling hands she pulled out the letter. She recognized Prudence's bold, sprawling script immediately.

Director Van Hopper—

Even as I write this, we are preparing for the final phase, and you may assure the Executive Commanders that Dr. Davenport and I will performing our duties on schedule. I trust that our efficiency will not be called into question again, as my husband sacrificed his own safety to ensure that Dr. Jones was removed from the project.

Regarding Dr. Jones—I am writing this to request that you send a team to his home to search for any missing pieces. Since we believe he had been suspicious of our activities, it is possible that he may have removed plans, notes, or other documents from the laboratory bunker. His wife is also very clever and he likely shared with her any notes he may have taken home. It is, of course, entirely your discretion, sir, if you wish to have her questioned or detained. I know that the Executive Commanders would appreciate the assurance of no loose ends.

Sincerely, Mrs. P. Davenport

The final envelope that Adelaide had taken was merely a water and waste bill.

The return address for cipher message and the personal mailings was a Los Angeles post office box number, with no name attached. And all three messages bore a stamp at the bottom of the page—the four uneven dots of the constellation Caelum. The calling card of an organization that was preparing for something far larger than a simple test run of an advanced engine. An organization that had directly and intentionally tried to kill her husband.

Cornelia rose up, dropping the letter onto her chair as she stood. Her mind whirled, and she felt suddenly sick. She crossed the room to the window, opened it, and leaned on the sill, letting the cool winter breeze pull away her tears and her breath.

She heard Adelaide come up behind her. "Cornelia, are you all right?"

She squeezed her eyes shut, and the wave of nausea subsided. "They tried to kill him. There was no accident—it was attempted murder."

"It's just so awful," said Adelaide quietly.

"The bastards," she snarled, not caring that she was using such offensive language in front of Adelaide. She should have had it out with Prudence days ago—or weeks ago, and that might have prevented this from happening at all. "I'm going to kill her."

"No, you're not." Adelaide's voice was suddenly strong and firm, and her hand clamped down on Cornelia's shoulder. "Cornelia, look at me."

She turned away from the cool air at the window, tears still burning in her eyes. The look on Adelaide's face gave her a start—her lips were tight with determination and her eyes blazed with defiance.

"What Prudence and Percival and these Caelum people did was absolutely awful," Adelaide stated. "But you're not going to kill anyone. They're the despicable murderers—you're not. Besides, you have to protect yourself now." She held up Prudence's letter. "They're going to come for you."

"Don't be absurd," Cornelia snapped—but even as the words left her lips she realized that Adelaide was right.

Adelaide waved the letter in front of her face. "'No loose ends,' she says. Cornelia, the post mark on the envelope shows that the letter was probably delivered yesterday, the day we broke in. It was already opened when I grabbed it, so this Director Van Hopper person had already read it. If your butler says that no one has come to the house yet to look for you or for any of your husband's papers, then that means someone could be here at any time." She flapped the letter again.

Cornelia turned to look back out the window at the lawn below, the green expanse broken by the winding gravel driveway and ornamental bushes. Just past the red oaks she could glimpse the stone wall at the edge of the property, and the front gate. They had a wall along the entire perimeter of their property, but always left the gate open, for their own ease of travel, and to welcome guests.

And now, she would welcome their enemies.

"We should call the police," Adelaide said. "You have proof now, proof that the disaster at the bunker wasn't an accident. They can arrest the Davenports, and put an officer here at your house to protect—"

"No." Cornelia spun around and snatched the letter out of Adelaide's hand. "We can't go to the police, at least not right now. Whatever this Caelum organization is, it's bigger than the police. This is a United States military laboratory. These people are above the law—at least above the law enforced by the local Los Angeles police."

She skimmed the letter again, heat burning in her chest. Prudence deserved every manner of public shame and private pain for what she'd done, for what she and Percival were involved in. Whatever the hell it was that they were involved in—this shadow group that was above the law and tried to murder the scientists who worked for them.

She slammed the window shut, then pushed past Adelaide and headed for the door. "Let them come. Let them send soldiers here, and I'll show them just how welcome they are." She stalked down the hallway towards the stairs. "No one is going to lay a hand on anyone in this house, or leave with so much as a pencil or a sheet of blotting paper. I'll shoot anyone who tries."

"Cornelia!" Adelaide scurried after her. "You can't do that! Be reasonable! Whatever this Caelum is, whatever they're up to—it's serious! You—"

Cornelia halted on the landing of the stairs and whirled on Adelaide. "Don't you dare talk to me about how serious this is! They tried to murder my husband! He's downstairs in a coma because of them!" Fury burned through her, and she wanted to smack Adelaide. She clenched her teeth to stop herself, and gripped the banister until her fingers hurt.

"I know that!" Adelaide shot back, rising up on her toes till her eyes were level with Cornelia's. "And I risked my life last night to help you save him! I know how serious this is! Which is why shooting people isn't going to fix it!"

Cornelia seethed, forcing herself to take a few deep breaths. Every last person who worked in that damn bunker deserved to die for what they did to John. And for what they'd tried to do to herself and Adelaide last night with their cursed automata. And for whatever the hell they were planning to do with all that radium. She heaved another deep breath as the red heat started to fade from her chest and her mind began to race.

A few seconds ticked by, hot and heavy, as Cornelia's brain kicked back into gear. If soldiers from a secret organization were coming to raid the house or take her away, simply shooting them all dead would only bring more of them down on her. If killing such potential attackers would even be as easy as that. They'd escaped from mindless machines only by the skin of their teeth. They either needed to hide, or somehow trick the Caelum goons.

Before she could manage to bring any of that into words, however, Adelaide yanked Prudence's letter out of her hand. "If you won't listen to me, Cornelia, then let's go talk to your butler. You'll listen to him, won't you? You said he's helped you with all of this, so let him help you with this, too." Adelaide marched past her and down the stairs to the foyer.

"Adelaide." Cornelia followed, and caught up to her at the bottom of the stairs, grabbing her arm. "I'm sorry. You did risk your life—voluntarily—to help me. I know that you know how serious this is." She swallowed as she felt sudden tears again. "I want..." She trailed off, and shook her head. She wanted too many things right now—most of all, she wanted for none of this to have ever happened. She loosened her grip on Adelaide's arm. "Prudence and Percival deserve to be punished for what they've done," she said finally.

"I know," Adelaide replied softly. "But you've got to stay alive and safe long enough to bring them to justice."

Cornelia nodded. Just like with the raid on the bunker last night, if she had any hope of seeking justice, curing John, or figuring out what the Caelum were doing, she needed a plan.

She took a deep breath, and touched Adelaide's arm again, this time giving a grateful squeeze. "You're right. Let's go talk to Rawlins."

AFTER DINNER, CORNELIA and Adelaide sat in the sitting room, drinking coffee and waiting. After Rawlins had read through the letters that afternoon, he had agreed that they should be prepared at any moment to receive some unwanted guests.

They'd spent the afternoon cleaning the house. All of John's notes and projects were cleared from his study and put in the basement. Cornelia and Rawlins then used salt and rue and an ancient Greek incantation to cast a spell on the basement door, shielding it from uninvited eyes. The basement door was not truly invisible—not to anyone in the house, nor to any potential invaders—but the shielding spell would cause an unwanted guest walking past the door to forget about it just as soon as they laid eyes on it.

Cornelia carefully planted a few sheets of notes about the gravity matrix engine on John's desk—notes that were either outdated, because the equations had long since been revised, or minor details that she already had a copy of elsewhere. If someone did come looking for information that John had supposedly "stolen" from the bunker lab, then they would be rewarded with a "successful" trip.

"So what do you suppose these Caelum folks are going to do with all that radium?" said Adelaide, sipping at her coffee. She was sitting in one of the russet armchairs, but Cornelia was far too anxious to sit still and was pacing in front of the fireplace.

"I don't know," she answered Adelaide. "But from what that Playfair cipher said, I have a feeling that your theory might be alarmingly close to the truth."

Adelaide raised her eyebrows as she set her coffee cup down on the serving tray. "What theory?"

Cornelia paused in her pacing to face her. "When we were in the storage room, looking at all of those crates of radium-197, you said that it was enough radium to power a city the size of Los Angeles and New York combined. The coded message mentioned a city. That must be what they're doing—building a city that will be powered by radium."

"But why?" said Adelaide. "Why not use electricity and gas like a normal city?"

"Because they're building this city in the middle of the ocean."

"A floating city?"

"Those coordinates that John wrote down are in the middle of the southern Pacific Ocean. That has to be what they're doing—building a city on the ocean, hundreds of miles away from everything."

"But why?" said Adelaide again.

"I don't know." Cornelia crossed her arms. "That's the piece we're missing. But it doesn't matter now." She uncrossed her arms and resumed her pacing. "Once we convince the Caelum that I know nothing and that John is dead, I can focus on healing him." She had absolutely no idea where to begin with that, but now that he was preserved and stable, she could take as long as was needed to figure out how to restore him.

"But Cornelia—" began Adelaide, but a light flashing through the partially drawn curtains interrupted her.

Cornelia went to the window and peered out between the gold silk curtain panels; headlights flickered through the trees and bushes as an automobile came down the driveway.

Rawlins poked his head into the sitting room. "Someone's coming, ma'am."

She turned away from the window. "I see them." She went over to the coffee table and picked up the silver tray with their cups and saucers. "Adelaide, go down to the basement. It's show time."

There was no reason for these Caelum people to suspect that Adelaide had anything to do with the bunker break-in or anything else involving the gravity matrix project. And Cornelia wanted to keep it that way. With the magical shielding on the basement door, anyone searching the house would go right past the door, and Adelaide would be protected, along with John.

Cornelia and Adelaide went down the hall; Adelaide turning left for the basement, Cornelia turning right to take the tray of coffee cups into the kitchen. "A few more dishes for you, Maggie," she said, setting the tray down on the kitchen counter.

The hot water tap was on, filling the sink with water, and Maggie was over by the ice box rearranging dishes and pitchers. "Very good, ma'am," she said. "So they've come, then?"

"Yes." Cornelia stepped further into the kitchen until she could see through the doorway into the dining room—Theda was in there sweeping off the tablecloth.

"Remember, both of you," Cornelia said. "If anyone asks you any questions, you don't know anything except that Mr. Jones is dead."

Maggie nodded, her round face solemn. Theda paused in her sweeping and also nodded. "Yes, ma'am," she said.

"Rawlins and I will do our best to keep you from being harassed at all. I'm not sure what to expect, but the more we appear to be a defeated household burdened by our grief, the less likely they will be to antagonize us." *I hope*, she added to herself.

Both Maggie and Theda nodded again, and Cornelia left the kitchen. She locked the basement door, tucked the key into the waistband of her black skirt, and walked back down the hall towards the sitting room. A loud banging of someone knocking on the door with a fist echoed through the house.

She hoped that with the notes they'd planted and a convincing display of grief over John's "death," the Caelum soldiers, or whoever they were, would leave with no fuss or violence. But just in case that didn't happen, Rawlins had Cornelia's little silver revolver in his trousers pocket and a knife in his jacket pocket. Cornelia had the Tesla gun, which was waiting in the sitting room under her black wool shawl.

Back in the sitting room, she draped the shawl around her shoulders, securing the gun in a fold of the fabric nestled against the crook of her left elbow. Then she settled herself in a chair near the door and pulled out her handkerchief. She was dressed all in black—a long black skirt and high-necked blouse, not her leather hellion-on-a-motorcycle getup—to put on a show of a wife in mourning. She heard Rawlins open the front door.

"We're from the Santa Monica Research Facility," said a man's voice. "We're here to retrieve property that was illegally removed from the facility."

"I'm sorry, sir, but there's no illegal property here," said Rawlins calmly.

"We'll be the judges of that. Where is the master of the house?"

"I'm sorry to say, sir, but Mr. Jones passed away this morning."

"Where is his wife?" The man didn't pause after Rawlins announced John's "death," nor did he sound surprised.

"May I ask who's calling for her, sir?" said Rawlins politely. "Mrs. Jones has been through a lot today, you understand."

"We're from the Santa Monica Research Facility," the man repeated. "We have a warrant to search the house."

"I'm sorry, sir, but—"

Time to let the invaders have their way for a bit, before things got out of hand. Cornelia got up and went to the doorway of the sitting room. "Who's at the door, Rawlins?"

"Some men from Mr. Jones' laboratory, ma'am," Rawlins said, looking over his shoulder in her direction.

"Let them in. I'll see them in the sitting room." Cornelia gave a weary wave with her handkerchief, and retreated back into the room to resettle herself and the Tesla gun.

"This way, sirs," said Rawlins.

He escorted three men into the sitting room. Cornelia had been expecting military personnel, but these men were all three dressed in plain black suits. If they were carrying weapons, they were concealed. None of them removed their black fedoras.

"If you're here to see my husband, you're too late, I'm afraid," Cornelia said to them in a sorrowful tone. "He's dead."

"We have reason to believe that Dr. Jones removed some property belonging to the Santa Monica Research Facility," said one man. "We're here to retrieve it."

"My husband was no thief," Cornelia said indignantly.

"We have a warrant to search your house, ma'am." The man flashed an official-looking document at her, returning it to his coat pocket before she could get a good look at it.

"Search my house? For what?"

"Items or documents pertaining to Dr. Jones' work at the Santa Monica Research Facility."

"My husband rarely brought his work home, so I don't know what you'd be hoping to find." She waved her handkerchief. "Show them to John's study, Rawlins. Maybe there's something on his desk that they're looking for."

"Yes, ma'am. Right this way, sirs."

Two of the men followed Rawlins out of the room; the one who had spoken stayed behind and stared at Cornelia.

"Where is your husband right now, Mrs. Jones?"

Cornelia glared up at him. "He's dead!"

"My condolences, ma'am," he said in a flat tone. "You said your husband rarely brought work home. Did he talk about his work?"

"Not much. So much of what he does—did—is beyond me. And he said it was classified work for the government, anyway." She dabbed at her eyes with her handkerchief, then looked up at the stoic man. "But if you're from the research lab, too, then wouldn't you know all of that? Why are you asking me about his work if you work there, too?" She tried to put as much confused innocence into her voice and expression as she could. No need to *sound* like she was trying to interrogate him, even though she was.

The man frowned down at her in silence for a moment, then asked another question. "Your husband was a well-known inventor. Was he working on any other projects at home in recent weeks?"

"Well, yes," Cornelia said slowly, frantically trying to think of something frivolous or innocuous that John had put together recently.

"Such as?"

"Well..." *Old Roberta's tea kettle*, she suddenly thought. "You'll think this silly," she said, dabbing at her eyes again. "But he built a tea kettle that whistles a little tune, instead of just the normal tea kettle whistle. The cook likes to sing while she works, you see, and it's awkward to have a gramophone in the kitchen." This tale was entirely true, except that John had put together the musical tea kettle when he was twelve, for his family's cook Roberta. The kettle resided in their own kitchen today, but Maggie rarely used it because she preferred to sing Irish folksongs while she worked, and the kettle played the old ragtime song "Hello Ma Baby."

"A tea kettle," the man said, sounding mildly annoyed. "Anything else?"

"Well, he's been reading a book about Fibonacci numbers." That should be another safe thing to say, since the Fibonacci sequence had absolutely nothing to do with the gravity matrix engine. "I don't quite understand it—something about circles." Hopefully she was doing a decent job of portraying the grieving and witless wife.

She heard Rawlins and the other two men coming back down the stairs. "What's down the hall there?" one asked.

"The dining room and the kitchen, sir," said Rawlins. "And the back door."

Cornelia buried her face in her handkerchief and bent forward as if crying, straining to listen as Rawlins and the two men went down the hall.

"When your husband did talk about his work, what did he say?" the man asked her.

She kept her face buried in her handkerchief a few moments longer, hunching her shoulders and pretending to cry, listening. Footsteps came back up the hallway; it didn't sound like they'd found the basement door.

"Mrs. Jones," her interrogator said loudly.

She lifted her head, keeping her face partly covered with the handkerchief. "I'm sorry, what did you ask me?"

"When your husband did talk about his work, what did he say?"

"Oh, he never bored me with the details. He said it was interesting and challenging work, and that was enough for me, knowing that he enjoyed it." She sobbed into her handkerchief again.

Rawlins and other two men came back into the sitting room. "We've retrieved the notes," said one man, patting his breast pocket. "Doesn't look like there's anything else to see."

"If you've gotten what you came for, then please just leave us be," said Cornelia wearily.

"This way, sirs," said Rawlins, gesturing towards the door.

The men seemed to hesitate, then as one they all followed Rawlins back into the foyer. Cornelia stayed in the sitting room, bent over her handkerchief, until she heard the front door close and the car engine start outside.

"They're gone, Miz Jones."

Cornelia looked up at Rawlins in the sitting room doorway. "What did they take?" she asked.

"Just the notes that we planted for them to see," he said. "They insisted on going into every room, including the bedroom and all the bathrooms, but they didn't open any drawers or rummage through anything."

Cornelia stood up, leaving the shawl and the Tesla gun in the seat of the chair. "That's good. And they bypassed the basement?"

"Yes, ma'am. They didn't see the door."

She exhaled quietly. At least that spell had worked.

Cornelia went down to the basement to retrieve Adelaide, while Rawlins brought another round of coffee to the sitting room for them.

"I'm so glad it went smoothly," said Adelaide, adding cream and sugar to her cup.

Cornelia sipped her coffee black, not bothering with her customary one cube of sugar. "As much as I wanted to throttle that man and make him answer all of *my* questions, I think playing the bereaved wife who knows next to nothing of her husband's career was the wise choice."

"I agree, ma'am," said Rawlins. "Let's hope it was enough."

"Why wouldn't it be enough?" said Adelaide. "You said they took the bait and left without a fight. It's over now. Right?"

"Right," said Cornelia. But as she met Rawlins' gaze across the coffee table, she could tell that he didn't think it was over, either. She wanted everything to be finished—no visitors, no distractions, no secret organizations or societal duties to pull her away from finding a cure for John. And after her performance, it should be over, as Adelaide had said.

Except she had a cold, uneasy feeling that whatever this was, it was far from over.

Chapter 8

Cornelia encountered Adelaide in the upstairs hallway the next morning.

"Thank you for letting me stay here another night," Adelaide said as they went down the stairs to breakfast. "But I'll head back home today. I don't want to wear out my welcome."

"You're most welcome to stay as long as you like," said Cornelia. "It's no burden at all, though I'm sure you'd like to sleep in your own bed and wear your own clothes again."

Adelaide gave a little laugh. "Yes, I suppose so. But your guest bed is gloriously comfortable."

"You can start without me," said Cornelia as they approached the dining room. "I want to check on John."

Downstairs, nothing was changed—which was a good thing, in this case. The preservation tank was doing its job, and everything was running smoothly. Cornelia returned to the dining room, and joined Adelaide for the breakfast of scrambled eggs, sausage, toast, orange juice, and coffee.

"Everything is good?" Adelaide asked, and took a sip of orange juice.

"The machine is running like clockwork," said Cornelia, taking a bite of egg. John had designed it perfectly. Hopefully very soon she could tell him how well his invention had worked.

They ate in silence for a few moments, and the Cornelia glanced up from buttering her toast as Rawlins came into the room.

"Begging your pardon, ma'am," he said, stepping up to the table. "The mail's just come. I know you prefer to wait until after breakfast to read through the mail, but I thought you might want to see this right away." He laid an envelope on the table beside her coffee cup.

The letter was addressed to John. In his own handwriting.

She laid down her knife and toast, and slowly picked up the envelope. It was not unheard of for John to mail something to himself—he often did it if he was out of town, or otherwise unable to keep track of copious notes about a project. But the timing of this mailing... She glanced at the postmark. January eighth, the day of the disaster at the lab.

Trying to keep her hands from trembling, she picked up the letter opener that Rawlins offered and sliced open the envelope. There were two sheets of paper inside: one, a large sheet folded over many times to fit into the envelope, and the other a sheet of plain rough notepaper of the sort that was usually on offer at telegraph and postal offices. She unfolded the letter.

John's normally tidy, willowy handwriting was scrawled and smudged, clearly written in a hurry, on both sides of the paper. The letter was dated January eighth, the same as the postmark. She held her breath as she read through it.

Cornelia darling—

If you are reading this, then I am dead. I am so sorry for the pain and grief you must be feeling right now, and I am also sorry for the added burden that I must place on you. I wish that I could call and speak to you, or drive home and see you, but I can't risk placing you in danger, as well. I drove into the city on my lunch break, but I know I am being followed.

For some days now I have suspected that there was a dark purpose behind the gravity matrix project. I hadn't told you of my misgivings, because I didn't want to worry you until I had more evidence. I now have the evidence, but I fear it is now too late, at least for me. The page I have included I found amongst Percival's notes this morning, and it confirms my fledgling fears.

A shadow group called the Caelum are the ones in control of this project. Their intention is not to use the perfected gravity matrix engine for progress in air travel, nor even for national defense in the event of another war. Their plan is to build dozens of these engines. I believe they have already begun the construction, based off of the work Percival and I have done so far. I don't consider our engine to be ready, even for a testing phase, but it seems that the leaders of the Caelum have decided otherwise.

They are building a city for themselves. It's to be a flying city, held aloft by a mass of gravity matrix engines. Not only was the gravity engine never intended to be used in such a way, but I fear that so many of these engines functioning in close proximity will have disastrous repercussions. Tidal waves, disruption of animal migrations, even potential earthquakes. They are also planning to power the engines with radium-197, which I have been opposed to from the start; and I fear that even with proper shielding, such a massive amount of radium being used in such a way will have detrimental effects.

My darling, please read these notes that I took from Percival—I know that you will understand everything. I'm sorry I haven't more time to write. But you must find a way, somehow, to stop the launch of this flying city. I wish that I could simply quit the project, but I know now that they suspect me, and if I don't return to the lab after lunch, they will hunt me down—and perhaps come after you, as well. I pray that I am wrong about all of this—and if I am, then I will intercept this mailing at home when it arrives in about a week's time, and you will never know about my erroneous suspicions. But if I am right, then I fear I must say goodbye.

Stop the Caelum, Cornelia. You must do something, or the entire world will suffer the consequences. I love you, always and forever. John.

A storm of emotions stampeded through her and the words on the page blurred as tears stung her eyes.

"Cornelia?" said Adelaide in a worried tone from across the table.

She didn't answer Adelaide, or even look at her. Wordlessly she handed the letter to Rawlins and pulled the other sheet out of the envelope.

It was a diagram, probably one of several pages, but this single page held enough information for her to see that everything that John had written was true. The diagram outlined the strategic placement of sixty gravity matrix engines beneath a circular platform measuring nearly a mile in diameter. Cornelia scanned through the equations and measurements written across the diagram and on the other side of the paper—height of buildings on the platform, weight distribution, altitude above sea level, average air temperature and wind speed.

Around the edge of the paper were notes written in a different hand—John's. He'd scribbled down a set of coordinates in the southern hemisphere—the same coordinates that she'd found in his fountain pen. He'd also written several equations about the exponentially amplified effects of the magnetic pulses and sound frequencies from so many gravity engines working at the same time in such close proximity to one another.

She looked up and met Rawlins' eyes. He'd finished reading the letter, and his black eyes glistened with the same tears she knew were in her own eyes. He angled his head subtly towards Adelaide, and she nodded. He went around the table and handed her the letter.

The silence stretched long as Adelaide now read the letter, and Cornelia showed Rawlins the paper with the diagram and equations.

At last Cornelia spoke. "This is what those men were looking for last night," she said, indicating the diagram sheet in Rawlins' hands. "If he took this from Percival's desk, then Prudence would have known it was missing. That's why she wrote that letter demanding that this house be searched for stolen documents." She picked up the envelope, and realized that John had mailed it via certified mail with a requested delivery date of today. Predicting the house would be searched, he'd used the postal service to hide the document.

Adelaide laid down the letter, then looked at the diagram page as Rawlins handed it to her. "What are we going to do?" she said in a hushed voice.

Cornelia didn't answer right away. She stared down at her plate of breakfast, which was suddenly no longer appetizing. This was her chance at revenge, after a fashion. Yesterday when she'd learned the depth of Prudence and Percival's villainous corruption from those stolen letters, she'd wanted nothing more than to hurt them as they'd hurt her and John. If they were hell-bent on living in some advanced city while the rest of the world burned because of it, then removing their opportunity to do so would certainly cause them pain. Hardly the same thing as the pain of having a nearly-murdered spouse comatose in a tank, but it was a start.

But more importantly, it was a sickening thought that an invention of John's was going to be used in such a horrifyingly selfish way. John was altruistic almost to a fault; anything he ever created was either for the betterment of humankind, or more simply just to see if it could be done. If he was conscious and able to take steps to stop this, he would. And he had, to the best of his ability, by writing her this letter.

But her first responsibility was to stay at home and find a way to bring John back to full health. She couldn't just go gallivanting off across the world after a bunch of madmen, even if they were corrupt murderers.

She stared at the diagram page again as Adelaide laid it on the table between them. Even if stopping the Caelum was John's final wish, how was she supposed to get to a spot smack in the middle of nowhere in the Pacific Ocean? If John were conscious and present, he'd figure out a way. But he knew that he wouldn't be here, and was counting on her to do something. But do what?

Tears burned in her eyes again as she lingered over the set of coordinates that he'd scrawled across one edge of the page. A strange thought niggled in the back of her mind as she remembered when she and Rawlins had first dug through the maps and atlases to pinpoint the location...

She stood up, nearly knocking her chair over with the abrupt movement. "Rawlins, I need John's notes for the gravity matrix machine, and some blank paper to do some calculations. Meet me in the basement library."

"Yes, ma'am," Rawlins said briskly, not questioning her as he turned and headed out of the dining room.

Cornelia grabbed John's letter and the diagram page and left the room as well, heading across the hall to the basement door.

"What's going on?" Adelaide's voice called behind her. "Cornelia, what is it?"

Ignoring her question, Cornelia hurried down the basement stairs, through the main lab room, and into the library. One of the maps where they'd circled the southern hemisphere coordinates was still lying on the table. She scanned the bookshelves along the walls until she found what she was looking for: *The Geomagnetic Atlas of Earth Currents and Subterranean Energies.*

"*Earth Currents and Subterranean Energies,*" said Adelaide, coming up next to her and peering over her shoulder. "Is that like ley lines? Currents of energy that connect landmarks and places across the earth?"

"That's right," said Cornelia, flipping through the pages till she found the map of the Pacific Ocean. "They often run in tandem with telluric lines, the low-frequency electrical currents that run through the earth. There's a telluric current that runs right through the Los Angeles valley." She laid her finger on the map, near the coast of southern California. "John has accessed the electrical energy for some of his experiments before, similar to the way early builders of telegraph stations used telluric currents to boost the telegraph signals."

"Golly," said Adelaide.

Cornelia glanced up as Rawlins came into the room, carrying a stack of paper in each hand. He laid John's notes down on the table, and the blank stack of paper beside it.

"Ley lines, ma'am?" he said, looking down at the book.

She nodded, and grabbed a pencil that was lying on the table. "I pray I'm wrong about this," she muttered, half to herself, and began plotting the exact location of the flying city on the earth-currents map. She prayed she was wrong, but she knew she was right.

She circled the spot in the southern Pacific Ocean, then trailed the pencil along one of the ley lines. It connected directly with Los Angeles.

"Telluric and ley lines aren't very powerful," said Rawlins, who no doubt knew where she was going with this. "The energy would barely transfer over such a long distance. Especially crossing the equator."

"I know," said Cornelia. "But they do connect." She pulled out a chair and sat down at the table as she reached for a blank sheet of paper. Then she shuffled through the pages of John's notes until she found the equations for the sonic and magnetic frequencies of the gravity engine, and frantically began to calculate.

The frequency output of one gravity matrix engine, multiplied by sixty, transferred into the lower frequency of the ley currents, adjusting for the diurnal shifts of the ley currents, then the exponential gravitational disruption caused by sixty engines functioning at once... She let her mind get lost in the math.

Eventually she had to lay the pencil down, as she realized that no amount of math would be able to fully prove her suspicions. Or fully disprove them. But she couldn't take that chance.

Rawlins picked up her sheet of scribblings and looked it over.

"I don't understand," said Adelaide. "What does all of this mean?"

"The disastrous environmental effects of the flying city that John mentioned in his letter are very real possibilities," Cornelia said, pushing back her chair and standing up again. "But one thing that he didn't calculate was that this city is situated directly on one of the most prominent ley lines in the Pacific. One gravity matrix engine operating in proximity to a ley line, or even a dozen engines all running at the same time, would not be a problem—if it were, John would never have built the thing in the first place. But since these Caelum people are planning to use sixty engines all together all at once, and for a sustained period of time, the energy will be enough to travel along the ley lines and disrupt electrical power and telephone lines halfway around the world." She laid her finger on the map.

"Los Angeles being one of the main places that would likely be affected."

"Golly," murmured Adelaide.

"But worse than that," Cornelia continued. "Is that John himself is suffering reversed and negative effects from the gravity matrix engine." She looked at Adelaide, and swallowed the sudden lump of fear in her throat. "Rawlins and I determined that something happened during this engineered 'accident' that caused the engine to reverse its field and create a matrix of increased gravity and density—that's why his organs are too dense to function properly. But because John himself is, in essence, already tuned to the frequency of the gravity engine, the energy from this flying city, traveling along the ley lines, could affect him even preserved in the artificial womb. If those engines turn on and this city launches, it could kill him."

There was silence. Rawlins laid down Cornelia's page of calculations, and leaned over the ley line map. Cornelia stared at the spot she'd circled, dead center in the middle of the southern Pacific Ocean—so far away, and yet now, with telluric and ley energy in the equation, so frighteningly close.

"So what do we do?" Adelaide finally asked in a small voice.

All Cornelia wanted to do was to stay here at home and restore her husband. But he wanted her to leave and somehow save the world. And saving the world was now the only way to save him.

She felt Rawlins lay a gentle hand on her shoulder, and she looked up at him. "Mr. Jones isn't going anywhere, ma'am," he said quietly, as if he could read her thoughts. "He'll be here, stable and safe, when there's time to cure him."

She gave him a grateful smile. What would she do without Rawlins?

She finally looked over at Adelaide, who was staring wide-eyed at the map and Cornelia's math. "You asked what we're going to do?" she said to the girl.

Adelaide looked up at her. Cornelia closed the book and gathered up all of the papers of notes, briskly stacking them together with far more determined confidence in her movement than she felt right now. "We're going to stop the launch of this flying radium city, that's what we're going to do."

"AND SO THAT'S WHY I'M leaving," said Cornelia. She sat in the back room of the Salon de Fontaine, having gone there after lunch to talk to Charlotte. Charlotte had left the other girls to manage the clients for little while, and invited Cornelia into the back room for some tea.

Cornelia took a heavy swig of her tea as she finished telling Charlotte everything that had transpired in the past few days—including the letter from John that she'd just received that morning.

"*Mon dieu*," Charlotte murmured, setting down her own teacup. "When you first told me about this, when you needed help from Lou, I had the feeling that this was perhaps bigger than you realized...but this?" She shook her head, blond curls bouncing. "How are you going to manage to stop such a thing?"

"I have no idea," Cornelia confessed. "I spent the morning making travel arrangements. We'll take a train to San Diego, then catch a steamer that's leaving tomorrow evening for

Panama. After that, I hope to catch another ship to get us most of the rest of the way to the southern hemisphere. And then..." She trailed off and shook her head. All of that traveling would take at least a week, probably more. If the city was indeed launching by January thirty-first, that didn't leave them a lot of time to stop it. But at least the long journey might give her the time to figure out *how* to stop it.

Charlotte leaned forward, one perfectly manicured hand resting on the white tablecloth. "We?" she said, looking at Cornelia, raising a slender eyebrow.

"Adelaide's coming with me. Against my better judgment."

"Ah!" Charlotte broke into a grin. "But it is perfect!"

"Not quite the word I'd choose for it. She did help me with the bunker break-in, though. And she found those letters and that coded message." And if Cornelia were perfectly honest with herself, she felt glad of the company. Having a wiling companion for a task of this magnitude and danger—however strategically unwise it might be—was a surprisingly comforting notion.

Charlotte continued to smile. "I knew she would be of help to you."

Cornelia responded to Charlotte's smile with a frown. "Why did you do that, Charlotte? She told me that you encouraged her to join me on my mad escapade. When I came to you for help and you told me about Lou Vincini, I wasn't anticipating that you'd share it with anyone."

She was no longer angry at Charlotte for spilling her secrets and involving Adelaide in the bunker break-in, but she didn't try to keep the hurt and confusion out of her voice.

The other woman didn't answer right away as she got up from the tea table and wandered slowly across the small room. They were in Charlotte's office at the back of the salon, which was a small cozy room full of pink frills, scattered papers, and a tiny window that looked out over the alley behind the building. The other back room, where Charlotte mixed her shampoos and magic potions, was larger, but less conducive to a close conversation.

Cornelia watched Charlotte cross the room to her desk, take a cigarette out of the gold box sitting beside the inkwell, and light it with a small silver lighter. After puffing a couple of times, Charlotte turned to face Cornelia.

"I apologize for breaking your confidence," she finally said. "I don't make a habit of doing such a thing if anyone shares with me a secret—least of all you. But when you came to me that night, telling me of a plan to break into a military facility, I knew that I couldn't let you do it alone." Charlotte leaned against the edge of the desk and gestured at Cornelia with her cigarette. "Adelaide is so very much like you, *ma chérie*. She's a wild bird with a lightning mind, and a passion bigger than all of Hollywood."

Cornelia opened her mouth, then closed it again, not quite sure what to say to that. Finally she just nodded.

"And she wants to learn from you," Charlotte continued. "She told me so herself. She sees you as a modern woman who can teach her how to be free."

Cornelia choked out a laugh. "A modern woman?" she echoed. "Charlotte, I'm a wife, a society heiress. I've never worked a job, and until I went to visit Lou Vincini the other night, I'd never been out in a public place wearing pants."

Charlotte laughed, too, a light tittering sound. "I know that. And Adelaide knows that, too. But you're so much more than that. You see the world differently, and so does she."

Cornelia could hardly argue with that. But even so... "So did you send Adelaide after me that night," she asked slowly, "because you thought I needed protecting? Or because you wanted me to teach Adelaide something?"

Charlotte smiled, an odd mischievous twinkle in her eyes. "Both, *ma chérie*."

"And what was I supposed to have taught her? How to avoid getting killed by mechanical guards? Or how to become a thief?"

Charlotte shrugged. "I was not there that night. But you taught Adelaide whatever it is that she might have learned."

Cornelia frowned again. "Charlotte, you're being more cryptic than usual, and it's beginning to annoy."

"Forgive me, *ma chérie*." Charlotte waved her cigarette, not sounding at all repentant. "Adelaide wants to learn. She wants to know. Yes, I could teach her the fine art of potion-making, but you can teach her so much more: herb-lore, the ancient history of witchcraft, science, technology. How to be free."

Cornelia stared at her, again momentarily at a loss for words. Some days Charlotte was merely her friend and hair stylist; other times, she was her confidant and potion-maker. But right now she was waxing philosophic like some wise old cunning woman of ancient times.

And she was right, of course. Except for one thing. The one thing that Cornelia hadn't realized at first, but now knew would prevent her from ever being a worthwhile teacher or mentor to anyone, ever.

Cornelia drew a deep breath.

"I have no right to teach Adelaide anything," she said slowly. "And would she even want to learn magic from a woman responsible for her own mother's death?"

"You were not the one who caused your mother's death," said Charlotte in a tone of finality.

"No, but I failed to save her, which amounts to the same thing." Cornelia stared hollowly into her empty teacup. In her head, she knew that Charlotte was right. Her mother had lost a long battle with illness all those years ago, and the fault didn't lie with any person—not even the useless doctors. But her heart still remembered the helpless frustration.

"It's not the same thing at all, *ma chérie*," said Charlotte, in a more gentle tone. "Have you told Adelaide any of this?"

Cornelia looked up at her. "No. How could I?"

Charlotte pulled slowly on her cigarette and blew out a long thoughtful stream of smoke. "You feel shame about this. But I don't think that Adelaide will see it that way at all."

Cornelia sighed. "Maybe you're right." She wasn't at all prepared, though, to reveal her deepest shame and failure to Adelaide, regardless of how the girl might respond. Especially not when Adelaide was trusting her to save the world with no preparation and no plan.

"Well, none of that really matters right now," Cornelia said decisively, after a pause. "We've both decided to embark on this mad quest, so there's no going back now. I do have a favor to ask of you, though."

"Anything, darling."

"I would like for you to stay in touch with Rawlins while I'm gone. Not constantly, of course, but I want to keep him updated on my travels, and... Well, I don't think it's entirely safe for me to be sending telegrams to my own address. Just because those Caelum men who searched my house the other night seemed satisfied with what we gave them, I don't think for a minute that they're going to just forget about me. No one outside of my own household besides you knows that I'm even leaving town—I used false names for both myself and Adelaide when I booked our passage. If the Caelum are keeping tabs on my mail, telephone, or telegrams, I don't want them even suspecting that anything is out of the ordinary."

Charlotte nodded. "A wise precaution to take, I agree."

"So I thought I could send you a telegram, addressed to the salon, every time we make port. Just to let you know where we are. I won't put my name or anything else incriminating in it. So if you could then communicate that to Rawlins, just to keep him updated..."

Charlotte nodded again. "But of course."

"And Charlotte..." she paused and took a breath. "If something happens, if I don't come back—I've left Rawlins in charge of everything. I want you to help him, however you can—I know you have your salon to manage, but..." She looked at Charlotte, still lounging against her desk just a few steps away. "You're the only other person who knows about John's condition," she said at last. "I'm not asking you to drop everything and try to heal him, I just...I just am hoping that you could make yourself available to Rawlins if he needs you." She felt guilty laying such a burden on Charlotte, but she also felt guilty leaving Rawlins to handle everything by himself.

"Cornelia, I'm honored that you would leave me to help manage your estate," said Charlotte with a smile. "I will do everything I can, and more, with joy. But I believe it won't come to that."

Cornelia didn't want it to come to that, either, but she had to be realistic about all this. The Caelum had already tried to kill her once, had tried to kill John, and was now preparing to all but destroy the world.

"I hope so." Cornelia swallowed, and glanced at her wrist watch. "I'd best be off so I can finish getting ready." She pushed her chair back from the tea table and stood up. "I sent Adelaide to our ladies' club's weekly bridge game. I have an excuse to be absent for a while a longer, but Adelaide doesn't, and I don't want anyone to get worried or suspicious. And if Prudence is there, hopefully Adelaide can glean something about her plans or her involvement with the Caelum. I just hope Adelaide won't ask too many direct questions and get herself into trouble."

Charlotte smiled. "I'm sure she'll be just fine. Oh, before you go..." She snuffed out her cigarette in the ashtray and went over to the small but overloaded bookshelf in the corner. She rearranged several stacks of books, and pulled down a small powder tin. Charlotte wasn't a disorganized person, and she kept the front room of the salon immaculately pristine and tidy; but her personal space was a bit more "free," as she called it.

Charlotte set the pink-and-gold tin on the desk and pulled off the lid. She lifted out a folded handkerchief, and handed it slowly to Cornelia.

"I always keep a few of these on hand, just in case. Not that I use them often, mind you, but it never hurts to be prepared.

And since you're going into danger, I think you might need them."

Opening the folded handkerchief, Cornelia saw a small collection of bobby pins. She gave Charlotte a questioning look.

"The tips are poisoned," the other woman explained. "Just a sedative, not a deadly poison. A simple touch to the tip can cause numbness at the point of contact, and mild disorientation. A jab that breaks the skin, even the tiniest bit, brings sleep for several minutes."

Cornelia stared at the bobby pins for a moment, then carefully folded the handkerchief back up. For at least the third time this afternoon, Charlotte had managed to surprise her. She trusted Charlotte's potions completely, and knew that these weaponized bobby pins would do exactly what she said they would. She shuddered, though, at the thought that she might have to use them. Firing a gun at mindless automatons was one thing, but...

She pushed those thoughts away. Plenty of time to plan and worry later. "Thank you, Charlotte," she said finally, putting the folded hankie in her purse.

"It's hardly magic on the same level as that seeker's potion that you said Lou gave you," said Charlotte. "That's why I sent you to him. He knows things and can find things that no one else can. Even if I'd had all the ingredients, I'm not sure that I could have given you a potion such as that. But these bobby pins will have to do for now."

"Any gift from you will help, I'm sure," said Cornelia. "And remember what I told you earlier: if I don't come back—"

"Shhh," said Charlotte, holding up a hand. "It won't come to that." She stepped up close to her and took Cornelia's hand. "It must not come to that."

Then Charlotte stood on tiptoe and air-kissed Cornelia's cheeks. "I will see you when you return. *Bon voyage, ma chérie.* And good luck."

<hr />

"IT LOOKS LIKE MISS Adelaide is here, ma'am," said Rawlins.

Cornelia peered around the base of the ladder to see a taxicab coming down the driveway. She and Rawlins were on the front porch, Rawlins at the top of the ladder with screwdriver in hand, affixing a small boxy frame to the underside of the porch roof. Cornelia's job was to judge the placement of the box and hand him screws when he needed them.

Adelaide climbed out of the car with a suitcase in hand, paid the driver, and then hurried up the wide porch steps as the taxi drove off. "What's all this?" she asked. "Did someone try to break in?"

"No, and this is to help make sure that no one ever does," said Cornelia. She looked up at Rawlins' work. "That looks good. A lick of paint to match the porch ceiling will help the box to be less noticeable. Not that many people will likely be looking up at the porch ceiling over the stairs, but still, any bit of disguising will help." She held up her handful of screws. "Do you need any more?"

"No, I think that's got it," said Rawlins. He put the screwdriver in the back pocket of his overalls, and Cornelia held the ladder steady as he climbed down.

Adelaide peered up at the installation. "What is that? It looks like an upside-down bowl."

"It's a crystal ball," said Cornelia. "Held in place by a wooden box, with a hole perfectly cut to allow just a little less than half of the sphere to protrude. That way there's no danger of the ball slipping out, but there's still enough of the ball visible to be useful."

"Useful for what?" asked Adelaide.

"This ball is connected to another crystal ball inside," Cornelia told her, opening the front door and leading the way into the foyer. She gestured at the large crystal sphere, resting in its onyx stand, sitting on the telephone table next to the brass candlestick phone. On the floor beneath the table was a small boxy device with wires and vacuum tubes visible.

"This is an amplitude modulation transmitter that's been modified to boost the connection between the crystal balls," Cornelia explained, pointing at the wires tucked between the ball and its stand that ran down to the transmitter box. "The crystal ball on the porch will see anything that moves below it, a bit like a moving-picture camera. And that image can be viewed in this ball." She laid a hand on the large volleyball-sized crystal sphere on the telephone table.

"Golly!" said Adelaide. "So you can see what's happening on the front porch without even looking out the window."

"Exactly. And we've just finished putting a crystal ball at each entrance to the house. This way, if there's any disturbance outside, Rawlins can see what's happening without opening a door or going near a window. This ball here in the foyer will even flash with light to get his attention if any of the peripheral balls detect movement."

"Golly!" said Adelaide again, setting down her suitcase and bending over to examine the large clear orb on the telephone table. "And you guys did all this today?"

"Well, John deserves most of the credit," said Cornelia. As he did for most things. "He came up with the idea some time ago," she continued aloud. "He'd already drawn up designs for the amplitude modulation transmitter, so Rawlins just had to put it together. And John and I had already placed the enchantments on all of the crystal balls." She remembered spending several evenings poring over books of spells and ancient treatises on the use of crystal balls, putting together the specific enchantment that would suit their purpose. For a time they'd kept one ball in the bedroom and one in the basement lab so that Cornelia could call John without having to traipse down two flights of stairs.

The distance between spheres proved too great, though, for effective communication, which had prompted John to come up with the idea of electronic amplification. Cornelia also had suspected that John was apt to ignore the flashing signal from the sphere when he was engrossed in work, which was not a problem that could be fixed with the addition of a wireless transmitter.

It was a little over a year ago that they'd last worked on this project. And now she was using John's idea to protect his comatose body while she took off across the world after his would-be killers.

The sound of Adelaide's voice brought her attention back. "I'm sorry, what was that?" she said, pulling her hollow gaze away from the sphere and focusing on the girl.

"I was just saying that I was awfully impressed, is all," said Adelaide with enthusiasm. "And here I thought crystal balls were just good for seeing the future."

Cornelia gave her a smile. "There's more myth than truth to that, I'm afraid." Rousing herself back into the role of a hostess welcoming a guest, she gestured for Adelaide to take off her coat and hat. "Some magical practitioners can develop the skills of a clairvoyant and use crystal balls to aid and enhance their work," Cornelia continued, hanging Adelaide's coat and hat in the coat closet by the base of the staircase. "But mostly the power of a good crystal ball is simply its ability to magnify energy. Personally, I've found them to be very effective at summoning ghosts."

"Ghosts?" Adelaide's eyes went wide. "Like at a séance? A friend of mine back in New York hosted a séance once, but I don't think anything happened. Certainly no actual ghosts turned up."

Cornelia smiled at her again. "If you know what you're doing and the ghost wants to communicate, you don't have to go through all the rigamarole of a séance. John and I spoke to his brother after he died. John's older brother Henry was killed in the War."

"Gee," said Adelaide sympathetically. "Did you use a crystal ball to summon his brother's ghost?"

"We did. But like I said, if the spirit wants to communicate, you don't even have to use a crystal ball or perform any sort of ritual. My grandfather died on the *Titanic*, but his ghost appeared to me later that year, on my birthday. He always sent me some little trinket from his travels for my birthday, so he came to me to wish me a happy birthday even though he could no longer give me a physical gift. We had a lovely conversation." Cornelia smiled at the memory—it had been years since she'd thought about that. She'd never been close to her grandfather, since he'd spent all his time traveling around Europe, but his letters and gifts had always been full of kindness and cheer. The one spirit she'd never been able to summon, despite her numerous attempts over the years, was her mother.

"Golly, that's exciting," said Adelaide. "So people can just come and go, or even stay around forever if they want to, after they've died?"

Cornelia gave a little shrug. "It seems that way. If the spirit has a reason to stay, I suppose."

Adelaide smiled, and carefully trailed a finger across the surface of the large crystal ball. "Could you teach me how to summon ghosts?"

"Not right now," said Cornelia. "I think we both have enough to think about what with trying to prevent John—and the rest of the world—from becoming ghosts." She noticed movement out of the corner of her eye, and turned her head to see Maggie coming down the hall towards the foyer.

"Dinner be ready, Mrs. Jones, Miss Adelaide," said Maggie, wiping her hands on her apron. "Beggin' your pardon, but Mr. Rawlins told me to announce dinner myself, seein' as how he's on his way to the carriage house to put away the ladder."

"Thank you, Maggie," said Cornelia, as she and Adelaide followed the cook back down the hall to the dining room. *I should have told Rawlins to leave the ladder on the porch,*

Cornelia mused briefly. Ronald or Joey could have put it away—Rawlins really didn't need to be man-hauling heavy things halfway across the estate.

After they were seated and had started eating, Cornelia asked: "So, how did it go at bridge this afternoon?"

"Not as well as we'd hoped," said Adelaide, as she bit into an asparagus stalk. She chewed for a moment, then looked at Cornelia. "Prudence wasn't there."

Cornelia sighed. "How convenient. I can't say I'm especially surprised, though."

"I was at a table with Hortense and Olive and Violet," Adelaide continued. "Hortense was the dummy, so she had plenty of time to talk. I started by asking how Prudence was doing and if her husband was recovered, and both Hortense and Violet said they didn't know. Hortense said that she hasn't seen or spoken to Prudence in over a week. And then she said that she'd heard that Prudence had closed up their house, laid off the staff, and left town."

"Where did she hear that from?" Cornelia asked.

"Hortense said that Geraldine had heard it from her housekeeper, who heard it from a Western Union telegram boy who delivers to both her house and the Davenports' house."

"Hmmp," Cornelia mumbled around a mouthful of potatoes. So Hortense had fourth-hand information—but even so, Hortense's gossip was usually fairly accurate.

"I could go over to their house and see, I suppose," said Adelaide.

"No." Cornelia shook her head. "It doesn't really matter. And it's probably true. If Prudence and Percival truly are part of this Caelum organization and are involved in the creation of this flying city, they're probably already on their way there."

They ate in silence for a moment, then Adelaide said, "Hortense and Violet asked about you, of course. Well, they asked if I'd seen or talked to you at all recently. I told them that I'd spoken with you a couple of times and that you were doing as well as could be expected. I tried to keep it vague, and they didn't ask for details about Mr. Jones."

Cornelia nodded. "That's good." While she wanted Prudence, Percival, and the Caelum to think that John was dead, she was not eager to announce such a falsehood to society at large. Ideally, she and Rawlins could figure out how to cure John very soon, and within a few weeks, months at the most, he'd be fully recovered and back in the public world. But first she had to make sure that the people who'd wanted him dead weren't around waiting to finish the job if and when they learned the truth. And even more importantly, she had to make sure that she, John, Adelaide, and the rest of the world survived past the next couple of weeks.

She took a large swallow of wine to clear her mind. No sense in worrying about all that right now—they had a long journey ahead of them, with plenty of time then for planning and worrying. "Ronald will be ready with the car at eight-fifteen tomorrow morning to take us to the train station," she said aloud.

"Okay," said Adelaide.

"Adelaide...it's not too late to change your mind."

The younger woman looked at her over the rim of her wine glass. "Cornelia, we've already been through this," she said, lowering the glass. "I'm coming with you. Why are you trying to talk me out of it?"

"Because it's dangerous—" Cornelia began, even though that wasn't really what she was trying to say.

"I know that," Adelaide interrupted her, giving her an impatient look.

Cornelia sighed. "I know. What I mean is...you have a family who care about you, and it's irresponsible of me to let you endanger yourself like this. What would your parents think?"

Adelaide slowly set down her glass, and her bright, determined expression grew serious. "You're wrong about that, Cornelia. My family doesn't care about me."

Cornelia opened her mouth to protest such a preposterous notion, but Adelaide continued talking.

"I suppose my parents love me, as dutiful parents should. But they don't like me one bit. Of course my parents wouldn't approve of me dashing off across the globe to stop a flying city. But they didn't want me coming to Los Angeles, either. They don't like it that I'm still unmarried at the ripe old age of not-quite twenty-one. They didn't like me spending my childhood escaping from my governesses so I could read books and explore the woods. They didn't like that I was born a girl instead of a boy."

Cornelia said nothing. The Victorian-minded old-money families of New England were legendary for their snobbery and strictness—at least that was her own impression, having met a few individuals who ventured westward to Chicago for visits when she was growing up. Adelaide hadn't talked much about her family, except to occasionally mention that she had no desire to ever return to the east coast.

"My brother is six years older than me," Adelaide continued. "So my father got his son and heir before I came along. I don't think he wanted another child at all, but especially not a girl. And then, to add insult to injury, I could never manage even to be a good daughter. I was never a proper lady." Adelaide's voice took on a hard edge, a tone Cornelia had never heard before. "I know how to behave at social functions, and I did sometimes—but even then, I was never quite good enough. That's about the only thing my parents ever said to me, especially as I got older—was how I was too wild, too improper, and was a disgrace to the family.

"My grandmother died right before my birthday last year," Adelaide then said, the harsh bitterness fading from her voice now. "I didn't get to see her very often, but I think she was the only one who truly loved me. I still have all of her letters."

"I'm sorry," said Cornelia with genuine feeling.

Adelaide smiled. "She willed me some money. Quite a lot, and her will stipulated that it was mine personally—not to be managed for me by my father or a husband. So I took that money and left New York. I knew that if I ever left home, unless it was to marry a man my parents approved of, my father would never financially support me. My grandmother must have known that, and she cared about me enough to give me money of my own. A chance at a life of my own."

Cornelia looked at her, understanding more deeply now why the girl had latched onto her as a mentor figure. That brought Cornelia's own shortcomings into the light more strongly than ever, though. She swallowed hard as she tried to squelch her fears.

"So that's why I don't care one bit what my parents might think of me or what I'm doing," Adelaide said, breaking into Cornelia's thoughts. Her tone was bright and energetic again, and she gave Cornelia an encouraging smile. "My grandmother gave me my freedom. And I'm never going back."

Despite her own fear and apprehension, Cornelia relaxed a little. The girl's optimism, quixotic though it might be, was infectious.

Adelaide continued to grin as she reached for her glass. "I'm ready."

Chapter 9

Cornelia stared at the papers strewn across the small wooden table. She'd packed every possible sheet of information that she thought might be needed: maps, John's notes and designs of the gravity engine, and of course the sheet of notes about the flying city that John had sent in the mail.

So many papers, so much information—and still so far from any feasible plan. She pushed her chair back from the table and began pacing across the small cabin, from the doorway into the bathroom and across to the round window that looked out over the deck of the steamship. It was after dinner now, though, so the sky through the window was dark and dotted with stars.

"Maybe we should go outside and get some fresh air," said Adelaide, who was still sitting at the table. The dinner dishes had been taken away by the porter, thus clearing the table for the papers. They'd been eating most of their meals in the cabin, but each time they laid out the papers again after a meal, answers and solutions were no closer than before.

Cornelia started to protest that they'd just gotten some fresh air right before dinner, but then she stopped her pacing and nodded. Walking the decks would be better than pacing in this tiny room; and after three days at sea, Cornelia just couldn't sit still and feign an interest in card games or reading in a chaise lounge.

She'd booked them a second-class cabin on the steamer *Estrella del Sur*, out of San Diego and bound for Panama City. She'd wanted to avoid the possibility of being recognized if she traveled first class, but couldn't quite bring herself to travel third class or steerage. Ordinarily she enjoyed a nice steamship voyage, and the second-class accommodations were comfortable. But right now, with so much at stake and time not on their side, the long days of travel were grating on her mind. If only steamships could travel faster. Ironically, the most effective way of getting them to the South Pacific the fastest would be an aircraft utilizing the very device they were on their way to destroy.

"Come on," said Adelaide in a firm tone, standing up. "Get your coat and hat and let's go outside."

Cornelia put on her long brown dress jacket and matching cloche, while Adelaide donned a burgundy jacket and black hat. Cornelia had insisted that they both bring the plainest clothes they owned and no jewelry, since the idea was to be as unobtrusive as possible and not look like they belonged in first class. She'd also packed her black bunker break-in outfit, although skulking around in robber's get-up wouldn't really provide the same degree of subtlety in this venture.

"They'll see us coming, you know," she said aloud as the two of them walked down the hall past the smoking room and the game lounge.

Adelaide looked at her. "Who?"

"The Caelum. Whoever is running this radium city. We'll have to rent a private boat to reach the coordinates out in the ocean. There's no way we'll be able to sneak up on anyone."

"I know." Adelaide pushed open the door to the outside deck and held it open for Cornelia. "So when we get there, we have to sabotage the vibration plates in at least half of the engines in order to incapacitate the city so that it can't take off. Right?"

"Well, that's one idea," said Cornelia, as they walked along the deck. "Though I sincerely doubt it'll be as easy as all that. The anti-gravity field is maintained by controlled magnetic harmonic resonance, using magnetic plates vibrating at a certain sound frequency. For all of those engines to work in tandem, they all would have to be vibrating on exactly the same frequency. The slightest change to even some of the engines would be enough to disrupt the gravity matrix energy field. In theory." They'd discussed this idea—and others—numerous times over the past three days.

She stopped talking as they passed another person out for an evening stroll; the older gentleman nodded at them and politely touched his fedora as they passed each other. Cornelia buttoned up her coat and snugged her hat tighter on her head. Even though the ship was nearing the equator, traveling at nearly twenty knots across the open ocean created a brisk breeze. Despite the chill, the rising moon and the salty air refreshed her.

"I've been reading those spell books you brought along," Adelaide said quietly, when the man was well past them. "They say that a full moon can enhance magic spells or make it easier to cast enchantments. There should be a full moon just as we're reaching the city, so that should help us if we need to use any magic. Right?"

"Generally speaking, yes," said Cornelia, pulling her mind away from thoughts about engines and speed. She wrapped her fingers around the little glass vial in her coat pocket. Before they'd left the house, Cornelia had burnt an herbal blend of star anise, bay leaves, and chamomile—the same collection they'd carried with them for protection and luck when they'd raided the bunker. She also was wearing the Eye of Horus pendant around her neck under her dress, and Adelaide had the Celtic knotwork amulet again. Hopefully all of those would help.

"I've been working on memorizing that incapacitating spell you showed me," Adelaide continued. "That's enough to stop someone who might try to attack us, right?"

"Just remember to keep both fists closed, with your thumbs tucked inside and your fingers pointing downwards until you've finished the incantation." Cornelia held up a gloved fist to demonstrate. "That position of your hands is what keeps the energy closed and locked down, which is what renders the recipient immobile."

"I will," said Adelaide, nodding.

"A word of caution, though," Cornelia continued. "A spell like that takes both strength and practice—it may not work the first time you try it. A simple charm like burning herbs for general good fortune is an easy task that even someone who knows nothing of magic can do if they simply follow the instructions of the charm." She pulled the little vial out of her pocket and held it up. "But something like manipulating energy and affecting another person takes a lot of mental strength and discipline. There's a cost to doing that kind of magic."

"A cost?" Adelaide looked at her.

"I've had spells leave me exhausted, or cause me physical pain. Or backfire in other ways—like produce a result that is the polar opposite of what I was trying to accomplish." She hadn't done magic of that magnitude for many years. She glanced at Adelaide. "I'm not trying to scare you. I just want you to understand that magic isn't a quick fix or easy defense for everything."

Adelaide nodded solemnly. "I was reading about a potion that can stop bleeding—even internal bleeding. Is that the sort of spell that—"

"That spell doesn't always work for everything," Cornelia interrupted her before she could stop herself.

"What do you mean?

Cornelia sighed and stopped walking, turning to rest her hands on the deck railing as she stared out to sea. She didn't want to talk to Adelaide about her failures, especially not now...

"Did you try that spell on John, before you put him in the artificial womb?" Adelaide asked quietly, stopping beside her and resting her own gloved hands on the railing.

"No," said Cornelia. "He wasn't bleeding internally, according to the doctor. I did think about modifying that spell, though, to try to lighten the density of his internal organs. But then we decided to build the tank, so all my time and mental energy went towards finishing that. When we get back home and I have time to work on healing him, maybe I'll try to come up with some sort of enhancement of that spell to...." She trailed off. *When we get back home,* she thought. *IF we get back home. Oh, John, did I do the right thing, leaving you and taking off with Adelaide on this madcap venture?*

"So what did you mean, then," Adelaide's voice intruded into her thoughts. "About 'that spell doesn't always work for everything'?"

Cornelia sighed again. There was no getting out of it now. "Adelaide...there's a reason that I've been somewhat reluctant to teach you magic. Yes, I know how to burn herbal incense for protection or how to summon a ghost with a crystal ball, but when it comes to doing magic that really matters, I'm a failure." She swallowed and looked out at the ocean, not wanting to look at Adelaide. "When it comes to saving someone's life with magic, I can't do it."

"But John—"

"I'm not talking about John," Cornelia interrupted her. "I'm talking about my mother."

Adelaide said nothing. Cornelia finally turned her head to look at Adelaide. The younger woman was staring at her with a sorrowful but expectant look on her face. Cornelia sighed again, and looked back out at the dark ocean.

"My mother died when I was sixteen. She'd been ill for many years before that. My father could afford the very best in medical care—she had all the best doctors, she stayed for a time in the very best sanatorium, and we even took a trip out to California from Chicago so that she could have the warm sun and the sea air. I decided that I wanted to live in California one day, after we spent the summer there with my mother." She smiled briefly at the memory: running barefoot through the surf on the beach, then turning back to see her parents resting side by side in wicker lounge chairs, smiling and waving at her.

"But none of the treatments lasted," she continued, her smile fading as the memories advanced into more unpleasant ones. "I did everything I could—I took over all of my mother's societal duties, handled all the household correspondences, managed the staff, as well as administering whatever medicines or treatments the doctors had prescribed at the time. And I read every medical book and witchcraft herbal I could get my hands on.

"I knew I couldn't learn more than the professional doctors simply by reading a few textbooks, but I wanted to better understand what they were doing to my mother and why they thought certain treatments would help. And I wanted to have some understanding of how the body worked so that I could combine the doctor's treatments with magical treatments. I tried dozens of potions and spells."

She paused as her memories continued to unfurl, letting Adelaide absorb everything she'd just said. The sleepless nights she'd spent reading book after book; the shopping trips she'd taken to parts of town where a young woman shouldn't have gone unescorted, searching for strange ingredients for spells...

"Did your parents know that you were mixing magic with the doctor's medicines?" Adelaide asked into the silence.

Cornelia nodded. "They did. They'd never discouraged me from pursuing knowledge of any kind—even magical lore. My father wasn't too keen on me actually casting spells on my mother and brewing potions for her to drink, though. At first my mother didn't object, but after a few years she tried to convince me to stop. I think at that point she'd given up, and she didn't want me to keep struggling in vain. But I kept at it anyway. But eventually, both medicine and magic stopped helping her, even a little bit, and she died."

"I'm so sorry, Cornelia," Adelaide whispered. "That must have been awful for you."

Cornelia blinked back tears and kept her gaze focused on the glint of moonlight flickering over the dark waves. "It was," she finally managed. "But my father and I got through it, and he let me leave home and attend college, and was so proud when John and I were married. And I've continued learning more about magic and practicing when I can, but..." She drew a breath and held it a moment. "But I've never tried to do anything big again. Anything important."

She swallowed hard and looked at Adelaide again. "I know that it wasn't my fault that my mother died, but...my magical knowledge and abilities couldn't save her. So I have no right to try to teach you how to do anything big or important."

"Oh, Cornelia." Adelaide touched her arm. "I'm so sorry that happened to you. And I can understand why you'd still feel awful about it, even after all this time. But I don't see you as a failure. There's so much that you can teach me, and I want to learn it. From you."

Cornelia couldn't bring herself to smile, but she felt a strange sense of relief, hearing Adelaide's words. At least the girl knew the truth now.

An unusually strong gust of wind came across the water, rustling their jackets and tugging at their hats. Cornelia snugged up the collar of her jacket, and Adelaide put a hand on the top of her hat.

"We'd best go inside, and try to get some sleep," Cornelia said at last. "We're supposed to be coming into port around midday tomorrow, and as soon as we disembark we need to find passage further south."

"I know we won't be staying long," said Adelaide as they headed back across the deck towards the door into the ship. "But I'm excited to see Panama City. I've never been to Central America before."

"Neither have I," said Cornelia. "Hopefully good fortune will be in store for us in Panama."

THEIR STAY IN PANAMA City was brief, but propitious. Cornelia found a telegraph office right after they disembarked, and sent a telegram to Charlotte's salon to update her—and thus Rawlins—on their progress so far. Not that there was much to tell yet, but she wanted to keep them informed.

Another steamer was scheduled to leave later that afternoon, bound for Valparaiso, Chile. The city of Valparaiso was the closest major port to the coordinates of the Caelum's city. From there they'd have to charter a boat for the long dangerous journey out to literally the middle of nowhere.

But they had another three or four days on the steamship to prepare for that. There was a second-class cabin available, even here at the last minute. Cornelia was glad that they wouldn't have to suffer in third-class accommodations for this leg of the trip.

She and Adelaide spent most of their time continuing to pore over the same books, maps, and schematics that they'd been studying on the previous ship. Cornelia filled page after page in a blank notebook with scribblings of ideas and calculations, but felt only vaguely more confident that any of the ideas she'd come up with would work.

Sabotaging the vibration plates on the engines was probably the most efficient way to prevent lift-off, as long as they could sabotage them in such a way that repairs would be out of the question. According to the diagram of the city that John had stolen from Percival, the engines were positioned underneath the city—which was logical. But would mean that physically accessing the engines would be a climbing feat worthy of a circus acrobat. There was also a central control building, the "cockpit" of the city, as it were. That would be another potential sabotage target that, while likely less physically demanding to access, would probably be more heavily protected.

And then there was the matter of what to say to anyone when they were inevitably spotted long before their arrival to the city. Adelaide's suggestion was to simply tell them the truth, or a form of the truth—inform the Caelum of the disastrous global impact their flying city would have, appealing to their moral humanitarian nature to halt the launch.

Cornelia was fully convinced that tactic would not work. Any person or persons smart enough to engineer this flying city was more than smart enough to know about any ill effects the city's presence might cause. And anyone who tried to murder the inventor of the gravity engine when he started to suspect their motives clearly had no higher moral nature to appeal to.

They still hadn't agreed on a good cover story yet when the ship pulled into the dock in Valparaiso, Chile. They arrived in the late evening, though it was still not fully dark yet, since it was summer time here in the southern hemisphere. The docks and seaside roads bustled with people, horses, donkeys, and automobiles. Adelaide had suggested that they change into their "adventuring duds," as she called their black thieves costumes. Adelaide had put together an ensemble of her own after their bunker break-in, and so they disembarked the steamer dressed in their most unladylike outfits. Cornelia felt more self-conscious than when she'd driven the motorcycle through Los Angeles and marched into Lou's speakeasy in this outfit.

But this truly was a cosmopolitan port and the residents jaded. No one gave the two women a second glance as they walked down the gangplank and melted into the crowd.

After finding the telegraph office and sending another message home to Charlotte, Cornelia scanned the shingles of the row of brightly painted shops bordering the wharf, looking for something that might indicate a boat rental. She could pick out a jumble of Spanish, Italian, French, English, and other languages in the buzz of voices all around, but all of the building signage was in Spanish. She saw no signs that indicated small boat rental.

"Let's try over there," she said, spotting a man farther down the wharf who appeared to be exchanging money with another man and pointing at a small dinghy bobbing in the water. Clutching the handle of her suitcase firmly to make sure that no one "accidentally" pulled it out of her hand in the jostling crowd, she headed down the wharf.

"Do you think we'll be able to row ourselves all the way out there?" Adelaide murmured in her ear as they threaded through the throng of people.

"I'm counting on finding someone with a slightly bigger and more powerful boat," Cornelia returned. "But that man is a good one to start with. And even if we do have to use a rowboat, I'm sure we can find someone to take us. A generous stack of American dollars should count for something."

A large man suddenly stepped out from between two little wooden shops and blocked their path; Cornelia halted just in time, but Adelaide bumped into him and gave a startled squeak.

"*Perdonanos, señor,*" Cornelia started to say, hoping her pronunciation was intelligible. As she stepped to the side to pass him, another man moved out from the shadows to stand beside him.

"*Let us pass, please,*" Cornelia said to the men in Spanish, giving them both an imperious glare.

"No need for Spanish, dear—they're Americans, too," came a voice. A very familiar woman's voice.

Cornelia felt her blood chill as Prudence Davenport stepped out to join the two men. "Welcome to South America, my dear Mrs. Jones. I wondered when you'd get here."

Chapter 10

Cornelia sat on the leather upholstered bench seat in the main cabin of Prudence's gasoline-powered yacht. Or the Caelum's yacht, or her bodyguards' yacht, or whoever owned the boat. One of the men was driving the boat. The other man stayed in the cabin, sitting on the bench across from Cornelia and Adelaide, while Prudence bustled around making tea. The boat rocked gently as they sped along, but Prudence didn't spill a drop.

"So, why don't you tell me why you're here," said Prudence in a false-cheerful tone that said she knew exactly why they were here. "Sugar?"

"One lump, please," said Adelaide in a small voice. Cornelia said nothing.

Prudence put one lump of sugar in both cups, stirred, and then handed the cups to the two women before fixing herself a cup and sitting down across from them. She was dressed in pants like they were—also black, though hers were perfectly tailored trousers instead of form-fitting riding pants. Unlike the black blouses and aviator jackets that they were wearing, though, Prudence wore a tan blouse and dark tweed vest with a tie. She would never appear in society dressed in such a mannish getup, Cornelia was sure—but they weren't in proper society right now.

"So," said Prudence, lifting her tea cup. "What's your story?"

"We came to join you," Adelaide blurted.

Cornelia gave her a sideways glance. On the steamer trip they'd briefly discussed that cover story, as well, but Cornelia had dismissed it as being even more useless than telling the truth. Especially now that they were face to face with someone who actually knew who they were.

Prudence laughed. "Well, that's a story, all right. So how did she manage to drag you into this little revenge quest of hers?"

"She didn't drag me, and it's not about revenge," said Adelaide.

"Not about revenge, is it?" said Prudence with another laugh, and looked at Cornelia.

Cornelia waited a beat to collect herself before answering. "What is all this about, Prudence?"

"You ought to know. You're the one who figured it out and traveled all the way down here."

"All I know is that you and Percival are completely mad as well as being murderers," Cornelia said darkly.

"So you came all this way to, what, bring us to justice?" said Prudence archly, then sipped her tea.

Cornelia wanted nothing more than to launch herself across the cabin and slam Prudence in the face, but the presence of the large man on the bench beside Prudence kept her from doing so. "Why are you doing this?" she finally managed. "Don't you know that your flying city is going to cause worldwide havoc? How dare you use one of John's inventions in such a way?"

"So this *is* about revenge, then. For us 'stealing' one of your husband's creations?"

"No, for what you did to him," Cornelia gritted in reply, not elaborating on that. Prudence and her compatriots needed to continue to think he was dead. "John was always willing to share his inventions and ideas, for the sake of progress and the betterment of humanity." Not a sentiment she entirely shared, and the only reason he held as many patents as he did was because she'd pressured him into filing for them. She was all for sharing knowledge, but hard work and creativity also deserved credit.

"But that's exactly what this is about, you see," said Prudence. "Progress and the betterment of humanity."

"But how is a flying city that will disrupt animal migrations, destroy electrical power, and cause tidal waves for the betterment of humanity?" asked Adelaide, her tone full of genuine puzzlement and curiosity.

"Because this city is to be a sanctuary," said Prudence in a warm, patient voice, looking Adelaide in the eyes. "A safe place for people like us—people who understand both science and magic, where we can live and work and create uninhibited by arbitrary rules of society and mundane people with no vision." She took a sip of her tea, then slowly set her cup back in the saucer before continuing. "Of course we know about the potential environmental repercussions of the launch of this city. We've taken every precaution to minimize risks and damages. But sometimes there is a cost to progress."

"So you're willing to sacrifice a few thousand ordinary people—and animals—so that you can live in a private kingdom in the sky," said Cornelia.

"Really, Cornelia," said Prudence with a melodramatic sigh. "We're not penny-dreadful villains who want to destroy the world for the sake of destroying the world. It would be wonderful if everyone thought the way we did. But most people scoff at the idea of magic, and don't give much more thought to science and technology. Oh, most people are happy with their motor cars and music on the radio, but they don't know—or care—that the ideas behind those inventions could do so much more than just provide mere lifestyle comforts. And the few that do support progress only want to create weapons. We lived through the most violent and hideous war in all of history thanks to mismanaged scientific progress."

Prudence took a delicate sip of her tea before continuing. "The Caelum believe in true progress—in blending the ancient arts of magic with the modern arts of science, and mastering the natural world for the benefit of everyone. Some old ways will have to fall by the wayside, and not everyone will make the cut to join us, but we truly do want what's best for humanity as a whole."

It was a compelling speech. And if Cornelia hadn't personally experienced what the Caelum were willing to do in order to make their grand humanitarian vision come true, she might have been swayed by Prudence's words. She glanced at Adelaide, and saw the girl's blue eyes shining with wonder as she gazed at Prudence. *Come on, Adelaide, don't fall for her pretty words,* she thought.

The large man who had been sitting silently on the padded bench with Prudence this whole time, who apparently was not worthy of introductions, suddenly rose and climbed the ladder up out of the cabin. For an instant Cornelia thought about rushing Prudence and attacking her. She and Adelaide together could certainly overpower her. Their suitcases—with Cornelia's utility belt and guns—were sitting at the other end of the small cabin. After knocking Prudence out, she could grab both guns and then it would be an easy matter to—

The man reappeared at that moment, climbing partway back down into the cabin. "We're nearly there, ma'am," he said to Prudence.

Prudence smiled, stood, and set her teacup down on the bar. "Come along, ladies. Let's go take a look at our city of vision." She gestured for Cornelia to precede her up the ladder, and the man waited for her at the top.

Placing her undrunk tea on the bar as she stood up, Cornelia then climbed up to the deck, with Adelaide behind her, followed by Prudence. The sudden brisk salty wind in her face made her hitch in a breath, but then her breath caught again as she saw what lay ahead of them.

The stars were bright in the cloudless sky and the moon nearly full, which only enhanced the well-lit spectacle before them. The Caelum's radium city sprawled across the water, the glinting chrome buildings awash with electric lights from dozens of windows. Spotlights on tall towers shone between the buildings, and the city itself was surrounded with brightly-lit pylons. The metal buildings and the surrounding water reflected all the lights like mirrors, and Cornelia had to squint. This man-made island, five times bigger than the largest steamships ever built, filled the horizon as they approached.

"It's beautiful," Adelaide murmured.

Cornelia had to agree. Very briefly, she forgot about the Caelum's underhanded secrecy and Prudence's treachery—this city was truly a triumph of modern science and engineering.

Their boat drew nearer, the dazzling lights looming before them. Prudence held out her hand towards the scene. "Welcome to the future."

CORNELIA PACED THE tiny empty room. She'd lost track of how long she'd been locked in here. Some hours ago, two armed men came and opened the door to deliver a tray of food and water, and a chamber pot. No amount of trying to question the guards, banging on the door, or shouting had resulted in any reply.

The room was approximately twelve-foot square, with a ten-foot ceiling, she had determined, after walking the space and measuring the walls with her hands. It was made entirely of metal, with no windows and only one door. The door was locked with a heavy arm bolt on the other side, so there was no lock on this side that she could try to pick. A single electric light bulb in the center of the ceiling provided light.

The only other opening to the outside besides the door was a ventilation fan at the back of the room up by the ceiling. Even if she'd been able to jump high enough to reach it, there would have been no point—the fan was recessed into the wall with a grate in front of the blades, and the opening was far too small for her to fit through.

She judged that she'd been in the room the entire night and into the day, because a small amount of daylight now slipped in around the fan. The temperature also rose quickly, making the room oppressively hot. Eventually the fan turned on, exhausting the stale humid air of her prison. It helped only slightly.

The jacket she'd removed some time ago, and now she unbuttoned the cuffs of her black blouse and rolled up the sleeves. She wondered if she'd be brought another tray of food and drink anytime soon. She wasn't feeling especially hungry, but with the heat of the day baking her little metal prison, she knew she was fast becoming dehydrated.

To conserve energy—and since she'd long ago established that escape was impossible—she sank down to the floor to rest. Leaning against the back wall of the room beneath the fan, where there was the vaguest hint of moving air, she closed her eyes.

For the hundredth time she replayed the events of the night before. Everything had happened so fast once the boat docked. Despite how well-lit the entire city was, Cornelia hadn't been able to get a good look at much of anything as she'd climbed a ladder from the deck of the boat up onto the deck of the city. And then her field of vision had been usurped by Prudence and one of her large bodyguards.

"Since you've come all this way, ladies, I'll give you a choice," Prudence had said. "You can join us, and learn how to truly change the world for the better. Or you can watch us change the world, like the rest of the ignorant populace, and wish you'd had the wisdom to join us."

"Go to hell," Cornelia had spat at her.

But then Adelaide had stepped forward, her face full of that eager youthful zeal that Cornelia had come to appreciate so much. "I want to learn."

And before Cornelia could protest or do anything else, she'd been grabbed by both of the large bodyguards, blindfolded, and escorted to this metal room.

So here she was, alone, trapped, and an utter failure. Even if by some miracle the launch of the city didn't demolish Los Angeles or kill John, she'd never get to see him again. It's not like Prudence and the Caelum were ever going to let her go. And Adelaide...she never should have encouraged the girl at all, and especially not let her join in on this mad quest. She had no right to feel hurt or betrayed—it's not as if Adelaide actually owed her anything. Everything Adelaide had done to help Cornelia was simply to learn, and now the girl had found someone who—she thought—could teach her more.

Cornelia didn't waste the energy—or water—by crying, but the hurt and anger and frustration squeezed at her throat and stung her eyes. She smacked her hand against the warm metal floor as she held in her tears. She had to get out of here. The next time a guard came to deliver food, she'd rush him—regardless of how many men there were or how many guns they might have pointed at her. Better to die trying something that just waste away in a prison.

She must have dozed off, because she was suddenly jolted awake by the sound of the heavy metal bar being removed from the outside of the door. Momentarily disoriented, she scrambled up, looking around. The solitary light bulb overhead cast a dim glow; the fan had stopped turning, and no light was visible around the fan blades. The door clanked again.

Cornelia rolled down her sleeves and grabbed up her jacket as she positioned herself against the wall next to the door. The door was hinged to open outwards, so as soon as there was a space wide enough for her arm to fit through, she would—

The door slipped open just a crack, letting in a tiny breath of refreshingly cool air. "Cornelia?" came a whispered voice.

She froze, her arms up and positioned to throw a punch the instant the door opened more than a crack. "Adelaide?" she whispered back.

The opening widened to reveal Adelaide's smiling face. "Oh, I'm so glad I got the right building. This place is a maze."

"Adelaide, how did you—"

"No time for that now," Adelaide interrupted her. "We should get out of the light before someone sees us."

Electric streetlamps illuminated the metal lanes like any civilized city, and a quick glance around showed Cornelia that every building, including the one she was in, had at least one light mounted over the door or shining down from the roof. Pausing only to close and re-bar the door to her prison, she then followed Adelaide around the building to a narrow passage on the back side that appeared to be more of an alley. There were streetlamps at either end, but since neither building had lights or lit windows on this side, the center of the alley was dark.

"Are you all right?" Adelaide asked quietly, peering at her in the dimness. "Did they hurt you? I asked them not to hurt you."

"I'm not hurt—just hot, cramped, and thirsty. But why—"

"I was worried that they might not keep their promise," Adelaide interrupted her. "I couldn't exactly hide a pitcher of lemonade in my pocket, so I'm afraid this will have to do for now." She pulled two oranges out of her jacket pocket.

Cornelia gratefully took the fruits and peeled one. The sweet juicy flesh refreshed her a bit.

"I smuggled away a couple of ham biscuits, too." Adelaide pulled a small bundle wrapped in a linen dinner napkin out of another pocket. "Oh, and I brought you this, of course."

With her other hand she reached down to her waist and undid a belt buckle, then held up Cornelia's utility belt—complete with the dark-vision goggles, both guns, and every other pouch that held all their tools and talismans.

Cornelia paused in peeling the second orange and stared at the belt, then Adelaide's face.

"What?" said Adelaide. "You didn't really think I was going to join the Caelum and let you rot in a locked room, did you?"

A strangely maternal swell of pride flushed through her as she took the belt from Adelaide. "I wasn't sure what to think," Cornelia finally said.

"Well, I figured I had to get close to them somehow. Those schematics we've been studying didn't show everything about the city. So I pretended to be interested in joining them so I could get more information."

Fastening her belt around her waist, Cornelia finally managed a smile. "Clever girl."

"Hopefully clever enough," said Adelaide. "Here, eat these while I explain my idea." She thrust the napkin bundle at her.

Cornelia quickly ate the two ham biscuits and then polished off the second orange while Adelaide talked.

"The city is still technically under construction. It's mostly finished, since they're on schedule to launch it in a few days, but they're still connecting the radium to some of the engines, and putting some last-minute touches on other things."

"Prudence told you all of this?" Cornelia asked around a mouthful of food. Even as egotistical as Prudence was, and as desperately as she seemed to want them to join her, Cornelia was surprised that she'd be that instantly trusting of Adelaide. Then again, she herself had started to doubt Adelaide's loyalty mere hours ago—much to her private shame now.

"Well, Prudence was with me, showing me around, but she didn't do a lot of the talking. Her husband told me a lot, and then I was introduced to Director Eli Van Hopper."

"Director Van Hopper. We saw his name on the letters when we broke into the Santa Monica bunker."

Adelaide nodded. "The Playfair cypher telegram was addressed to him. But I don't think he's the ultimate man in charge. Both he and the Davenports referenced the Executive Commanders, who will be coming to the city in a few days, right before the launch."

So this Caelum organization was even bigger than they'd realized. Possibly a world-wide organization, with shadowy fingers in the upper echelons of governments in addition to the United States. That was an alarming thought.

"I'm not sure that any of them completely trust me yet, or believed that I truly wanted to join them and had no doubts about it," Adelaide continued. "I was given a private apartment in one of their residential buildings, but after we all said our good-nights, Prudence locked me in. I guess she didn't think I could climb out of a third-story window."

Adelaide grinned, and Cornelia smiled at her, again gratified and impressed. None of the buildings in this city were taller than three stories—to reduce wind shear, no doubt—and with enough bed linens roped together, three stories was an easy matter for a determined young woman.

"But even if they didn't fully trust me," said Adelaide. "They still gave me the grand tour and showed me the main control center. I don't think we need to try to sabotage the individual gravity matrix engines—I think we can stop the city from the control room."

"I was hoping we'd be able to do something like that," said Cornelia, wrapping her orange rinds up in the napkin and stuffing the bundle into her pocket, as she pulled out her black gloves with the other hand. No need to leave any evidence that someone had been surreptitiously snacking in a dark alley. "The schematics we have didn't show any details about the control center, only where it was located. Was the building guarded?"

"I didn't see any guards, but it was locked. Percival had a key," said Adelaide, and then smiled. "But now that you have your belt again, so do we."

"Quite true."

"Another thing that the schematics didn't show," Adelaide then said, "is the floating framework that's keeping the city level and floating right now, before they launch it into the air."

"I'd figured there had to be something like that, to keep the city afloat and out of the water," said Cornelia. "I tried to look at everything beneath the platform of the city when the boat docked, but it was so dark and Prudence's guards were rushing us so. But I knew that they'd have to have a way to keep all of the gravity engines out of the water. Even with extra shielding around the engines to protect them from the elements up in the air, they couldn't be submerged. And the workers would have to be able to access the engines."

"Exactly," said Adelaide. "The 'floor' of the city is twenty feet above the water, and is supported by this huge floating framework, with pylons that extend out into the water to help stabilize everything. They have these huge bladders of air on every pylon to help keep it all afloat. It's easier to see in the daylight, of course." She paused. "I wasn't lying to them when I told them how everything was so amazing and how excited I was to be able to see such a scientific marvel."

"It is amazing," Cornelia agreed. "I just wish that it hadn't been created by such a villainous group of people."

Adelaide nodded. "And I wish they weren't using it for such a selfish purpose. With all this knowledge and ability, they could be helping people, instead of just running away and letting the world burn behind them."

"So we have to stop them," said Cornelia. "If the city is above the water to keep the gravity engines dry and accessible, then instead of sabotaging the vibration plates or another part of each engine, we could simply drown the engines."

"Exactly what I was thinking," said Adelaide. "The air bladders aren't just balloons that are filled up and tied off—there are hoses that run to each one and connect back to an air pressure engine so they can control the air in each bladder to keep the city level. Percival told me all about it. I think he helped to engineer it—he was very proud."

Cornelia rolled her eyes. "Of course."

"The controls for the air bladders are in the main control center," Adelaide said. "If we deflate them all at once, we can do more than just drown the gravity engines. I think we can drown the whole city beyond repair."

Cornelia smiled. "You are indeed a clever girl. Let's go find the control center."

Chapter 11

They crept through the streets, keeping to the shadows as well as they could. Adelaide informed Cornelia that it had been nearly two a.m. when she climbed out of her third-story window, so the late hour reduced their chances of encountering anyone. Cornelia had memorized the schematics page during their sea voyage, but right now she was having a hard time matching the two-dimensional pen-and-ink blueprint to the darkened real-life city around her.

Adelaide pointed out a few buildings as they hurried down the metal lanes, from shadowed spot to shadowed spot. "That's one of their greenhouses, for growing their own food. That one over there is one of their water reclamation towers, I think, so they can filter rain water and sea water to make it drinkable."

"I saw three of those water towers marked on the schematics," said Cornelia.

"That's right. That one is the main power plant complex—where they generate and store all the electricity to run this place." Adelaide indicated a narrow three-story building with a spider-web network of pipes and cables extending from the top to the other buildings surrounding it. The electricity then traveled from there through wires beneath the floor of the city, instead of along power lines on tall poles like a traditional city, Cornelia remembered from the schematic. She also knew that the roofs of the connected buildings supported dozens of wind turbines, which is how the power was generated—though in the dark those weren't visible.

"And over there is the airplane hangar—I think it's that building, or maybe that one." Adelaide pointed at two different long low buildings. "Prudence said that they have over twenty airplanes that they use for bringing people to the city and bringing in small supplies."

"Let's remember how to get back to that building," said Cornelia. "A plane would be a better escape vehicle than a boat."

"That's a good idea," said Adelaide. "I hadn't actually thought that far ahead yet." She stopped walking, and shrank against the wall. "Okay, here we are," she whispered. "That's the main control center. Nuts—it's guarded now."

"Apparently they don't completely trust you," Cornelia whispered back, giving a small smirk. "Is that the only door to the building?"

"No, there's another door on the opposite side."

"That's probably guarded, too. So we should take them both out at the same time in case the other guard notices and raises an alarm."

"All right. How?"

How indeed? There was only one Tesla gun. Cornelia had a vial of flash powder in her belt, but that would be better for a distraction scenario, or temporarily blinding a pursuer. Flash powder was too bright and noisy for a quiet break-in. The regular gun would be too noisy, as well—and she was reluctant to actually shoot someone in cold blood. They merely needed to distract or incapacitate the guards for a short time.

Incapacitate... Cornelia reached up to her hair, suddenly remembering the poison-tipped bobby pins that Charlotte had given her. She'd put several into her bun when she and Adelaide had changed into their black outfits, right before disembarking in Valparaiso. Using them would mean she'd have to get dangerously close to the guard, but it was the best option they had.

"We could try that incapacitating spell that I was practicing on the steamer," Adelaide whispered, holding up her hand in a fist, thumb tucked inside as Cornelia had showed her.

Cornelia shook her head. She didn't want the girl's first try of magic of that difficulty to be a true life-or-death situation.

"Here, take this." Cornelia pulled the Tesla gun out of its holster and handed it to Adelaide. "Twist the dial twice and then squeeze the trigger. He should be out for a good ten minutes. Try to get as close as you can before shooting to maximize the electrical charge. But not too close—don't put yourself in danger. I'll go around the building and take the other guard with this." Cornelia pulled one of the bobby pins out of her bun.

Adelaide's eyes widened. "Oh, those poison-tipped hair pins you told me about. You had them in your hair?"

"Where else would one keep a hair pin? I have them in my bun, so there's no chance the tips will touch my scalp." Then she dug in another pouch on her belt, glad that she'd thought to pack some twine. She handed the bundle to Adelaide. "Tie up his hands after you've stunned him. It's just twine so he'll probably be able to break it when he revives, but it should at least buy us a little more time."

Then she gestured at the wide-barreled Tesla gun in Adelaide's hands. "Give me about a minute to get to the other side, then shoot."

Cornelia set off through the shadows of the surrounding buildings, grateful for the rubber soles of her boots that made very little sound, even on the steel "pavement." The control center had fewer windows than many of the other buildings, which was good—that would hopefully make their presence that much less noticeable.

Sure enough, there was a guard at the other door. Both guards were large, intimidating-looking men—perhaps the same men that had been Prudence's guards on the boat, but Cornelia couldn't recall their faces well enough to be sure. If they were armed—which they probably were—no weapons were visible.

Taking a deep breath, Cornelia positioned the bobby pin firmly between her gloved index finger and thumb of her right hand, and then slunk along the wall of the building. As soon as she reached the edge of the puddle of light above the door, the guard turned his head towards her.

"Stop—" he started to say, but she surged forward and stabbed at his face with the bobby pin.

He swatted her arm away with surprising force, knocking the pin from her grip, but then he crumpled to the ground with a heavy thud. *Thank you, Charlotte,* she thought. *Whatever the hell you put in that potion, it works.*

She knelt down beside him and pulled off her black gloves. Focusing on his body and his slow breathing, she held out both hands above him, fisted tight with her fingers pointing downwards. *"Vita vinculum,"* she whispered three times in a row, and then, "*Sopor cerebrum.*" Her hands warmed as she finished the incantation, culminating with a sharp tingle in her fingertips and the backs of her wrists.

Between that spell and Charlotte's sleeping potion, he should be out for a while.

She put her gloves back on and pulled her lock picks out of her belt pouch. Unlocking the door was an easy matter. The control building was just one large room, filled with consoles and terminals; she hurried through the expansive room to the other door and opened it. Adelaide was tying up the other guard's wrists.

"So you got him?" Adelaide asked as she slipped inside and closed the door behind her. "Charlotte's bobby pins worked?"

"It worked, all right," said Cornelia. Adelaide handed the Tesla gun back to her as they moved into the room. "So, where do we begin?"

"Percival showed me several things in here, but he was most proud of the floatation pylons," said Adelaide. "Let's see, which console was it... Over here, I think."

The overhead lights were off, but every console and panel had lit buttons or small lights over the dials and gauges, so they were able to navigate with little difficulty. Everything in the room was chrome and copper and glass and glittering with dozens of tiny lights—Cornelia was again momentarily awed by the technological wonder and scientific beauty of it all. It seemed a shame that the best way to stop these mad people was to destroy such a marvelous creation.

"This is it," said Adelaide, stopping at one of the consoles. The console was conveniently labeled "Floatation" embossed on a brass tag at the top corner of the control panel. Numerous dials controlled air pressure and direction of air flow for ten different pylon balloons. "So if we reverse the air flow to the air bladders, they should deflate and—"

"No," Cornelia interrupted her as Adelaide reached for a dial. "I have a better idea. Pump more air into them. Overfill them. If they burst, then the damage can't be fixed. And the force of all the bladders bursting should destabilize the city, in addition to lowering it to the water. If one edge of the city dips below the surface—"

"It will start flooding and sink that much faster," Adelaide finished for her, and grinned. "That's brilliant." She reached for the dial again, then stopped. "Wait, I have an idea. You do the air—I want to find the console for the power plant."

Cornelia stepped up to the console as Adelaide moved through the room. "I'm setting all the hose pumps to full," Cornelia said, twisting the dials to the maximum. She had no way of knowing how long it would take for the balloons to burst, so the sooner they started the process the better.

"Here it is," Adelaide called from across the room. "If we can overload the power plant, the explosion will rock the city that much more, not to mention cutting off the electricity to everything. It will be easier for us to escape if everything's dark."

"Will that affect the gravity engines, though?" Cornelia asked, turning the last of the air pump dials. "The schematic we have didn't show that the gravity engines were connected to anything else in the city, but unless we can be sure, we shouldn't take that risk. We don't need overloaded gravity matrix resonators exploding beneath our feet. Or blasting magnetic resonance along the ley lines back to Los Angeles. We came here to prevent that."

"No," said Adelaide, working at the console. "The gravity engines aren't connected to anything else in the city. They're powered by radium and all they do is make the city fly—everything else is powered by the electrical power plant here. Percival explained all that to me during my tour."

"That's good," said Cornelia. "Let's overload the power, then."

The air pressure gauges for the pylon balloons all had needles in the red now, and the hoses were still pumping. Any moment now...

A red warning light began flashing on the panel, and abruptly one of the air pressure needles dropped down to zero. "One of the air bladders just burst," Cornelia reported. Sooner or later, anyone near the edges of the city would hear the bursting and sound an alarm.

Another air pressure needle dropped to zero and this time Cornelia felt a faint shudder run through the floor. "It's working. We should go. How are you coming with the power?"

"Almost," said Adelaide. "I'm setting all the storage batteries to maximum output." Another shudder, more noticeable this time, ran through the floor. "Okay, I think that's done it. Once I hit this button, all the batteries will release, and the whole building should explode." She held her hand over a switch. "But that will kill the power to the air pumps, too. We should wait for a few more of them to burst. How many are left?"

Cornelia scanned the gauges as she felt another vibration and the floor shifted ever so slightly. "Six left to go," she said. "No, five."

A sudden crash came from the door across the room, and three men burst in. Automatically Cornelia ducked down behind the console. At almost the same instant, the other door crashed open, admitting three more men. All six wielded large guns.

They swung their weapons to bear on Adelaide. Apparently Cornelia had hidden herself quickly enough. She pulled out the Tesla gun and peered out from behind the console.

"Hands in the air!" shouted one of the men, brandishing his gun. Thompson submachine guns; Cornelia recognized the weapons. It seemed that the Caelum was fond of using prototype inventions that had been created for the Great War but not put into use in time—first John's gravity matrix engine, and now these Thompson guns that had been intended to replace the Browning Automatics.

The floor tilted again, very slightly, as Cornelia crawled forwards. If she set the gun on the maximum charge, and got a little closer, she could probably knock out at least four of the men with the blast, if just for a few moments. A few moments might be enough...

"Hands in the air!" the man shouted again. "And step away from the console!"

"Or what?" Adelaide returned.

Cornelia paused to look up at her. The men all had their backs to Cornelia's position, and so Adelaide was facing her. The girl wore a determined expression, which Cornelia had seen before—but she had a strange glint in her blue eyes. Her hands still hovered over the control panel.

"Or what?" Adelaide repeated. Her eyes flicked down at Cornelia, ever so briefly, then she stared defiantly back at the men facing her.

"Hands in the air, or we'll shoot you!" the man yelled, and all six cocked their guns.

Adelaide's eyes met Cornelia's again, and she mouthed a word: *Go*. And then slammed her hand down on the switch.

All six men opened fire. Adelaide crumpled under the hail of bullets, disappearing behind the console.

"No!" Cornelia shouted, lunging out from her hiding spot.

The men spun on her, guns still blazing. She squeezed off a shot with the Tesla gun as she dove for cover behind another console. The distant boom of an explosion shuddered through the air. The entire room jolted, and all of the lights went out.

"Get her!" shouted one of the men.

Cornelia scrambled in the darkness, trying to figure out where Adelaide had fallen. A spray of bullets narrowly missed her and she flattened herself to the floor.

"The blonde one's dead," said another man. "We need to get the other one, too. Spread out, men!"

The floor tilted again, and the door banged open with the movement. "Over there! Get her!" shouted a man, amid another shower of bullets. Cornelia stayed still, lying on the floor and trying not to breathe, as she heard several of the men run past her and out of the swinging open door. At least three of them, she calculated, based on the sounds of their pounding footsteps. At least three, she hoped.

Cornelia couldn't see a thing in the pitch black darkness that surrounded them, but the remaining men were not being particularly quiet as they shuffled nosily around the room. "Mick, use your flashlight," said one of them, almost directly above Cornelia. "We need to make sure that the other dame isn't hiding out in here still."

Giving one twist to the knob on the Tesla gun, Cornelia aimed it at the direction of his voice and squeezed the trigger. He gave a strangled grunt and fell to the floor. She slithered back away from him as one of the other men snapped on a flashlight. The blinding beam raked the room, gliding well above Cornelia as she lay on the floor behind a console.

"Don?" called Mick the flashlight man. "What was that? Where are you?"

Cornelia risked a peek around the pedestal of her console, and glimpsed one man standing beside Mick and his flashlight. She held her breath a moment, didn't hear any movement anywhere else in the room, and twisted the Tesla gun knob twice for the higher electrical discharge.

As the flashlight beam swept past again, Cornelia stood up and fired. The blast caught both men and they went down. They'd been a good ten feet or more away, though, so at that range, even the higher setting wouldn't stun them for very long.

The floor tilted again, making her grab onto the nearest console to keep from falling over. Mick's flashlight rolled across the floor towards her. She quickly holstered the Tesla gun and snatched up the flashlight.

A quick sweep of the room with the light showed Adelaide crumpled on the floor where she'd fallen. Staggering around the control consoles as the floor heaved beneath her, Cornelia hurried across the room and dropped down beside her.

"Adelaide," she said, her voice sounding hoarse to her ears as she rolled the girl over. "Adelaide...oh God."

Blood oozed from over a dozen bullet wounds across her torso, and trailed out of her mouth, pooling on the floor. Cornelia closed her eyes briefly to choke back a wave of nausea, then opened them again to get a better look at her in the flashlight beam. Holding the flashlight in her left hand, she touched the girl's face with her gloved right hand.

"Just hang on, Adelaide," she muttered. "I'll get you out of here." How? She pushed a lock of blond hair back from the girl's face, and her glove came away bloody. What was that spell that could stop a flow of blood? She couldn't remember any of the words. Or there was that spell that could pull out bullets because it focused on magnetism, but that needed a lodestone, which she didn't have, and she'd never memorized the incantation for that one.

Adelaide's eyelids fluttered in the beam of the flashlight. "Cor—" she started to say, but then choked on the blood in her mouth.

"Shh, don't try to talk." Cornelia cradled the girl's head. "I'm going to get you out of here."

"No..." Adelaide's eyes drifted closed, then she sucked in a raspy breath and opened them again. "Go."

"I'm not leaving you here." Cornelia laid the flashlight on the floor and slid an arm under her body.

Adelaide made a choking sound, but then grabbed Cornelia's arm with a startling grip. "No," she rasped softly. "I'm dead. You...go." She heaved in another breath, shallower this time. Her blue eyes looked foggy. "Go, Cornelia...go save the world." Her blood-covered mouth moved in a small smile, and then her eyes closed.

"No." Cornelia felt her go limp. "Adelaide, no!" This couldn't be happening. After all they'd been through, this couldn't be the end. Tears blurred her vision as she groped at Adelaide's neck for a pulse. Nothing. She yanked her glove off and pressed her bare fingers to the girl's skin. Nothing.

Another distant explosion rocked the room again. The flashlight skittered away and Cornelia tumbled backwards against a console pedestal. She heard one of the men she'd stunned groan and shift around. Across the room, the door swung open again with a metallic bang.

Cornelia hesitated for just an instant. *Forgive me, Adelaide.* She scrambled up and made a dash for the sound of the open door.

The entire city was plunged in darkness, but the stars glittered bright overhead and the moon shone full and round. And a brilliant orange blaze was shooting high into the sky from a nearby building.

You did it, Adelaide. How can I leave you? Cornelia turned to go back into the control room, but another lurch of the "ground" sent her stumbling and sliding into the wall of a building across the street.

There was no time. The platform of the city was at a pronounced angle now, and shuddering with movement. She staggered as she tried to stand upright. Shouts of alarm and panic came from all around, and she heard one of the Thompson machine guns go off again.

They'd done it. The city was sinking. Adelaide had sacrificed herself to make sure it went down. And now it was time to leave.

Using the wall for support, Cornelia pushed herself standing. She scanned the moonlit buildings, looking for the airplane hangar; she finally spotted the low building, thankfully the opposite direction from the blazing power plant.

She hurried along the streets, hugging the walls of buildings and freezing every time she saw running figures or heard nearby voices. If anyone noticed her, they were more intent on their own escape than anything else right now.

The floor of the city continued to lurch and tilt more dramatically, and over the yelling voices and the roaring of the power plant fire, she could hear the sound of sloshing water, very close by. Several men and women ran into the airplane hangar through a personnel door; Cornelia stayed in the shadows until they all were in, then dashed through the door.

A dozen or so small open cockpit bi-wing planes filled the space—modified army planes left over from the War, by the looks of them. The ear-piercing revving of engines made her head throb. She crouched down behind a row of large metal fuel drums; she struggled to focus and let her eyes adjust to the darkness inside the hangar, but all she could see was Adelaide's bloody body.

Focus, Cornelia. You have to make it. For John. For Adelaide. She took a breath and peered out from behind the fuel drums.

The planes held two passengers each, and as she scanned the people clambering into seats and pulling on flight goggles, she realized that all of the planes were full—except one.

The plane nearest her had only one man in the rear pilot's seat. One of his compatriots had started his propeller for him, then climbed into another plane. The lone pilot was just pulling on his flight goggles. It was now or never.

Cornelia dashed out from her hiding spot and yanked the Tesla gun off of her belt. With a running start, she scrambled up onto the lower wing and fired the gun at the man's head. He slumped in the seat.

Climbing up onto the top of the plane, she nearly fell, and banged her shin against the edge of the upper wing. Pushing away the pain, she pulled the goggles off the man's head and slung them around her neck, then grabbed him under the arms, feeling a faint tingle of the residual electrical blast from the gun. Grunting and panting with the effort, she finally hauled him out of the cockpit and pitched him over the side of the plane. He landed with a thud, then slid towards the wall with the tilt of the floor.

He might not regain consciousness before the city fully flooded. Cornelia couldn't let herself feel responsible for his death, however—or the deaths of any of the Caelum people who didn't manage to escape. Anyone who called themselves Caelum was a murderer by association—they'd tried to kill John, planned to kill thousands more across the world, and had just killed Adelaide.

She forced those thoughts away as she slid into the seat and studied the dashboard. She knew how to fly a plane, in theory—she'd seen schematics of numerous types of airplanes. Unfortunately, knowing how the cockpit controls were wired or how the engine was constructed was not at all the same thing as actually knowing how to fly.

This dashboard was unlike anything she'd ever seen before, though, and she quickly figured out why. This plane was powered by a gravity matrix engine. All of the planes were. In front of her, several of the planes were lifting off—they rose up vertically into the air, like a toy plane lifted by a string, before flying out the open doors at the far end of the hangar.

This had been the original plan for the engine, when John was first commissioned to build it during the War. A small engine that could be attached to the normal engine of a fighter plane, allowing the pilot to fly and maneuver normally when needed, or to fly higher and faster than any other aircraft could. Had the Caelum been behind the project then, too? What else had they orchestrated during the War?

As she latched the shoulder harness and fitted the goggles over her eyes, she glanced up at the remaining planes in the hangar. A few yards away, the closest plane, propeller whirring and head and tail lights glowing, had a man in the rear pilot's seat and a woman in the front seat. Percival and Prudence.

Cornelia fumbled at her belt, grabbing her revolver. It would be an easy shot, she thought, as she leveled the gun over the edge of her cockpit. At this range, with a stationary target, she couldn't miss. Prudence and Percival could pay for all that they'd done.

Her arm wavered. She wasn't a killer. But they were. She slipped her finger back into the trigger loop.

With a high-pitched revving of engines, their plane lifted off the hangar floor. At that instant, Prudence turned her head and looked at Cornelia.

It was impossible to be sure, of course—the plane was several yards away, and the hangar was dark except for the planes' running lights and the ambient moon light coming in the open door. But there was no mistaking that it was indeed Prudence in that seat—Cornelia could make out her perfectly-coiffed light brown hair and her narrow chin, recognizable even under the flight goggles. And she was sure that Prudence had recognized her, too.

Then the hovering plane bolted out the open hangar door.

She had to catch them. Stowing her gun and flipping the switch to activate the gravity engine, Cornelia felt a strange surge of lightness as the field of reduced gravity enveloped the plane. She slid the acceleration lever forwards, and her plane shot out of the hangar.

Damn, this thing was fast. She fought with the direction controls as the plane hurtled into the night sky. She hardly felt the motion at all as she pulled the plane lower again and circled back around to look at the city.

Over half of the circular platform of the city was below the waves now. With the bright full moon and the shining inferno spreading through the buildings, the spectacle was nearly blinding.

Pulling her plane up again, she scanned the sky all around, hoping to spot Prudence and Percival's plane. At this speed, it would be nearly impossible to recognize one goggled pilot from another; but she did see a collection of dwindling lights headed into the deep sky away from the city.

Cornelia angled her plane to follow them. Glancing at her dashboard, she saw that they were heading south-west. Where would they be going? Another base of some sort, no doubt. The Caelum had to have other bases or staging areas for a project of this scale. The radium had been stored in Los

Angeles, but they probably wouldn't have shipped all of their equipment and supplies from there. She could find out where they were hiding, and take them all down. Or at least catch up to Prudence's plane and pull out her gun and shoot her and Percival out of the sky.

But not with less than a tank of fuel, she abruptly realized. The gravity engines of these planes, unlike the engines for the city, were powered by regular gasoline, not radium. That had been John's original design, but he'd quickly started exploring other power options, because the gravity engine burned through gasoline at an accelerated rate.

This plane's fuel tank was larger than standard for a plane this size, probably to accommodate the fuel-guzzling gravity engine. Her fuel tank was a little more than three-quarters full, but she'd be lucky indeed if it was enough to get her back home. Or enough to follow the escaping Caelum planes to their hidden base—which could be as far away as the Falkland Islands or even Antarctica, based on their heading. But certainly not enough fuel to do both.

Cornelia wheeled the plane around. She had to make it home. She glanced back down at the sinking city once more as she flew by. The blazing buildings reflected on the water, a shimmering coppery inferno that was slowly winking out as the ocean overtook it all.

Tears blurred her vision, but she didn't remove her flight goggles to swipe at her eyes. *Goodbye, Adelaide. I'm sorry, so very sorry.*

The full moon sat on the western horizon, and the eastern horizon glowed with the pink of dawn, washing out the stars.

MRS. JONES AND THE RADIUM CITY

She pointed the nose of the plane northwards and headed for home.

Chapter 12

She was going to crash. What a way to die—succumbing to gravity in an airplane designed by her husband to subvert the laws of gravity.

"No," Cornelia said aloud. She couldn't die, not after everything she'd been through. Not after what Adelaide had done.

The gravity matrix engine had taken her from the South Pacific to southern California in just under ten hours—astounding, considering it had taken her over a week to traverse that distance by boat. But now she had to land safely before she ran out of fuel and crashed.

The lights of Los Angeles glittered below. So close now. If she could find a public park, or even a farm at the edge of the city... The engine sputtered and heaved on its final dregs of fuel; she struggled to decrease speed and altitude without coming to a sudden stop in midair. Frantically she scanned the view below her, looking for a patch of darkness amid the lights that might indicate a park or a field. Having never seen an aerial photograph of the city before, it was difficult to tell exactly where she was; and the fact that it was after sunset and growing rapidly dark didn't help.

Suddenly the *Hollywoodland* sign loomed ahead of her, garish and blindingly bright against the mountainside. Never had she been so happy to see that hideous sign. Nudging the plane to the right, and angling the altitude lower, she headed for home.

The turret of Ivystone Hill Manor came into view. A small light had been installed on the top of the tower when they'd had the house built, just in case a low-flying plane were to sweep over the neighborhood. The turret was the height of a three-story building, which John had judged to be sufficient for his telescope. Ordinarily, even a low-flying plane would not be that low. But right now, Cornelia was very glad that they'd had that warning light installed.

So now the only trick was to land without smashing into the house or killing herself. She pulled back on the acceleration levers and lurched forward into the seat straps as the plane slowed dramatically and plummeted several dozen feet. Perhaps that was too much too quickly. She tried to compensate, but at that moment the blinking fuel light turned a solid red and the engine shut off.

The bubble of reduced gravity that surrounded the plane vanished. Cornelia didn't need any of the gauges on the dashboard to tell her that, though, as a sudden invisible crushing weight enveloped her and the plane abruptly lurched towards the ground. She fumbled with the seat straps—if she could jump from the plane just before it hit the ground, then maybe—

With a hideous shuddering crunch, the plane landed in the bushes that ran along the outside edge of the horse pasture fence. She tumbled out of the plane and rolled down the wing, landing face down in the mulch and dirt. Wheezing and coughing, she tried to push herself up but she couldn't get her arms to move.

Was she suffering from broken bones or torn muscles, or just struggling with the disorientation of a return to full gravity and no longer being airborne? She smelled smoke and heard sparks hissing from the plane.

Get away from the plane, get away from the plane, was all she could think. She hadn't made it all this way just to die in an explosion. Or wind up like John, if the engine hit her with some sort of reverse gravity field like it had him.

Adrenaline surging through her, Cornelia pushed herself up to her hands and knees and crawled away from the wreckage. Temporarily disoriented, she wasn't sure which direction the house was, but surely Rawlins had seen or heard the plane crash. Or Ronald and Joey had noticed, since they lived in the apartments above the carriage house, much closer. She doggedly crawled across the grass, hoping that she was moving faster than it felt like. If the plane exploded, then a distance of only a few feet away wouldn't make that much difference.

She tried to stand so that she could travel more quickly, but as soon as she got upright, her head swam and her knees buckled. She collapsed and retched into the grass. After coughing and trying to catch her breath, she resumed crawling. Which way was the house, and which way was the crashed plane? She didn't smell smoke anymore, but she also couldn't see much of anything, either. Was it getting darker? She tugged off her flight goggles and tossed them aside.

Faint voices floated in the distance. In the increasing darkness clouding her vision, she saw two men running towards her. Rawlins and Joey. She was saved.

But Adelaide never would be.

"Miz Jones!" Rawlins shouted, and both men dropped down beside her.

Her arms gave out and she collapsed in front of Joey. "Adelaide," she mumbled.

"Stay with her," Rawlins said to Joey, and he took off towards the remains of the plane.

Cornelia struggled to stay conscious as she lay in the grass. Joey cradled her head, his warm gardener-rough hands on her temples a comforting sensation. Rawlins appeared above her.

"Where is Miss Adelaide, ma'am?" he asked breathlessly. "I don't see her in the plane."

"Dead," Cornelia croaked. She felt something warm and wet on her face, but had no idea if it was tears or blood. "At the bottom of the ocean. She's dead."

Rawlins disappeared from her field of vision and she heard other voices nearby. Then Rawlins was beside her again, kneeling and gathering her into his arms. "Ronald has gone to call the doctor. Just hold on, Miz Jones—everything will be all right."

She tried to say something, though she wasn't quite sure what. Nothing was all right, and it never would be. But the warm support of Rawlins' arms lulled her; she sagged her head against his chest and let herself drift into unconsciousness.

CORNELIA AWOKE ABRUPTLY, and blinked in disorientation at the bright light assaulting her eyes. Squinting, she tried to look around, and then realized that she was lying on her back.

She pushed herself up on one elbow, then collapsed back down with a grunt as pain lanced through her chest and left shoulder. She was lying on something downy and comfortable. Blinking again, she came more awake and realized that she was in her own bed.

"No, lie still, darling," said a soft high voice beside her, and Cornelia rolled her head to see Charlotte's smiling face.

"Charlotte?" she rasped in surprise, and then coughed. Her throat and mouth felt parched.

"I have water," said Charlotte. She bent over Cornelia and helped her to sit up a little, tucking another pillow behind her. She then picked up a glass of water from the bedside table and held it to her lips.

Cornelia drank gratefully, letting Charlotte hold the glass and support her head, as pain still throbbed through her shoulder and neck.

"Thank you," Cornelia said, her voice feeling stronger, as Charlotte set the glass back down. Cornelia saw that Charlotte had pulled the teal-and-gold brocade chair from across the room over to the bedside; there was a thick book of French poetry lying on the seat. An empty tea cup sat on the bedside table next to the water glass. Apparently Charlotte had been here for some time. "What are you doing here, Charlotte?" she finally managed.

"Looking after you, of course," Charlotte said with light laugh. She removed the book from the chair seat, setting it on the table beside the water, then sat back down. "I've been here all day."

"All day?" Cornelia echoed. "What time is it?"

"Well, it's only two in the afternoon, actually," said Charlotte. "But I've been here since late last night, just as soon as Rawlins called me. He said your plane crashed in the back garden at about seven yesterday evening."

The door across the room opened, and as if on cue, Rawlins stepped in. "Miz Jones!" he said, his face brightening as he hurried over to the bed. "You're awake. How is she, Miss Charlotte?"

"Wide awake and hungry as a horse, I should think," said Charlotte with another tittering laugh. "Aren't you, *ma chérie?*"

"I suppose." Cornelia didn't really want to think about food. Right now, she wanted answers. "Rawlins, what happened?"

"We all saw the air plane heading towards the house," he said. "I called the boys in the carriage house, and went outside. And then the plane crashed in the horse pasture. We all went running—I was hoping it was you, but we didn't know for sure. We found you and brought you inside, and called Dr. Huett. You were unconscious and bleeding badly. I called Miss de Fontaine, as well, just in case you'd been hurt with a magic spell or anything. And I knew she'd want to see you.

"Dr. Huett said you had a gunshot wound in your left shoulder, as well as scrapes and bruises, and a sprained ankle and cracked ribs. Blessedly no other broken bones from the crash—just a mild concussion, he said. He said you'd lost a lot of blood and were very dehydrated—we've been trying to get you to drink water, but since you've been unconscious, you haven't swallowed much." He glanced at the half-empty glass on the night stand. "Dr. Huett said to call him if you hadn't woken up by dinner time, so I'm very glad to see you awake, ma'am. He's prescribed lots of fluids and plenty of bed rest, and he's coming back tomorrow morning to look at your shoulder." He folded his hands behind his back and gave her a solemn look. "It was probably the gravity matrix engine that saved your life, ma'am. Dr. Huett said that ordinarily an impact like that would have been fatal."

Cornelia absorbed all of what he'd just said. It could have been worse, so very much worse. And it had been for Adelaide. She gestured at the water glass, and Charlotte helped her to drink some more.

"We accomplished our goal," she said finally. "We stopped the Caelum from launching their flying city." She then recounted everything that had happened. At first the memories seemed jumbled, but as she talked, everything cleared in her mind and she recalled it all with perfect clarity: the smell of salt air and burning electronics as the city sank, the cold wind on her face as she flew across the endless ocean, the sound of machine gun bullets, the weight of Adelaide's bleeding dying body in her arms. "So the world is safe," she finally concluded, her voice breaking. "And so is John."

After a moment of somber silence, Rawlins spoke. "Miss Adelaide will be greatly mourned and missed. You need your rest now, Miz Jones. Maggie prepared some chicken broth this morning, so I'll bring up a bowl."

Cornelia gave a weak nod. "And some more water, please. Or perhaps hot tea."

He gave a little bow. "I'll bring both, ma'am." He turned and left the room.

Exhaustion tugged at her, even though she'd just woken up. Her shoulder throbbed, where apparently one of the gunmen had hit her. She'd ask Rawlins for some aspirin or laudanum when he came back. She should be grateful that all she'd suffered was bruising and a wounded shoulder, but all she could think about was Adelaide.

She turned her head and looked at Charlotte.

"More water?" Charlotte asked, reaching for the glass.

"It's your fault she's dead," Cornelia growled, anger at the unfairness of it all rising suddenly in her mind.

"My fault?" Charlotte cocked her head to one side in that bird-like manner she had, a genuinely puzzled expression on her face. "What do you mean?"

"You started this whole mess by sending Adelaide after me when I went to get the radium. You encouraged me to teach her magic. And this is the result!"

"The wicked people of the Caelum killed her," Charlotte said softly. "I did not. And neither did you."

Cornelia glared at her. Why didn't Charlotte get angry? If she raged and shouted and tried to defend her innocence, then Cornelia would have an excuse to hit her. She needed to hit something. Not that she could right now, since she couldn't even sit up by herself, but still...

When Charlotte's calm silence stretched on, Cornelia turned her head away. "You have no idea how I feel."

She felt Charlotte lay a hand on the blanket. "But I do."

Cornelia rolled her head back to glare at her. "How dare you. I failed her as a friend, as a mentor, as a protector."

"I know how you feel," Charlotte said, "because, as you said, I encouraged you to teach her. Like you, I bear some of the responsibility. Not *fault*," she added with emphasis. "But responsibility."

With a jerk, Cornelia turned her head away again, the tears in her eyes blurring out the view of the framed Monet landscape on the wall that she wasn't really looking at anyway. "Rawlins said that John's gravity matrix engine saved my life. Maybe that Eye of Horus protection talisman helped, as well." She felt at her neck, her fingers finding only the lacey collar of her nightgown.

She heard Charlotte clinking something metallic, and turned her head to see her lifting the medallion and its chain from the small cut-crystal trinket dish on the nightstand.

"*Oui*, I am certain this helped to shield you from bullets and all the others dangers of your journey," Charlotte said in a thoughtful tone, fingering the gold *wadjet* eye medallion. "It is very ancient, and very potent with magic."

"I didn't know if it actually had any magic," Cornelia said, watching the light glinting off the gold. "I wore it mostly because John gave it to me." She paused. "Adelaide had a protection talisman, too. Lou Vincini gave me one—a Celtic protection symbol, carved on a stone medallion. Alabaster, or maybe soapstone. I already was wearing the Egyptian talisman, so I gave the Celtic knotwork one to her." She swallowed hard and blinked away more tears. "Lou gave me a fake talisman," she gritted. "He got Adelaide killed."

"Lou deals in only real magic," Charlotte said, her voice still calm, almost soothing. "The protection talisman he gave you was probably just as powerful as this one, maybe even more so."

"Well, it sure didn't work," Cornelia choked. "I know she was shot by six guns point-blank, but shouldn't it have done something? Couldn't she have lived long enough to..." Her chest tightened with the injustice of it; her cracked ribs sent a spear of pain through her, and she held her breath.

"A protection spell or talisman," said Charlotte after a moment, "is at its strongest when the wearer believes in its power, lets the protective magic do its work."

"So you're saying Adelaide didn't believe enough?" Cornelia said with a glare.

Charlotte shook her head. "Adelaide's belief in magic, in you, in the cause of your quest, was strong. The hot fire belief of the young and pure. But no protection spell of any power could have saved her in that moment. From what you told us happened, I would say that she was not killed—she gave her life on purpose. No protection talisman can stop self-sacrifice."

Cornelia felt fresh tears spilling down her face, and closed her eyes. She wanted to contradict Charlotte, but she knew the other woman was right. "I miss her."

Charlotte moved her hand from the edge of the blanket to rest on Cornelia's arm. "I miss her, too. And I almost lost you."

Cornelia opened her eyes. Charlotte's normally bubbly demeanor was suddenly gone, making her petite, fine-boned frame seemed suddenly shrunken and frail. Cornelia reached out and gripped Charlotte's arm, feeling like she needed to keep her from crumpling out of the chair.

Charlotte leaned closer and embraced her; her hold was strong and reassuring. Charlotte wasn't frail, and she wouldn't shatter. Gratefully, Cornelia returned the embrace as best as she could.

"I'm so sorry that Adelaide is gone, *ma chérie*," Charlotte murmured. "But I'm so very glad that you came back home."

Cornelia didn't try to stop her tears as she hugged her friend. "So am I, Charlotte. So am I."

"I KNOW YOU CAN'T HEAR me, John, but I wanted to tell you anyway. We did it. We stopped the flying city."

Cornelia stood in John's basement chamber, looking up at his body floating in the tank of the artificial womb. Rawlins had kept the machine running smoothly while she was away. Now that she was finally able to get out of bed and manage the stairs, she came down to see him and talk to him.

He couldn't talk back, of course, but it was comforting to say his name and see his face, even covered by the breathing mask.

"Today is January thirty-first," she continued. "The day the Caelum were going to launch their city and use your gravity engines to wreak havoc on the world and kill you. We stopped them. Adelaide stopped them."

She wandered around the room as she talked, walking with the cane that Dr. Huett had given her to take weight off of her still-recovering twisted ankle. She let her eyes rest on every instrument and gauge along the walls, and trailed her hand across the glass wall of the tank. That was as close as she could get right now to touching John. But just for now—one day soon, he'd be fully restored and healed.

Eventually she left the room and made her way down the basement corridor, then through the main lab room. One of the long tables had been cleared off to make room for the pieces and parts of the gravity engine from the plane. It had not exploded, thankfully, although both the plane and the gravity engine were damaged beyond repair. The gravity engine could be rebuilt, though. Cornelia had all of John's schematics and designs.

She slowly climbed the stairs, taking her time on her ankle. Her shoulder wound was also healing nicely, though it still hurt. Dr. Huett had given her several exercises to do twice a day, to keep the muscles from becoming stiff with scar tissue. Her cracked ribs seemed to be slowing her down the most, though, since she couldn't move or bend normally, or take deep breaths.

Upstairs in the hallway, she met Rawlins as he was just coming out of the dining room. "Luncheon is almost ready, ma'am," he said.

"Thank you, Rawlins. I'll be there in a few minutes."

"Very good, Miz Jones," he said with an incline of his head.

Cornelia headed down the hall towards the staircase, but paused in the foyer as she glanced at the large crystal ball sitting on the telephone table.

This wasn't over. The radium city was sunk, and John was safe, but whatever the Caelum might be up to was far from finished. And Prudence knew that she had escaped the city. The magic crystal ball spy cameras should stay up outside, and maybe they should even install more, like at the gate and around the perimeter of the property. Sooner or later, Cornelia knew that she'd be seeing the Caelum again.

She went over to the ball and trailed a finger across the cool smooth surface. Adelaide had asked her to teach her how to summon ghosts. Had there been a particular person that

Adelaide had wanted to see again, to say goodbye to? She would never know now.

Ghosts...Perhaps she could talk to Adelaide one more time. The girl had died so young, so full of life—even dying a sacrificial hero's death didn't necessarily mean she had closure on her life. Cornelia knew how to summon even a reluctant spirit with a good crystal ball. Surely Adelaide would be fairly easy to summon. Even if she did feel closure at her own death, mightn't she like to see Cornelia one more time?

Cornelia turned and went into the sitting room, where they kept a smaller crystal ball. On a shelf between a silver candelabra and a Royal Albert decorative plate was a small wooden box, carved with a delicate floral pattern. She leaned her cane against the wall as she picked up the box; it was the perfect size to hold a small fist-sized crystal sphere, resting on a cushion of red velvet.

As Cornelia lifted the lid of the box, she felt a strange draft of cold air brush past her neck. She glanced at the windows, but they were all closed. Then she looked back down at the crystal, still resting inside the box. An image flickered briefly in the ball, like her own inverted reflection, but not quite. She turned around.

Adelaide was standing beside the sofa. She wasn't wearing the black costume she'd died in—she was dressed as Cornelia had first seen her, before she'd gotten to know her at all. Adelaide had come to a ladies' tea shortly after arriving in Los Angeles, where Hortense had introduced her to all the women. She'd worn a sunny yellow frock, the frilly asymmetrical hemline hitting just below her knees, low burgundy pumps with gold buckles, and a pale pink cloche. She grinned. "Hi, Cornelia!"

Cornelia shut the lid of the wooden box with a snap, and set it down on the lamp table next to her, partly to steady herself by touching something solid like the tabletop. "Adelaide." She swallowed. "I was just about to try to summon you."

"Oh, crummy timing on my part." Adelaide's face fell. "I can leave, if you want to keep your summoning skills sharp, and come back when—"

"No, you silly girl." Cornelia took a step towards her, then halted again. "It's good to see you again. I wanted..." She swallowed the lump in her throat. "I wanted to tell you I'm sorry."

"Sorry for what? You're not blaming yourself for my death, are you?"

Cornelia didn't trust her voice at the moment, so she gave a weak nod.

Adelaide gave her a sorrowful look. "Please don't. I certainly don't blame you. Oh, Cornelia, I don't want you moping around, sadly contemplating about how our adventure cost me my life. Because it was just that—a grand adventure—and it didn't cost me anything. I willingly gave my life—I gave it for something important, something that mattered." She smiled. "I got to be a heroine."

Cornelia managed a faint smile, but then stepped forward so she could sink onto the sofa. She wasn't surprised to hear Adelaide say these things, not really—but actually having her spirit standing there saying them was somehow more than she felt ready to handle at the moment.

Adelaide came around the arm of the sofa and sat down beside her. She looked solid, but the gold cushion didn't sink beneath her; and Cornelia could feel a faint pocket of cold air beside her where Adelaide sat.

"Of course I didn't want to die," Adelaide said quietly. "But it was the only way. And I don't regret it. And I don't want you to regret it, either."

Cornelia swallowed again, blinking back tears, and wished she had a handkerchief with her. "Adelaide...I'm sorry I left you behind."

The girl gave a small smile. "You didn't."

"Your body is at the bottom of the Pacific Ocean now. I've robbed you of a proper burial and funeral." Every time Cornelia tried not to think about that, it was all she could think about.

Adelaide's smile was gentle. "That's just my body. I don't need it anymore."

Cornelia blinked through her tears, not sure what to say to that. "Prudence and Percival got away," she said finally. "Most of them did."

"I know. And that's good. I didn't want anyone to die, not even them. The world is safe. And so is John." Adelaide put her hand over Cornelia's. The touch was cold, but Cornelia felt the pressure. Tentatively she covered Adelaide's hand with her other one. It felt like a normal human hand, just icy cold.

"John is safe, isn't he?" Adelaide then asked, a crease of concern on her brow.

"Yes. The gravity engines never turned on, and so no backlash from the city reached him. I don't think there was any energy from the city powerful enough to travel along a ley line.

The Caelum had planes powered by the gravity engines—that's how I escaped. I flew it home, and now we're repairing the engine. We're going to try to use it to reverse the effects of John's injuries—reduce the mass of his internal organs." She drew a breath. It was a risky long shot, and would require a lot of math to make sure the experiment would be safe, but it was something. "And if that doesn't work, we'll try something else."

"That's good," said Adelaide with a smile.

"Wait. So...you didn't know any of that already?" Cornelia had never fully bought into the theory that deceased spirits could predict the future or impart more knowledge than what they'd known in life, but she'd also never had the opportunity to bring it up with any ghost she'd talked to.

Adelaide chuckled. "How would I have known that? I've been dead for days. Or has it been longer? It's hard to keep track of time when you no longer have a social calendar and don't need to eat."

Cornelia smiled in spite of herself. "It's been five days."

"Five days. Golly, no wonder you're still so upset." She patted Cornelia's hand, a strange clammy pressure that was still comforting. "Oh, you were thinking I might have some arcane knowledge beyond normal human ken now that I'm dead. I don't think it works that way, really. I feel like I...*understand* some things better than before, and so many things seem less important than they used to. But I don't think I know anything new. I'm certainly not omniscient."

"But you're tangible." Cornelia patted her hand in return.

"It's because I wanted to be able to touch you," Adelaide said, smiling. "I've gone intangible and popped through a few walls, too, though. That was a neat experience. I had no idea that wiring for electric lights in a building was so complicated."

Cornelia laughed.

"I visited my parents," Adelaide then said. "To tell them what happened to me."

"You did?" Cornelia blinked at her. She'd been agonizing over writing a letter to Adelaide's family, informing them of her death, since she was the only one who even knew that the girl had died. She hadn't been able to bring herself to write anything yet, though, and had no idea what to say. "I was going to write them a letter," she said. "But I hadn't yet. I know you weren't very close to your parents, but they needed to know..."

Adelaide nodded. "I know. I realized the same thing. We were all happier with me away from home, but I still felt that they deserved to know what had happened to me; that I'd never be coming back to New York, and why. I'm not sure if they believed me when I told them I was a spirit and had died saving the city of Los Angeles from some very dangerous people. Maybe they thought they were dreaming." She shrugged. "But I wanted them to know. So don't worry about writing any letters."

Cornelia nodded, feeling tears again. "I haven't told any of the ladies what happened," she then said after a pause. "I telephoned Hortense the other day to tell her that I would be absent from events for some time, while I nursed John." She also had no desire to show up at a bridge game or a charity dinner limping with a cane and sporting a bandaged shoulder. "I told Hortense that you'd decided to travel, and had no plans to return to Los Angeles." She looked at Adelaide's tangible and very alive-looking face. "I know you were a heroine, but Hortense and the other ladies wouldn't understand."

"I know," said Adelaide with a smile. "It's okay. So is Prudence back in town?"

Cornelia shook her head. "The Davenports are gone for good, gone to wherever the Caelum are hiding. Hortense said that their house is for sale."

There was a tap at the sitting room doorway. "Begging your pardon, Miz Jones," came Rawlins' voice. "But I was wondering if you—Miss Adelaide!"

Cornelia looked over her shoulder to see Rawlins in the doorway, gaping at them. He was usually so stoic, and he'd encountered ghosts before, so Cornelia was surprised at the vividly stunned expression on his face.

"Hello, Rawlins," said Adelaide with a grin.

"Miss Adelaide, it's a pleasure to see you again," he said, pulling himself together and giving her a little bow of his head. He looked at Cornelia. "A crystal ball, ma'am?"

"No, I beat her to it and just showed up," said Adelaide. She released Cornelia's hands and stood up. "But now I should be going. I'm glad you're all right, Cornelia." She looked back at Rawlins. "I'm glad all of you are all right."

"I will be," Cornelia said, slowly standing up.

"I know you will be," Adelaide said, giving her a little smile. "Keep fighting, Cornelia. For knowledge and education, for opportunities for women, for your husband. For everything good in this world." She gave them both a little wave. "I'll see you around sometime." And then she vanished.

Cornelia sank back down onto the sofa. Rawlins came over to her; laying a warm living hand on her shoulder, he produced the handkerchief that she'd been wanting earlier. Her tears flowed freely now, and she covered her face.

"Miss Adelaide's right, ma'am," he said softly after a moment. "You're a fighter, and you've got to keep fighting."

"I know," she said into the handkerchief. She mopped at her eyes, then looked up at him. "I haven't given up, and I won't. It's just a hell of a way to begin the year, is all."

Rawlins smiled. "I agree with you there, ma'am." He went over to the wall by the shelf to retrieve Cornelia's cane, then returned to the sofa, handing her the cane and offering her his arm.

She took the cane in one hand and his arm in the other and stood up, more steadily this time. She was glad Adelaide had come. Despite what anyone said, though, she had to add the girl to the list of people whose deaths she hadn't been able to prevent. But John was not going to be on that list. She would keep fighting.

She squeezed Rawlins' arm as they walked out of the sitting room. "Thank you for everything, Joe. Everything you've done, and everything you're ever going to do. Let's go bring back John."

Epilogue

Two years later

Cornelia pulled the motorcycle to a stop beneath the porte-cochère. Switching it off, she left the key in; she crunched across the few feet of driveway gravel and then up the stone steps to the side door.

Rawlins was waiting for her in the hallway. "Good evening, ma'am," he said, holding out his hand to take her utility belt from her.

She'd already unbuckled it, and she gratefully draped it over his outstretched arm, glad to be rid of the weight of it. Dark vision goggles, screwdriver, lighter, revolver, Tesla gun, knife, extra bullets, lock picks, poison, flash powder—the belt felt heavier every time she wore it.

"I told you that you didn't have to wait up for me," she said, pulling off her driving goggles and cap, and handing those over to him as well. "I knew I wouldn't be back until at least three." She pulled off her black driving gloves, then began unbuttoning her leather jacket. "What time is it, by the way?"

"Ten minutes to four," Rawlins said calmly. "And I wasn't about to let you come home to a dark and silent house."

Belatedly she realized that he was still in his full butler's livery, albeit with his tie loose and his cuffs undone. She sighed and shook her head, but gave him a little smile.

"Was the night's mission a success?" Rawlins then asked, holding out his other hand to take her jacket and gloves.

"After a fashion," she said. "It's been a long, exhausting night, but I suppose we can call it a success. Though I still feel I have nothing to show for it." She sighed and rubbed at her temples, trying to think about nothing. "I'll give you the full debriefing after breakfast, if that's okay."

"Of course, Miz Jones. I had Maggie leave a bit of food out for you, in case you were hungry. Do you want anything, or will you be heading straight up to bed?"

"I'm exhausted, but I'm too keyed up to sleep just yet. I'm not hungry, though—perhaps just a drink."

"Coffee or scotch?"

She wanted to say "both," but then she'd definitely never get to sleep. "Scotch, I suppose. Could you bring it to the basement? I want to see John."

"Of course, ma'am. Let me just put these away and I'll bring it right down." He started off down the hall with the armload of motorcycling gear.

"Thank you," Cornelia said. "And Rawlins? After that, please go to bed. I'll get the rest of the downstairs lights when I go up."

He paused to look back at her and smiled. "Yes, Miz Jones."

Cornelia headed down the slate steps and navigated her way through the darkened basement, switching on only one of the lights in the main room on her way through.

The lights were always on in John's Vault. She stood for a moment looking up at him, then began slowly walking around the tank, glancing at all of the instruments, as she had every night for the past two years.

"I know I'm very late tonight, John," she said aloud. "Or very early, depending on how you look at it. I'll tell you all the details later." She ran a hand across the glass of the tank as she walked, feeling the subtle thrumming of liquid, air, and electrical impulses traveling to and from the tank and the instrument panels. "I wish the Caelum never existed," she added with a sigh.

But if she was too tired to talk about her adventure tonight, then she was definitely too tired to think about it anymore. Rawlins would be down with her drink in a moment, and then she should follow her own advice to him, and go to bed.

She'd nearly completed the circuit of the tiny room when a flashing red light caught her attention. Instantly wide awake, she stared up at the panel on the wall. The flashing light was the heart rate monitor. She scanned the bank of gauges. Heart rate, respiration, blood pressure, electrical impulses from the brain—all were abruptly elevated.

Her own heart pounding in a panic, she turned around and looked up at John's body. He looked as he always did, naked and floating motionless in the pale blueish liquid.

Except that his eyes were open. And he was staring directly at her.

THE END

ABOUT THE AUTHOR:

Grace E. Robinson is a lover of stories—real and imaginary. She is a lover of words in any language; a lover of travel and the music of the world. Born and raised in Virginia, Grace studied English and creative writing at Hollins University. She lives in north Idaho with a cat and a lot of books.

Read Grace's blog at her website, StorytellerGirlGrace.com[1].

You can connect with Grace on Facebook[2], Twitter[3], Instagram[4], and Pinterest[5].

---

1. https://storytellergirlgrace.com/

2. https://www.facebook.com/storytellergirlgrace

3. https://twitter.com/StorytellerGRL

4. https://www.instagram.com/grace_storytellergrl/

5. https://www.pinterest.com/storytellerGRL/

www.ingramcontent.com/pod-product-compliance
Lightning Source LLC
Chambersburg PA
CBHW070908180626
46817CB00003B/971